AWARD-WINNING CANADIAN FICTION

ARTHUR ELLIS

A W A R D S

An Anthology of Prize-Winning
Crime & Mystery Fiction

D1433059

AWARD-WINNING CANADIAN FICTION

ARTHUR ELLIS

A W A R D S

An Anthology of Prize-Winning
Crime & Mystery Fiction

edited by
Peter Sellers

CRIME WRITERS OF CANADA

The publisher gratefully acknowledges the support of
The Canada Council for the Arts and the
Book Publishing Industry Development Program
of the Department of Canadian Heritage.

ISBN 1-55082-265-9

Design by Susan Hannah.
Typeset by Robert Stewart.
Copy edited by Mandy Chan.
Series Editor: Edo van Belkom.

Printed and bound in Canada by AGMV Marquis,
Cap-Saint-Ignace, Quebec.

Published by Quarry Press Inc.,
PO Box 1061,
Kingston, Ontario,
K7L 4Y5, Canada.

www.quarrypress.com.

THE CANADA COUNCIL FOR THE ARTS   LE CONSEIL DES ARTS DU CANADA

CONTENTS

Introduction

The entire history of crime fiction, the millions of books and the billions of words they contain, began with a single short story. "The Murders in the Rue Morgue," by Edgar Allan Poe, introduced some of the genre's most venerable institutions, including the sleuth of vast intellect with uncanny powers of reason. The foundation of the detective story that Poe established was brought to full life by another legendary short story writer, Arthur Conan Doyle in his tales of Sherlock Holmes. In Canada, mystery and crime writers like Grant Allen, Robert Barr, and Harvey O'Higgins worked primarily in the short story format in the late nineteenth and early twentieth centuries. Later, Canadian authors like H. Bedford Jones, Frank L. Packard, and R.T.M. Scott were staples of the pulp magazines. And, following the demise of the pulps, the two Canadian mystery authors with the largest regular readership were short story specialists James Powell and William Bankier, each of whom has published dozens of stories, primarily in the pages of *Ellery Queen Mystery Magazine*. Their careers continue unabated.

With a few exceptions, however, the people who get most of the attention in the crime fiction field in recent years are not short story writers but novelists. During the 1980s in Canada, Howard Engel sent Benny Cooperman out to prowl the mean streets of Grantham (a.k.a. St. Catharines, Ontario). Ted Wood placed former Toronto cop Reid Bennett in the cottage country town of Murphy's Harbour. And Eric Wright created Charlie Salter, who brought a human face to the Toronto police force.

There were others, too, who made contributions in those years. L.A. Morse's novel *The Old Dick* won the Edgar Award for Best Paperback Original in 1981. John Reeves launched a series of four novels about Toronto cops Coggins and Sump with a case of murder at the CBC. Both William Deverell, in 1979, and Tim Wynne-Jones, in 1981, won the $50,000 Seal Books First Novel Award for crime novels, the former for the thriller *Needles* and the latter for *Odd's End*, a story of psychological suspense. And writing crime fiction spread nationwide when authors such as L.R. Wright, Gail Bowen, and Laurence Gough brought murder to British Columbia's Sunshine Coast, the Prairies, and Vancouver, respectively.

This sudden and rapid growth of crime and mystery writing led to the creation of the Crime Writers of Canada in 1983, a national organization established to support the professional writing community in this genre. The inspiration for, and driving force behind, the CWC was Derrick Murdoch, the long-time mystery book reviewer for *The Globe & Mail*. Derrick was highly respected for his urbane and insightful commentary on the genre. He was also a highly regarded non-fiction author of books, including the Edgar-Award-nominated *The Agatha Christie Mystery* and a book about Canadians who vanished under mysterious circumstances called *Disappearances*.

One of the first major decisions of the CWC was the creation of an annual award recognizing the highest level of achievement in crime, mystery, or thriller writing by a Canadian author. Thus, the Arthur Ellis Award was born. Named in dubious honor of Canada's long-serving government hangman — a man whose zeal was matched only by his comparative lack of finesse — the first Arthur Ellis Award was handed out in 1984. The Arthur Ellis Award is unique among literary prizes. In further tribute to its namesake, the award has been designed as a fifteen-inch-high wooden gibbet on a plinth to which an inscribed plaque is attached. From the top of the gibbet hangs a genderless human form, a noose around its neck. The arms and legs dangle loosely with wooden pins at the shoulders, hips, and knees. There's also a string hanging down the figure's back. Pull it and the arms and legs jerk up and down like a child's toy. The award ceremony itself has become the stuff of fiction in a story written by Edgar Award winner Edward D. Hoch called "The Unpleasantness at The Arts and Letters Club," published in the program for the 1992 awards and re-printed by way of an introduction in this anthology.

In 1984, there was but one category in competition for the soon-to-be coveted trophy: Best Novel. The inaugural Arthur went to Eric Wright for his landmark book *The Night the Gods Smiled*, which introduced Charlie Salter to an appreciative public. (Eric went on to win a second Best Novel Arthur two years later for the third Salter book *Death in the Old Country*, as well as two Best Short Story Awards, making him the reigning champion.) Included among the list of finalists for 1986 — a list featuring novels by Maurice Gagnon, Anthony Hyde, John Reeves, Eric Wright, and L.R. Wright — was one non-fiction book, *A Canadian Tragedy*, Maggie Siggins' compelling study of the notorious Thatcher murder case in Saskatchewan. This book was honored with a special Arthur, paving the way for the development of a full-fledged non-fiction category. Best First Novel was added in 1987. And one year later, the Best Short Story Arthur was born, fuelled by the publication of the first book in the *Cold Blood* anthology series.

Prior to the publication of *Cold Blood: Murder in Canada*, there was no regular market for original short crime fiction in this country. A few anthologies had appeared, including the CWC collection *Fingerprints* in 1984, but there was nowhere for authors to submit their stories on any kind of regular basis. *Cold Blood* changed that and soon inspired the publication of several other anthologies, some using reprinted stories, some using original work, some using a combination of both. With the stories that appeared in the initial *Cold Blood* book, plus tales from both *Ellery Queen* and *Alfred Hitchcock* mystery magazines, there were enough entries to establish an award category. With a fitting symmetry, Eric Wright's "Looking for an Honest Man" — from *Cold Blood: Murder in Canada* — captured the inaugural Best Short Story Arthur. Eric's Arthur also came with a handsome cash prize of $1,500, donated by Douwe Egberts, the makers of Amphora pipe tobacco.

Douwe Egbert's President David Salem had been approached with an elaborate presentation that outlined the long standing link between pipe smoking and crime writing. Conan Doyle and

Sherlock Holmes; Georges Simenon and Inspector Maigret; Frederic Dannay and Manfred B. Lee who wrote as Ellery Queen; Raymond Chandler, John D. MacDonald — the list of pipe smoking crime writers and fictional detectives goes on and on. Unfortunately, changing government regulations prevented Douwe Egberts from giving out their prize the following year — but it did help get the Best Short Story Arthur Ellis Award off to a great start.

Now, there are a dozen winning stories to feature in this anthology. The list of authors is diverse and impressive. Included are top names with powerful resumes like Peter Robinson and Eric Wright (with his two winning stories) and fast rising stars such as Mary Jane Maffini, Rosemary Aubert, and Scott Mackay. You'll also find work by both Nancy Kilpatrick, one of Canada's leading horror writers, Josef Skvorecky, one of our most respected literary authors, and Robert J. Sawyer, best known for his award-winning science fiction. Seventeen years in the making since the founding of the Crime Writers of Canada, *The Arthur Ellis Awards* is a collection of work that shows the richness and strength of Canadian crime and mystery writing.

For more information on the Arthur Ellis Awards, and the Crime Writers of Canada, visit the CWC web site at www.crimewriters.com.

The Unpleasantness at the Arts and Letters Club

Barney Hamet had never been to Toronto before, but he liked the city as soon as he saw it from the air, circling to land at the international airport. He could see a grouping of islands in the harbor, and then the giant geodesic dome just offshore, and the sliver of a tower that seemed to reach to heaven. Next to the tower he could see the city's new baseball stadium with its retractable roof sliding gently open to the afternoon sun, and beyond it there were scores of modern buildings that dominated the skyline and looked as if they'd been built only yesterday, their glass and metal sides reflecting the warm May sunshine.

The view from above had been somewhat deceptive. The city wasn't all new, he realized as he passed through older sections whose street signs were in Chinese. There were even trolley tracks on some of the downtown streets, though the trolleys themselves were long slender vehicles that could bend in the middle and moved along their tracks more quietly than any Barney remembered. Out the window of his hotel he could see both the new and the old — the curved, modernistic buildings of the new city hall across the street from the dark stone fortress that had been the old city hall, complete with a clock tower that marked the hours with a tolling bell.

Barney was looking at these when a knock on his door signalled the arrival of his welcoming committee. He opened the door with a smile and admitted a short, blond woman in her early forties who seemed to be a bundle of energy. The tall balding man who trailed behind her said nothing at first.

"Mr. Hamet? Welcome to Toronto! I'm Dora Pratt from the Crime Writers of Canada. It's a pleasure to have you up here for our awards dinner. I've admired your work for a long time."

Barney couldn't return the compliment because he wasn't really familiar with anything of hers. "Toronto is a lovely city," he replied. "I can't imagine how I've avoided coming here this long."

"Well, you're here now, and —" She suddenly remembered her companion. "Oh, this is Roger Yourly. He writes the Captain Collins books."

Barney had read those. "A pleasure, Roger," he said, shaking hands. "I've enjoyed your work, especially *One Home Free*."

The tall man managed a shy smile. "Coming from you, that's a very nice compliment. I sometimes wonder if anyone reads them outside my family."

"I thought I'd run over tonight's dinner with you," Dora Pratt said, resuming her conversation. "As you know, it's at the Arts and Letters Club on Elm Street, a fine old building."

"So old it's being renovated," Yourly interjected. "We hope it'll be finished in time for next year's awards dinner."

"How many do you get for the awards?" Barney asked. He was used to the Mystery Writers of America's Edgar dinner in New York, which sometimes attracted close to a thousand people.

"Only about a hundred," Dora Pratt replied. "I believe there were ninety-eight last year. We don't always have a speaker. Often we just present the awards and it's over. But when you were so gracious as to accept our invitation —"

"Believe me, I'll keep my remarks short."

"You've not only been a private detective and a successful mystery writer, but I understand you've solved a couple of mysteries in recent years."

"There was a killing at the Edgar dinner many years back, and a death at the New York hotel where the Bouchercon fan convention was being held. I helped out on those."

"So that's why you wanted him!" Roger Yourly said, addressing the woman. "You think he can protect you." Dora Pratt blushed and Barney said, "What's this?"

"Her life has been threatened, Mr. Hamet. Someone wants to kill her, probably tonight."

Barney Hamet sometimes wondered how he got so involved in other people's troubles. Though Dora Pratt strongly denied the connection, there did seem to be some relation between the anonymous threats to her life and the invitation she'd extended, as chairman of the dinner committee, for him to speak at the CWC awards dinner.

"I don't take them seriously," she insisted. "A few letters to the newspaper where I work, that's all. I'm a critic, really, and one with a passion for mysteries. I do a mystery review column for the weekend edition, every Saturday. Some months back these notes started arriving, threatening to kill me on the night of the CWC dinner."

"Someone didn't like her reviews," Yourly commented dryly.

"That's nonsense! If anything, I'm too kind to the mysteries I review. I rarely dislike anything."

"Any other enemies?" Barney asked. It was merely a casual question. He didn't really plan to get involved.

"None of whom I'm aware. But then I suppose everyone has enemies."

"I'm surprised they allow critics into CWC."

"I wrote a true crime book ten years ago, about executioners — the Sanson family in France, Arthur Ellis in Canada. He was our hangman, you know. The CWC awards are named after him."

"She's very active in the organization," Yourly explained. "Dora is a great publicist for the mystery."

"What time do things start tonight?" Barney asked.

"The bar opens at 6:30 and dinner is at eight. They beat a wonderful gong for dinner, just like in an Agatha Christie mystery."

"Fine, I'll be there. And don't worry about my boring the guests. I'll speak no longer than fifteen or twenty minutes."

"Then we'll look for you this evening."

Barney shook hands with them both and saw them to the door.

He dressed in the new gray suit his wife had insisted he wear, and set off across Nathan Phillips Square by city hall. He'd wanted Susan to come with him to Toronto, but she had a writing career of her own to pursue. Just then she was involved in a project to start a new slick magazine for women over forty, and it was taking all of her time. Barney was lucky if he saw her one evening a week for dinner.

Dora Pratt had given him directions to the Arts and Letters Club, and he cut through the Eaton Centre, a multilevel shopping mall that ran on for several blocks, its vaulted glass ceiling reaching to the sky like a European galleria. He left Eaton Centre at Dundas Street and walked north on Yonge, which seemed to be the city's liveliest thoroughfare. Elm Street was just two blocks north, and the dark brick building of the Arts and Letters Club was halfway down the block on the north side. Barney mounted the stone steps to the big wooden door with its brass nameplate that was the club's only identification.

Just inside the door was a registration table where an attractive, efficient young woman greeted him. She must have recognized him from his pictures because she immediately said, "Welcome to Toronto, Mr. Hamet. I'm Constance Quinn, with CWC. It's a pleasure to meet you at last. I've enjoyed your books for years."

She made him feel like an old man, but he smiled graciously and told her, "It's a wonderful city you have here."

Constance handed him a blank card. "We have open seating for dinner. You can write your name on this card and place it where you'd like to sit. There's a cash bar now, and a free drink for everyone after the awards."

"Thank you." He glanced around for a familiar face. The entrance hall had a scattering of people and he recognized Ted Wood, a former member of the Toronto police force whose Reid Bennett mysteries were popular in the States. He shook hands with Ted and then turned back to the young woman at the desk. "Has Dora Pratt arrived yet?"

"She has. In fact, she was the first arrival. I spoke with her while I was setting up my table around six o'clock."

He nodded. "I'll find her."

The rooms just off the entrance hall seemed to be a library, though just now the bookshelves were bare and the center of the two connecting rooms was filled with large sealed boxes. A discreet sign asked the members' indulgence while renovations were under way.

Barney purchased a glass of white wine at the bar at one end of the room and went to join Eric Wright and Howard Engel, both of whom he knew well from their attendance at the Edgar dinners in New York. He was chatting with Howard about the Canadian TV films made from a couple of his mysteries when Eric introduced him to Medora Sale, CWC's president.

He was still talking with them when Mary Frisque from New York came up to speak with Eric Wright about the next gathering of the International Association of Crime Writers, of which Mary was the North American executive director. Barney had known Mary for several years, since she'd been executive secretary of MWA. He saw that another New Yorker was in attendance too — Carol Brener, who recently sold her Murder Ink bookstore to a new owner.

In the midst of all this conversation, Roger Yourly appeared, looking concerned. "Barney, have you seen Dora Pratt around?"

"I've been looking for her myself. She's here someplace."

Yourly shrugged. "I'll keep looking."

From the hallway a gong sounded. He followed the others into the Great Hall where the tables were set for dinner. It was a relatively small room by New York standards, but its high cathedral ceiling and dark wooden beams, set off by colorful banners and leaded glass windows, looked like something from an English castle. There was a stage at the far end of the dining hall, but its maroon curtain was closed and the rostrum for the evening's speeches was set on the floor in front of it.

Barney found himself seated with Jack Paris and his wife. Paris was a Toronto advertising man who edited an annual anthology of new Canadian mysteries. Each table was set for ten, and he was pleased to see an old acquaintance, James Powell, with his wife. Powell was a Canadian short story writer who lived in Pennsylvania. Across the table were a couple of Toronto booksellers, Al Navis, owner of the Handy Book Exchange, and J.D. Singh from the highly regarded Sleuth of Baker Street. They and others had donated books as door prizes, and Barney won a copy of *The Suspect* by Vancouver novelist L.R. Wright. The novel had won an Edgar a few years back and she was present to give one of the evening's awards. He sought out her table and introduced himself, and she signed the copy of her book.

Uniformed waitresses were already bringing around plates of smoked Atlantic salmon as the appetizer and Barney was just sitting down when Yourly intercepted him again. "She's nowhere in the building!"

Barney was nothing if not practical. "Did you check the ladies' room? Come on, I'll help you search again."

Constance Quinn was just leaving her desk at the front door and they enlisted her to check the ladies' room downstairs by the coat rack. It was empty and she invited Barney in to take a look himself. He checked the men's room too, a bit surprised to find a large reproduction of the *Mona Lisa* on one wall.

"You're certain she didn't leave by the front door?" Barney asked Constance. "Perhaps you were busy with someone —"

"No, no," she insisted. "I'd certainly have noticed Dora."

They checked all floors of the building, squeezing by boxes that lined the hallways in preparation for remodeling. The small stage area was completely empty, cut off from diners by a beige curtain. Downstairs in the kitchen the catered meal was being arranged on plates for serving. "What's the main course?" Barney asked.

"Roast duck," Yourly replied.

The supervisor from the catering firm, a buxom woman named Clare, assured them that no one had left through the back service door, the only other way out of the building. "I've been here all the time. None of the guests came down here except Mr. Yourly."

Barney turned to Constance Quinn. "What was Dora wearing tonight?"

"A peach-colored wrap-around dress. It really looked good on her."

"Notice anyone like that?" Clare shook her head. "How many dinners are you serving tonight?"

The woman glanced at a typed sheet with penciled corrections. "Ninety-eight. There are a hundred places set but two are unoccupied."

Barney turned to Constance. "Who's missing besides Dora?"

"The only one not checked off my list is William Sloefoot. He's a Mohawk writer from the St. Regis Indian Reservation."

"The St. Regis Reservation straddles the U.S. and Canadian border," Yourly explained. "You've probably read about their troubles over gambling. Some people have been killed. Sloefoot is working with Dora on a true crime book about it. He came to Toronto with another Mohawk writer."

"Is the other writer here tonight?" Barney asked.

"He should be."

Constance nodded. "Harold Norfolk. I remember checking him off."

"Let's see if we can find him," Barney suggested. "He may have had some conversation with Dora."

They went back to the Great Hall where Barney discovered he'd missed most of the meal. It reminded him of the time he'd missed the meal at an Edgar dinner while helping to search for a lost carton of MWA Annuals, the glossy program book that should have been at everyone's place. Those had finally been located in the hotel kitchen's walk-in freezer, mistaken for a delivery of frozen food. There'd been no place in the kitchen here that was large enough to conceal Dora Pratt.

Constance wove her way between the tables with Barney following along. She paused once, uncertain, then plunged forward to tap a large blackhaired man on the shoulder. "Mr. Norfolk, I'd like you to meet Barney Hamet. He's come up from New York to speak to us tonight."

Harold Norfolk rose to his feet, towering above Barney's near six-feet. He had the chiseled features of a native American, with deep dark eyes that seemed to be watching something just over the horizon. "I'm honored to meet you, Mr. Hamet. You're a fine writer."

"It's a pleasure to be in Toronto. This is quite a lively organization up here. I don't want to take you away from your dinner, but I wanted to ask you about William Sloefoot. I understand you came here together for the awards dinner, and to see Dora Pratt."

"Willy's back in the hotel room," Norfolk said with the hint of a smirk. "He said his stomach was upset. Maybe he was expecting a visitor, though Dora told us not to tell anyone what hotel we were at."

"What about Dora? Did you speak with her?"

The tall Mohawk shook his head. "Haven't seen her since I arrived."

Dessert was finished and the CWC president was about to introduce Barney as the evening's speaker. "I'll see you after the awards," he told Norfolk.

The Crime Writers of Canada did not have a speaker every year, though Barney knew that Julian Symons had spoken at one of their dinners a few years back. Medora Sale introduced him most graciously and he was greeted with a welcoming round of applause. All through the next twenty minutes, as he spoke about the ties between Canadian and American writers, and the future of the mystery novel, he kept expecting to see Dora Pratt come through the door. There was no sign of her, and nobody but Roger Yourly seemed unduly upset at her absence.

After his talk, the awards themselves were presented. A wooden figure with hinged arms and legs, suspended from a miniature gallows by a hangman's noose, the Arthur Ellis Award was presented for the best novel, first novel, nonfiction and short story by a Canadian writer. The awards in Canada were different from the Edgars, having sponsors like Parker Pen, Worldwide Library and Sleuth of Baker Street Books who contributed cash prizes. When the brief ceremony was concluded, Barney sought out Harold Norfolk again.

The tall Mohawk was easy to spot in the crowd at the bar. Barney drew him aside and asked, "What is this book your friend and Dora are working on?"

Norfolk sighed, as if tired of telling the story. "It's about the trouble over gambling at our reservation. You've probably read about it in the American press. The St. Regis Reservation straddles the border up by the St. Lawrence River, and on the American side there are eight gambling casinos. The tribal council ruling the U.S. side supports the casinos, but there is a strong anti-gambling element there as well. This has led to shootings and killings on both sides. Willy has been writing a book about it, and Dora offered to help. She'd had a true crime book published some years back —"

"About executioners."

"Right! So he thinks he can use her help writing it and getting a publisher. She's already shown the manuscript to one company."

"She told me earlier today that there'd been some threats against her life."

"We know about those. We've all had them. Willy and me both."

"Some of your fellow Mohawks?"

"Well, we live on the Canadian side of the reservation. We're not with the gamblers, but there are times when you can understand their viewpoint. Unemployment is high on the reservation. There's very little for a young man to do unless he wants to work on high steel in New York, building skyscrapers. The casinos give them jobs. Unfortunately they also lead to prostitution and drug-running. It's relatively easy to bring drugs in on the Canadian side and cross over to the American side of the reservation."

"The threats said something might happen to Dora tonight, at the awards dinner."

"Nothing did."

"Except that she disappeared."

Barney took his drink and wandered back into the Great Hall where the dinner had been held. The caterer's people were cleaning up now, collecting plates and silverware and glasses. In Dora's unexplained absence, Constance Quinn was supervising things. She glanced up and saw Barney staring up at the ceiling. "This is quite a room, isn't it?"

"Very impressive," Barney agreed. He could imagine sword fights in a room like this, but then he'd always had a vivid imagination.

"What about Dora?" she asked. "Any word?"

"No. I suppose she just fell ill and went home. She might have been in the ladies' room for a time, then left by the front door after you quit your station to help us search."

"No. I spoke with three people who were in the front hall or seated in a direct line of vision with the door. They all swear no one went out, and they all know Dora well."

"Well," he decided, "maybe I should look some more." A stray thought crossed his mind. Was this all some sort of game they were playing, to baffle the great American mystery writer? No, they didn't seem like that sort, nor had Dora.

He went back to the bookless library and glanced around. Both rooms were small, made even more so by the boxes piled in their center. But now at least the crowd was smaller as people called out their goodbyes and headed for home. He noticed a row of books on a bottom shelf, overlooked by the renovators, and bent to examine their titles. Still in that position, he heard a voice in the entrance hall say, "A body has been found."

Barney rose so quickly he almost bumped his head. In the outer hall, by the doorway, stood two men in suits who could only have been police officers. One of them was speaking with Roger Yourly.

"What's going on?" Barney asked. "Is it Dora?"

"This man is Sergeant Baxter," Yourly said, introducing Barney. "He's looking for Harold Norfolk."

The tall Mohawk must have heard his name spoken. He stepped out from a room across the hall. "I'm Norfolk. What is it?"

Baxter turned to him. "Are you occupying room 425 at the Summit Hotel around the corner?"

"Yes I am."

"With a Mr. William Sloefoot?"

"Yes."

"I'm sorry, sir. We'll have to ask you to come with us. William Sloefoot has been found dead in your room. It appears he's been murdered."

It was Roger Yourly who first raised the question of a connection between Sloefoot's death and Dora's disappearance. "Did someone from the reservation follow Sloefoot and Norfolk here, to kill all three of them?"

"We don't even know that she's dead," Constance pointed out. Some of the others had gathered around too, having overheard the detective's announcement. For the first time, word of Dora's disappearance began to spread. An elderly man who seemed to be a member of the club rather than the CWC was heard to mutter something about "this unpleasantness."

"I want to look one more time," Barney said. "I'm convinced she's here somewhere. After all, if she didn't leave, she *must* be here!"

"And now it's more crucial than ever that we find her," Yourly said. "She might be lying wounded somewhere."

"How was Sloefoot killed?" someone asked.

"Shot in the head," Barney answered. "The detective said he managed to knock the phone to the floor and gasp something to the operator. When security investigated, they found his body, shortly after eight o'clock. They didn't know where his roommate was until Baxter found the unused dinner invitation in the dead man's pocket. That's when they came here and located Norfolk."

There were about a dozen of them still remaining from the dinner, and Barney split them into teams to search the building once more. He and Constance took the main floor, but found nothing new. He was about to abandon the search when his eyes strayed to the big sealed boxes in the library. "Constance —"

"What is it?"

"Dora's quite small. I think she could even fit into one of these boxes if her legs were folded."

She shook her head. "The boxes were sealed like that when we arrived."

"But notice that row of books on the bottom shelf. Couldn't someone have emptied a box to make room for her body?"

She motioned toward the bartenders at the end of the room. "They would have seen it."

"You told me you arrived a half-hour early, and Dora arrived while you were setting up your table by the front door. The bartenders wouldn't have been on duty yet at that time."

"But I was at my table, not twenty feet away!" she argued.

"You can't see in here from the front door. You wouldn't have noticed what was happening." Already he'd taken a little pen knife from his pocket and was slitting the tape that sealed the top box.

Barney had an instant fear of what he might find as he lifted the cardboard flaps, but he needn't have worried. There were only books inside.

"Try the other boxes," Constance suggested.

They were all the same. Whatever had happened to Dora Pratt, the answer was not to be found here. Frustrated, Barney lifted out the top book in one of the boxes and saw that it was Chesterton's *The Innocence of Father Brown*. "He would have known what to do with this mystery," Barney commented. "But I certainly don't."

Yourly and his team of searchers came down from the second floor. "She's nowhere up there," he announced. The gong in the hallway sounded and he glanced at his watch. "Eleven o'clock. I think they want us out of here."

Barney moved reluctantly toward the front door. "Where could she be, Roger?"

Yourly glanced around and lowered his voice. "You're overlooking the most obvious answer. Dora was never here in the first place. We have only Constance Quinn's word that she arrived."

"Why should she lie?"

"I don't know," he admitted.

Barney paused at the front door, remembering something. "Before we go, let's check one more place."

"Where's that?"

"The curtain on the stage."

"We looked on both sides of it."

"Yes, but it's maroon on this side and beige on the other. It could be a lining, or —"

"Or what?"

"There might be two curtains with a little space between them. Let's take a look."

Barney crossed the Great Hall and leaped onto the low stage, pulling open the heavy maroon curtain. The lighter beige one was about a foot behind it, and in the space between them he saw Dora Pratt's body. He'd never been so sorry about guessing correctly. "She's here!" he shouted back to Yourly. "Get help!"

"Is she dead?"

Barney could smell the pungent traces of chloroform on the rag by her feet. "She might be alive. Give me a hand with her."

Someone had already called an ambulance and the others gathered around while Barney did his best to revive her. "There's a pulse, at least. That's something."

"Who would have done such a thing?"

"Perhaps the same person who killed William Sloefoot."

❖

Barney was awakened in his hotel room early the next morning by the ringing of the phone. It took him a moment to remember where he was, in this unfamiliar bed, and then he rolled over and reached for the phone. It was barely past eight o'clock.

"Hello?"

"Mr. Hamet? This is Sergeant Baxter. We met last night."

"Yes, Sergeant. How is Miss Pratt this morning?"

"She's fine. They kept her overnight at the hospital but she'll be released this morning. I understand you're the one who found her and I wonder if we might have a cup of coffee together. I'd like to get your opinions."

"I'm a writer, not a detective, but I'll be glad to tell you what little I know."

"Fine. Shall we meet in your lobby? Say, twenty minutes?"

Barney agreed and then scrambled out of bed to shower and dress in the allotted time. He was only a minute or two late and Baxter was waiting. Barney needed breakfast but the detective just ordered a cup of coffee as promised. "They tell me, Mr. Hamet, that you've had some success with detective work in the past."

"I was a private detective for a time before I became a writer. I wouldn't call that a success, though."

"I was thinking of one or two more recent occasions."

Barney grinned. "Someone's been talking to you."

"They say you figured out where that woman was last night, after the building had been searched several times."

"I was lucky."

"Could you figure out who chloroformed her, and why?"

"Someone wanted to get her out of the way, either temporarily or permanently. Enough chloroform could kill a person, you know."

Baxter nodded. "You see this as connected with Sloefoot's murder?"

"I never met any of these people before yesterday, Sergeant. In fact, I never met Sloefoot at all before he died. But he was working on a true crime book with Dora Pratt, about the killings at the St. Regis Indian Reservation, and it would be quite a coincidence if two different assailants chose last night to attack them both."

"I spoke to her in the hospital. She tells me her life was threatened. Do you know anything about that?"

"Just what she told me. She reviews books and we kidded about her having given some author a bad review." He took a sip of his orange juice. "Did she tell you what happened to her last night?"

"She arrived early at the Arts and Letters Club to check on arrangements. Constance Quinn was the only one she spoke with. The others were just beginning to arrive when she went backstage to see if it would be possible to open the curtains and move the rostrum up on stage. That's when someone grabbed her from behind —a man, she thinks — and she woke up on her way to the hospital."

"Does she know about Sloefoot?"

"I told her. She couldn't suggest a motive for it, unless the pro-gambling forces back on the reservation want to keep the book from being published."

"I suppose that's a possibility," Barney admitted.

"Any other ideas?"

"Not really. I could speak to the other Mohawk, Harold Norfolk, again. And I should see Dora before I return home. If I learn anything I'll let you know. One question — how does the timing work out on the two attacks?"

"Near as we can tell, Miss Pratt was chloroformed around 6:30. She said other people were just beginning to arrive for drinks before the awards dinner. Sloefoot's death is pegged at 8:05, although it's possible it could have been somewhat earlier that the actual shot was fired."

"Why is that?"

"He was near death and had to crawl to the phone. The call to the hotel switchboard came at 8:05, but we're not certain how long he might have lived."

"What does your medical examiner say?"

"That he couldn't have lived at all with that wound, but the doctors are often wrong, too."

Baxter finished his coffee and departed, pausing only to ask Barney when he'd be returning to New York. "Tomorrow noon," Barney told him. "I have to get back to my writing."

❖

He caught Dora as she was about to leave St. Michael's Hospital, just a few blocks from the Arts and Letters Club. "I'm waiting for Constance to pick me up," she told him, seated on the bed in her room.

"You had quite an experience. Do you think it was the person who threatened you?"

"I don't know. I feel terrible about William. He never believed the threats that his life was in danger."

"What about Harold Norfolk? Is he working on the book too?"

"Not on the actual writing. He's given us some valuable research and background material, though."

"Do you remember anything at all about your assailant that could provide a clue?"

"Not really —"

"Sergeant Baxter said you thought it was a man who attacked you."

"Well, yes. It was a strong person, and taller than me. But I suppose that could apply to many women as well."

Barney frowned. "The problem, as I see it, is that if the same person chloroformed you and shot Sloefoot, as the police believe, how did he or she leave the Arts and Letters Club? When we were searching for you last night, we pretty much established that no one could have left the Club without being seen."

"Sort of like Chesterton's invisible man."

He remembered the Father Brown volume he'd seen in the opened box of books. Just then Constance Quinn arrived, looking tall and cool in the flowery blouse and dark skirt. "Ready to go home, Dora?"

"I certainly am!"

Constance turned to Barney. "It's been a pleasure meeting you, Mr. Hamet. I hope you haven't gotten the impression that CWC's affairs are always like this. We're quite a staid group most of the time."

He left them and headed for the Summit Hotel where the two Mohawk writers had been staying, but at the desk he learned that Norfolk had checked out. As he came out of the lobby he recognized a woman just getting out of a little car halfway down the block. It was Clare, from the catering service, with whom he'd spoken last night.

"Oh, Mr. Hamet, isn't it?"

"You have a good memory for names. Are you catering another affair today?"

"Not at the Arts Club. I think they'll be pretty much closed down until they finish their renovations. No, I just came by to pick up one of our big serving trays that they forgot last night."

She went in through the unlocked backdoor and Barney followed her. The kitchen area was quiet now, though he could hear the sounds of workmen on the floor above. Clare picked up the tray and glanced out through the swinging door at the stairs that led up to the Great Hall. "Oh, one of the girls left her uniform. I'd better take that too." She lifted the hanger from its rack. "Size six. One of the smaller girls."

"The queer feet," Barney said, half to himself.

"What's that?"

"Just thinking out loud. Do me a favor, will you, and leave that here for a little while."

"What for?"

"I think someone else might come by for it."

"Well — all right. I suppose it's the responsibility of whoever left it."

She went out with her tray and Barney went around behind the staircase, out of sight of anyone who entered. For a time, silence descended on the club's lower level, broken only by occasional hammering from above. He had just about decided to give up the wait when he heard the street door open and someone quietly enter.

"Good morning, Mr. Norfolk."

The tall Mohawk turned, startled to hear Barney's voice. "What are you doing here?"

"I might ask you the same thing. I was looking for you at your hotel."

"I checked out. I'm heading back to St. Regis."

"Is this on the way?"

"Willy's manuscript was missing from our room. I thought it might be here someplace."

"The manuscript he and Dora Pratt were working on? Why would it be here? To my knowledge the dead man never set foot in the Arts and Letters Club."

"If the killer took the manuscript, and the killer was someone from here, he might have brought it back here."

"You know who killed your friend, don't you?"

"I've got a good idea."

Barney heard the street door opening again and pulled Norfolk out of sight behind the staircase. For a moment there was silence, and then the swinging door was pushed open. Norfolk broke free of Barney's restraining hand and dashed forward.

"You killed him, didn't you? You killed Willy!"

"Stay away from me."

"I'll make you pay for it!"

Barney had wanted the scene to play itself out, but then he saw the gun and knew he could wait no longer. He leaped forward and brought his hand down hard on Dora Pratt's wrist. The weapon flew from her grip and clattered onto the floor.

"No more killing, Dora," Barney said. "Once was too much."

It was Norfolk who supplied the motive when Sergeant Baxter had arrived to make the arrest. "She'd stolen his manuscript," he said. "Willy wrote that whole thing about the Reservation killings without any help from her. She took the manuscript and tried to pass it off as her own. That was what she meant by collaboration — he wrote it and she collected the money."

"Is that true?" Baxter asked her.

Dora Pratt stared off into the distance. "I'll wait for my lawyer before I answer any questions."

"Lady, if this is the gun that killed William Sloefoot, your lawyer won't do you much good."

"That's the gun, all right," Barney said. "She had this briefcase with her too, and inside you'll find the other copy of Sloefoot's manuscript. She took it from the room when she killed him. See this tag on the briefcase? She put the manuscript and gun inside and then checked it with a bellman in the lobby on the way out. When she got out of the hospital this morning, and as soon as she could get away from Constance Quinn, she returned to the hotel to pick up the briefcase. Then she came here to get this uniform."

Baxter seemed puzzled at the mention of the uniform. "What's that got to do with it?"

"The uniform explains how she could leave this building and re-enter it without being seen, or at least without being noticed. This whole affair seemed like something out of Chesterton and it was. Not *The Invisible Man* but *The Queer Feet*. Remember that Father Brown tale about the thief who was mistaken for a waiter by the guests and for a guest by the waiters? This was a bit different, but it worked on a similar principle. Dora came to the awards dinner early, making sure she was seen by at least one person — Constance, in this case. Beneath her wrap-around dress she wore a duplicate of the uniform worn by the caterer's waitresses. After speaking with Constance, she shed the dress in an instant downstairs, hiding it somewhere near the ladies' room. Then she walked into the kitchen, where a dozen other women, wearing the same uniform, were preparing to serve the first course. They'd been hired for the occasion. Most of them probably knew each other, but no one would think twice about an unfamiliar face. Even Clare, the woman in charge, might not spot her immediately as a fake. And of course Dora didn't linger. She simply walked across that room and out the door, as if she were going after more food."

Baxter turned to stare at Dora Pratt but her expression didn't change. "Then she killed Sloefoot?"

"Exactly. The hotel was just around the corner, remember. She killed Sloefoot, checked the briefcase, and returned to the Arts and Letters Club exactly as she'd left, through the kitchen. This time she had to change in the ladies' room because she couldn't be wearing the waitress uniform under her clothes when they found her unconscious. She hung up the uniform and probably emptied a small vial of chloroform onto a rag. The vial was flushed down the toilet and she took the rag upstairs with her, backstage. She hid between the stage curtains, took a sniff of the rag and knocked herself out. She was counting on someone finding her, of course, and helping establish her alibi. The supposed threats on her life were more of the same advance planning."

"How did you know all this?" Baxter asked.

"Sloefoot skipped the dinner and remained in his room, which implied an appointment with the person who killed him. On the surface none of the people at the dinner seemed able to have left the club without being seen, but I kept looking for a way.

I was present this morning when Clare came upon that extra uniform, and it showed me an almost Chestertonian way in which it could have been done. But the uniform was an extremely small size, which really eliminated a man or a tall woman like Constance Quinn. In fact, the only small woman we knew about with ties to the dead man was his collaborator, Dora Pratt. Was there verification? Yes, in at least two areas. You told me yourself, Norfolk, that Dora didn't want anyone to know what hotel you were at. Yet the killer knew. And second, there's the matter of the dying man's phone call which the medical examiner says he couldn't have made. If he didn't make it the killer did. Why? Because it was essential to her alibi that the time of death be recorded. No one at the dinner had a better alibi than Dora, unconscious behind that curtain."

"You'll have trouble proving all that," she said.

Sergeant Baxter shook his head. "We've got the gun, and the stolen manuscript. And I'll bet we can find a hotel bellman who remembers a short woman in a waitress's uniform checking a briefcase last evening."

Back at his hotel the phone was ringing as Barney entered his room. It was James Powell, calling to see if he was enjoying his stay in Toronto.

Looking for an Honest Man

When Fred Dawson's wife proposed a week in the sun before the Canadian winter set in, she was surprised at his immediate agreement. Dawson had always balked at do-nothing holidays. He liked travelling, enjoyed sitting in foreign cafés, talking to strangers, riding on ferries; but lying on a beach, trying to avoid skin cancer, surrounded by women of his own age (fifty-seven) wearing nose-guards, was something he found boring and ignominious. This time, though, he said yes, so long as they chose a beach that did not have to be heavily-guarded to keep out the poverty-stricken natives. He agreed on condition he chose the island they would go to.

For Dawson had a hidden agenda. A holiday in the Caribbean was an opportunity to satisfy a dream that had been growing for twenty years. At his age he was reconciled to the setting aside of most of his early ambitions: he accepted that he would never now try sky-diving, or ride a racehorse in a steeplechase, or jig unself-consciously in a disco, or make love in a shower. But if he chose the right island, he would, finally, be able to visit a casino.

Dawson was a gambler, modest but dedicated, who lived in Toronto, where the opportunities for gambling are very limited. He visited the two race tracks occasionally, but his family and other interests made competing demands on his time on the week-ends, and he was not so addicted that he was prepared to upset his life in order to bet. Sociologists tell us that a man who "needs" one drink a day before dinner is an alcoholic, and by this criterion Dawson should have been a member of Gamblers Anonymous. He needed a small bet from time to time to stay happy. For him off-track betting would have been ideal — half an hour to study the morning line, a call at the betting shop in the lunch hour, and the excitement of opening the next day's paper to check the results. But Ontario politicians fear the issue and handle it by proliferating government lotteries. Dawson bought tickets to all the lotteries that were available and he played poker every Friday with a group of accountants and customs brokers where the maximum raise was a dollar except for the last hand when it was five. Dawson did not repine. He could satisfy his needs, more or less, and he was wary of his ability to control himself if Toronto ever became the Atlantic City of Canada. But he did want to visit a casino before he got too old to travel, without the expense of flying down to Vegas with the big players. A week, he thought, was probably just enough time for him to get settled in, find out where the casino was, circle the idea conversationally for a few days, and make the plunge, probably on the Friday before they returned.

He spent most of an afternoon in a travel agent's office where he was able to read his way through all the brochures, and he narrowed his choice down to three islands, all of which mentioned casinos. He suspected there were others but none of the publicity he read made much fuss about the availability of any form of gambling, from which he surmised that casinos were like the kind of night-life available in pre-Castro Cuba: anyone interested knew all about them, and the resorts could safely rely on word of mouth. So he raised the subject, casually, with his Friday night poker group and sure enough got a firm recommendation which he passed on to his wife, without telling her where the recommendation came from. He did mention, as an afterthought, that he would like to drop in to a casino for an hour, and she shrugged cheerfully enough. His gambling had been the smallest of hobbies within the family, no more expensive or time-consuming than if he played in an amateur string quartet, and beyond forgetting occasionally to leave his Fridays clear, she hardly thought about it. It was enough for her to be going on vacation. For his part, Dawson was as excited as he had been twenty years before when he had visited an English racecourse and learned how to bet with the bookmakers on the course.

They arrived on Saturday and spent the weekend establishing themselves in their room and on the beach. Dawson was more gregarious than usual, hoping by chatting up the other guests to meet someone who knew casino etiquette (Was a tie required, as at Monte Carlo? Did you have to watch your wallet? Did you pay to go in?) and on Sunday evening, at the bar by the pool, he struck up a conversation with an amiable piston-ring manufacturer from Wilmington, North Carolina who raised the subject himself. He had just come back from the casino after "dropping a couple of hundred" and Dawson was easily able to find out much of what he wanted to know. He couldn't conceal his interest, or his innocence, sufficiently to fool the manufacturer who recognized a fellow addict and offered to take him along the next night and show him the ropes. Dawson backed off: Monday was too soon because it involved the risk that if everything went well Dawson would go back Tuesday and every evening of their stay. He also wanted to go alone, as he went to the races, not wanting to discuss his betting with anyone else, and he therefore stuck to his intention of going on Friday, the night before they were to return, and told his wife so in order that she wouldn't make any social arrangements with any of the other guests. Friday, they agreed, was his night.

When the day came, Dawson had made all his decisions. Minimum stakes, of course, and only blackjack and the fruit machines. He planned to lose two hundred dollars (if he won that much he would quit), but just in case, he had another two hundred in his sock, held in place with a rubber band. He left his wallet and his credit cards in his room so that the worst that could happen to him would be that his pocket might be picked of the two hundred, and he could afford that. He had made similar arrangements on the one and only time he had visited a prostitute in Paris, thirty years before, guessing what she might charge, doubling it just in case, then putting an equivalent sum in his shoe to avoid haggling. He had underestimated the price that time, but had still emerged without having to take off his shoes. Now he added ten dollars for cab fares and made his way to the hotel lobby. The rest was easy. There was a line of cabs in front of the door, all of them going to the casino, and Dawson shared a ride with three other men.

He was stunned by the casino at first. The intensity with which the front of the building was lit was intimidating, but he allowed himself to be carried through the doors by the continual surge of arriving gamblers, and only caught his breath inside the door. The scene before him went far beyond what he had imagined. Literally hundreds of fruit machines glittered in rows like a giant supermarket, shining, spinning, spewing out coins; dozens of blackjack tables; half a dozen dice games ringed with shouting players, and at least four roulette wheels; while in a corner, railed off from the crowd, a group of baccarat players were silently absorbed in the ultimate purity of the quest.

When he became used to the hubbub, Dawson began to circle the room, watching. He was apalled and excited by the twenty-five dollar minimum of the first blackjack tables he came to — a poor run of luck would wipe him out in five minutes — but he was getting most of what he came for just by watching, and he changed the limit of his loss to four hundred, all he had. It was going to be worth it. Then he came across a blackjack table with a five dollar limit and sat down to play.

In five minutes he had lost fifty dollars, and he played automatically for a couple of hands while he tried to calculate how best to maximize his pleasure. Losing the money was only slightly less exciting than winning, but he worried about using himself up too fast. If he carried on at the present rate he would only last about half an hour, and now he wanted to stay at least until midnight. There were the fruit machines to be tried, and now, just possibly, a try at the roulette table after all. Already, watching was no longer satisfying enough. Having written off the four hundred to clear his emotions, he now allowed his mind to play with the possibility that tonight was his night, that he might make a killing. It didn't matter if he didn't; but it would be terrific if he did.

While he was sorting himself out, his luck turned and ten minutes later he had won back his fifty and seventy-five more. He moved to a table with twenty-five dollar stakes and lost fifty on the first hand and paused, twenty-five dollars ahead, to calm down. He needed a drink but he was not sure how to go about it. Waitresses appeared regularly to take orders; money changed hands, but not always, and he couldn't tell if the drinks were free, and the bills being dropped on the tray were tips, or if some of the players were running a tab, so he left the table and made his way to one of the bars. He bought a roll of silver dollars and fed some fruit machines along the way, but got nothing back, and by the time he was seated at the bar with a drink in front of him he was seven dollars ahead. This is the life, he thought. But the thrill of being inside a casino had subsided and been replaced by the desire to make a killing.

Another man appeared on the stool beside him — a good-looking, carefully-groomed man in a dark-gray suit with a slightly metallic lustre — like a television actor playing a banker — and nodded to him. "How're you making out?" he asked.

"I'm ahead," Dawson said. "Some," he added. He had meant to say "a few dollars" but "some" sounded more colloquial in a casino.

The banker looked pleased for him and ordered them both another drink. "This your first time? On the island, I mean."

Glad that the man did not mean "in a casino," Dawson nodded.

"Pretty nice casino," the man said. "Better than Atlantic City."

Dawson agreed. "Quieter," he suggested tentatively.

"That's it," the man said. "I think they mute the bandits a little. Nice."

They sipped their beer in silence for a few minutes, two old gamblers taking five. Then the man said, "I think you're the guy I've been looking for. You want to make some money?"

Dawson wanted to leave immediately and be translated back to North Toronto. He forced himself to respond. "What do you mean? How am I the guy you're looking for?"

"I need a partner. All you have to do is play a slot machine. When it pays off, pick up the money and meet me back here for the split."

Dawson looked around the bar, hoping to see someone he knew, but there were only two other drinkers, neither within earshot.

"Okay?" the banker asked.

"Okay what? I don't know what you're talking about. Why me?"

"Keep your voice down. You look like a guy who'd stay cool, but I could be wrong. I'll spell it out. One of the machines is going to pay off with a small jackpot soon. How do I know? Let's just say I've captured the circuitry." Here the man took out a small black box from an inside pocket. It was about the size of a compact disc container with a set of buttons on one side, numbered from one to ten. "I can punch up the jackpot anytime I want. But I need a partner." He put the box away. "They see me out there with this thing, I'm a dead man." He smiled reassuringly. "Not literally. They don't do that here. But I can operate remote. I've been working this thing up a long time."

Dawson swallowed some beer. "Let me be sure what you're saying. I go out there, operate one of the fruit machines, and you make it pay off. Right? Then I give you half."

"That's right."

"How much? How much will it be?"

"It'll pay off three thousand; fifteen hundred each. Just enough not to be too conspicuous. You cash in and meet me back in here."

"What are you?" Dawson blurted out. "The Wizard?"

The banker laughed. "I'm a guy who has figured out how to beat the odds, that's all."

"Christ," Dawson said. "Jesus Christ." Then, "How will you know it's me working the machine?"

"We'll time it. I can make that baby pay off any time I want. You got a good watch?" He looked at Dawson's wrist. "Not that thing. Here, take this." He unstrapped a watch from his wrist, an old-fashioned watch with a sweep second hand. "Now we're synchronized. Let's make it you'll be on the machine at nine twenty-seven exactly. Get there at nine twenty-two: play a few coins slowly until the time."

"What if someone else is playing it?"

"It's a risk, but it's not a popular machine and five minutes should be enough."

Dawson looked at his newly acquired timepiece. "Where will you be?"

"You don't need to know that. Out of sight. That's why we have to get the timing right. I won't be able to watch."

"Then I come back here . . ."

"No. Then you cash in the metal for thirty one-hundred dollar bills. Then you come back here and give me fifteen. There may be a few dollars over. You can have that."

"You do this every night?"

"You don't have to know that, either. Let's just leave it that this is my living. Are you on?"

Dawson sipped his beer, making it last. He was deeply frightened and just as deeply excited. Every instinct but one told him to stay away from this shark-suited stranger lest he wind up contributing to the pollution in the bay, but the remaining instinct, greed, kept him examining the proposition. He could see no risk in it whatever. All he had to do was play one of the machines, pick up the winnings (if any — he still didn't quite believe all this) and cash them, then pay this man his share. "Which machine is it?" he asked.

The banker explained. "There is a row of dollar machines on the right of the front door. My machine is the third one from the end. It's a straight fruit machine — cherries, oranges, you know. The machines either side of it use playing card symbols. Okay?"

"Yeah," Dawson said. "One more beer first, though."

"Right. Make it nine forty-seven, then. Exactly." The man slid off his stool and disappeared.

At nine thirty Dawson looked around the gambling hall, getting his bearings. Five minutes later he was standing near the rigged machine, sweating. An old man was feeding the machine a handful of dollars and then, as if on cue, at nine forty-four he ran out of money, cursed the machine and wandered away. Dawson positioned himself in front of the machine and put in his first dollar. Playing slowly he put in six dollars and then, as the second hand swept up to the time, he put in the crucial coin and stood back. He was prepared for two things. He had kept in mind that the man in the bar was simply a practical joker (but a joker who gave away wrist watches for laughs?).

He also worried that if it worked, three thousand dollars would pour all over the floor of the casino. What actually happened was that the lights went up on the machine, a bell rang, one of the attendants hurried over, checked the amount of the win, and gave him a note for three thousand two hundred and eleven dollars. "The cashier will pay you off, sir," he said. "Congratulations."

For about a minute, a small crowd gathered, wanting to play the machine, but he was soon left alone with a note in his hand for over three thousand dollars. The cashiers were stationed beside the door for the convenience of arriving players and Dawson joined the line-up at the nearest cage. He cashed the note and then looked around to see where the bar was. Then he hesitated. The bar was at least fifty yards away, out of sight on the other side of the room. The door was about six paces in the other direction. Dawson made his decision and walked straight through the door to a taxi which whisked him back to his hotel. He stayed in his room all evening and returned to Toronto the next morning. On the plane, his wife said, "Did you win anything last night?" He told her about the jackpot, but he never told her or anyone else about the banker, and he never went into a casino again.

When Dawson was putting the winning dollar into the fruit machine, three men were watching him on a row of cameras in a room above the ceiling of the casino. As the second hand reached nine forty-seven, the banker pressed a button on the console in front of him and the fruit machine sign lit up. The three men watched as Dawson collected his money and left the cashier's window. As Dawson hesitated, the banker urged him on as if he were watching a horse race. "Over to the bar," he shouted, unheard through the ceiling. "Over to the bar. I'm waiting for you, for Christ's sake. There he goes, Joe."

"Run for it, dummy," Joe, one of the other men, said.

The old man who had been playing the fruit machine before Dawson laughed. "You two are crazy, you know it?" he said.

"There's the door," Joe called. "Run for it. Now!"

Dawson hesitated, looking around for the bar, and the banker shouted in triumph. "He's going over, see. He's on his way."

"Run for it, dummy," Joe yelled. "Go, go, go!"

The three men held their breath as Dawson paused, then, as he dashed through the door, Joe shouted, cheering him on his way. "That's it baby. Don't let me down."

Dawson was gone.

"Son of a bitch," the banker said, taking a roll from his pocket and handing over ten one-thousand dollar bills to Joe. "I was sure of him."

"I'm sure of everybody," Joe chuckled. "You might as well

quit, Tony. You ain't gonna find one."

The banker gritted his teeth. "Double or nothing?" he asked.

"Sure," Joe said. "This is the easiest money I've ever made. You spotted another one?"

"That guy, watching the roulette wheel."

Joe didn't even glance at the screen. "Anyone at all, Tony. Off you go. Set it up. But you're wasting your time."

"I'll find one," the banker said. "I'll find one, for Christ's sake."

1988 WINNER

ERIC WRIGHT
"Looking for an Honest Man"
Cold Blood: Murder in Canada

Nominees:

TONY ASPLER
"Murder By Half"
Cold Blood: Murder in Canada

JAS. R. PETRIN
"Magic Nights"
Alfred Hitchcock Mystery Magazine

JAS. R. PETRIN
"Prairie Heat"
Alfred Hitchcock Mystery Magazine

TED WOOD
"Pit Bull"
Cold Blood: Murder in Canada

JAS. R. PETRIN

Killer in the House

"**Y**ou *will* be all right, won't you, Nanny?"

Course, I will. Go out, and have fun, and leave me at home with a killer!

Nanny sat in her wheelchair, silent, angry, swathed in her blanket, watching her grand-daughter Gwen fuss in and out of the bathroom, the bedroom, putting on her clothes, her scent, and her face, while her husband Will leaned his head in at the door and called with annoyance, "The car's warmed up and running, the Arabs are getting rich, are we going to the damn restaurant or not?"

"I'm coming, can't you give me a minute's peace? I've only got to put on my coat and see if Nanny needs anything!"

Gwen came stumping across the living room, shaking the floor, and bent over Nanny. She smelled like a harlot's picnic. She was a good girl, though, Gwen was, more considerate of Nanny than her sister Liz had ever been. Considerate and caring, but none too bright. She was a stupid, and so was her husband. They were both stupids.

"Nanny," Gwen whispered, "we're leaving now. You know I'll worry about you the whole time we're gone. We may go to a movie after din-din, we may not. I don't know. But if we're late, you mustn't worry. Louie will be along. I made him promise to skip the bar at the Red Lantern tonight, to come home early and fix your dinner. So you'll only be alone for an hour or so. Now tell me, darling, if there's anything you want before we go."

She was studying Nanny's lips, and Nanny's eyes swam from the scent of her perfume.

There's lots I want, Nanny thought. *I want you to stay right here and not charge off and leave me alone with that murdering Louie, and I want Will to go on out to that freezer Louie brought here with him when he moved in and crowbar that lock open and get your frozen-stiff sister Liz out of it and thaw her out and bury her proper and Christian, and I want Louie dragged out of here by a policeman, kicking, and a rope got around him, and him hung up high until he's dead, dead, dead!*

But when a stroke comes along and hits you like a runaway wagon the way it had Nanny last fall, you were lucky if you could still draw breath.

She could feel Gwen's eyes on her face. Out in the driveway Will was revving up the Dodge like he was part of a getaway. Which maybe he was. A getaway from Nanny.

Nanny struggled to shape the words on her lips.

Killer, she mouthed, *in the house! Look . . . the freezer!* Gwen straightened, puffing out her fat cheeks and laughing.

"Oh, Nanny, don't start up with that again."

"Don't start up with what?" It was Will poking his head in on a blast of winter air.

"I think she's going on about Louie's freezer again. You know how it upsets her. She thinks he's got Lizzie Mae's body inside it. I wish you'd make him open it and give Nanny a look inside so as to set her mind at rest."

Will sighed a long weary breath and rolled his eyes in his best God-give-me-strength expression.

"Look. You know I talked to Louie, and you know I explained it all to Nanny a dozen times. He keeps the freezer locked so those kids you baby-sit don't go trapping themselves in it and suffocating; he keeps it running so it doesn't get to smelling all skunky inside; and she doesn't need to look in it anyways because, like I told her another dozen times, me and Louie seen Liz at the mall. I seen her myself with my own two eyes, walking large as life through the Easton Mall. Now if all that don't satisfy her, nothing will. Can we go now?"

Gwen's eyes flashed with sudden annoyance.

"I wish you'd stop talking in front of Nanny like she wasn't even here. It wouldn't hurt Louie to let her have a little peek. It wouldn't hurt anybody one bit." She bent over Nanny again, with a look of concern. "There's nothing for you to worry about, darling, everything's fine. You'll see."

She kissed Nanny's forehead — lightly, so as not to smear her lipstick.

Then the big door banged and they were gone.

Nanny would have stamped her foot in frustration if it were possible. Nothing to worry about!

Everything's fine, is it? But you haven't seen Louie kneeling by his freezer, reaching down into it and speaking softly and crying. No you haven't, have you?

Leaving her alone with a killer! Did they think Nanny shouldn't have fears, simply because her welfare was entirely in their hands? Neither of them had never awakened in the night with eyes stretched wide as sealer rings, sweating, wanting to scream, run, turn over and cry out to someone, but only able to lie there with her body wrapped around her like a steel clamp and silently shriek into the dark.

A killer in the house!

Being paralyzed, she'd learned fear, all right. Fear such as she'd never known before in her life. Fear of fire. Fear of being at the mercy of some cruel person — like a killer. And even, because it was always present, the fear of falling! Except for the killer, that was the worst. Even sitting quietly here at home in her chair held a terror that made her head reel. Falling out of her chair was a horrifying notion. The nightmare of it woke her every night. The slow weightless launch into space and the floor hurtling up to smash her. It was the old childhood dream of falling, falling, falling, and not being able to raise an arm to save yourself. She shuddered.

And now they'd invited a killer to stay.

Louie.

With his freezer.

The cold they'd let in was making the oil stove groan; it whirred its fan in the corner and creaked its joints at her. She wished she had thought to ask Gwen to turn it up a notch or two; she wished she could just reach out herself and give the dial a damn good twist.

But she'd have to lift her arm to do that, and it was all she could do to lift her fingers. She lifted a finger now to the little control wand on her chair, and the motor hummed and crept her across the kitchen. It hesitated before it went; the switch wanted cleaning again. She stopped a few feet from the stove and let the heat soak into her.

Her eyes were still bleary from that horrid perfume Gwen had been wafting around. She blinked once, twice to clear them; it was an awful thing to be unable to rub your eyes when you wanted to. Her eyesight had always been good. She could read the chrome letters on the stove that spelled CHAMPION, she could read the spine of the telephone book on the stand by the back doorway, she could read the name ARCTIC through the partly opened door on the . . .

FREEZER!

It was visible there in the open doorway, hulking, one hard angular white shoulder in the dark.

Louie's freezer.

The one with Lizzie Mae's body locked inside it like a frozen pork roast.

Damn it, Gwen, you could at least have thought to close that door before you went off to enjoy yourself. Nanny moved her finger to hum the motor to turn the wheelchair away and not look.

And Louie saying he had seen Liz at the Mall. What rubbish. Did he think he could fool Nanny with a comment like that? Liz couldn't be in two places at the same time and she sure as heck hadn't clambered out of that freezer, what with it being locked and all, and her lying at the bottom of it stabbed or shot or strangled, with a glaze of ice over her and her lips all blue. And Will, who had backed Louie up, had only caught a glimpse from the barbershop window where he had sat breathing with the rest of the men, all of them lathered up like mad dogs, watching the women's legs go by. It wasn't as if he'd actually spoken to her.

But Will, listening to Louie, thought he'd seen Liz, and so neither he nor Gwen would consider the real truth. They weren't surprised at Liz staying away; it was just like her to cut them out. They assigned no blame for the marriage breakup, and they let Louie go smiling on. They liked him. Thought he was the cat's whiskers. It was only Nanny who had seen him, when Gwen and Will were gone for groceries and he thought she was asleep, kneeling over that open freezer like a monk, bowing and talking into the frost and sobbing.

Louie was a clothing salesman, or had been. Best in the business, he liked to brag. He'd made his managers jealous, on account of, with his commissions, he made more money than they did. Or so he said.

Nanny had never warmed to him.

She hadn't liked him from the day three years ago when Liz had waltzed him in the door, hanging all over him, announcing to a shocked silence that she was marrying him the very next day. Liz had always been impulsive like that. Taking up with any half-cracked lunatic that came smiling out of the sun. She'd found three husbands that way before Louie came along, and though all three of them had been stupids, Louie had been the only one who had struck Nanny as being totally . . .

BAD!

So Nanny had done some phoning — she wasn't all seized up then — and found out some very curious things from her friend Emma Parker in Youngerville. *They'd* had a fellow just like Louie working in their clothing store — Casey's on Third Street — and he had been simply the *strangest* man! Folks had seen him on warm evenings, parked on Lover's Lookout — which was the hill over the river where the young folks liked to go — and he had a different girl with him every single time. One night a blond, next night a redhead — always somebody different. The gossip had gone round about it, and the next thing anybody knew, he'd got the sack from Casey's and had left town. Folks had pried away at Casey with crowbars for weeks, but he wouldn't say a word about it. Said he wouldn't bring disgrace on his store.

That same night, after the phone call, Nanny had woke up screaming because she had looked on death in a dream. And the next few times she saw Louie, she saw death following one step behind him, or peeking around him, or standing next to him and holding his arm like a bride. That dream was prophetic.

He'd killed Liz, all right. Nanny had seen it coming from the first. And now here was the proof, if anybody would bother to look. In the back room. Under lock and key. In the freezer.

Of course she'd tried to warn Liz, but Liz had only turned all huffy and cold and gone for her coat wanting to leave right away. Then she'd begun staying away altogether, which was that Louie's doing for sure, whispering evil in her ear.

Right about then the stroke had hit Nanny, and that had been Louie's doing too, just as sure as sheep-dip. He'd hexed her. Who else had the evil to do it, after all?

Oh, Louie was trouble, all right, and nothing but. In the end, Nanny had been proved right.

Just take that night Liz had phoned. She must have been crying up a storm, Gwen was so sympathetic with her. And later Nanny had overheard Gwen telling Will about it:

" . . . lost his job at the store."

"How come?"

"She wouldn't say exactly. But they caught him red-handed at something . . . something pretty bad. Louie wouldn't talk about it, so she phoned the manager and he told her what it was. She was ashamed to tell me too much, but I think it was because he would-n't leave the female customers alone. Liz said she'd always had her suspicions about that, and now she was going to leave him . . ."

So things hadn't worked out too well down at the clothing store. And after Louie bragging how he'd been too good for all those other stores, too — he'd worked in half a dozen. It told Nanny a lot. He hadn't been victimized by jealous managers at all. It was just the old wandering fingers problem.

And suddenly Liz had stopped phoning. Just like that, no more calls. Very suspicious. Nobody saw hide nor hair of either one of them until Louie showed up at the door with his battered suit-case and his freezer. And wasn't that just the darndest thing? A freezer! Most men would have brought their TV or their liquor cabinet, but here comes Louie with a freezer.

He'd explained with his easy smile that he and Liz had bro-ken up, that Liz didn't want to be bothered with it, and he'd brought it because it was the only thing in the house they owned free and clear. And if anybody believed that story, they'd buy a raffle ticket with the World Trade Center as first prize.

He hadn't fooled Nanny. Not one bit.

And now here they were. All of them under the same roof. Liz in her frozen sleep; Gwen, foolish Gwen, suspecting nothing; Will, who liked having a man in the house to talk sports with; and Nanny in her chair.

And Louie.

Hating her. No, *despising* her!

He made no secret of that, either.

Only a week ago there had been just the two of them in the living room, watching TV, Louie seated on the end of the couch, cursing her under his breath. Oh, he was quiet and cute about it, speaking feather soft so that Gwen shouldn't hear in the kitchen, keeping his murdering hands in his lap, his murderous eyes on the television, barely moving his lips.

"Nanny, Nanny, hard old Nanny, mean old Nanny, Nanny the witch." He'd gone on like that for twenty minutes. Oh, he was confident with her so seized up from the stroke he'd hexed on her.

Nanny closed her eyes, tried not to think of the freezer in the dark in the room behind the wall. After a while she rested.

What woke her was a thump at the door.

Somebody cursing, fumbling, laughing.

Louie was home, and tight as a tic. So he had stopped at the Lantern, after all. Nanny felt her pulse pick up a beat from somewhere, then settle itself again.

Louie was home.

Louie the killer.

And no Gwen!

Nanny waited in her chair by the stove, and at that moment the blower shut off, sighing to a stop and impressing her with the silence of the house when Louie wasn't around. Sober or drunk, he had a loud way about him. Too friendly when sober, laughing too harshly and smiling too broadly and always standing one step too close to you; and too stupid when drunk, playing the clown, telling rude jokes and mimicking famous people to turn those around him purple with laughter.

There was a crash from the steps outside, and a loud groan. A tinkle of broken glass.

He didn't fool Nanny, though.

Nanny could see the real Louie behind the smokescreen of jokes and laughter. She had known a lot of Louies in her time. He was a type. The sort you got a glimpse of sometimes when a fresh wind gusted the smoke away, and you were always strangely shocked to see just what you'd expected, like a glimpse of hard white bone in a deep red wound.

You learned a thing or two in eighty-two years.

Now she heard the jangle of keys at the lock. Louie seemed in awful shape. He was fumbling around out there badly. Despite what Gwen had said, he must have started earlier than usual today down at the Lantern, and run into some generous friends, too.

Then the door crashed open, and there stood Louie, smiling.

"Hello — Nanny!"

He swayed in the doorway, more concerned with holding himself up than in shutting out winter with the door. He had brought two cases of beer home with him, one tucked up high under his arm, the other clutched tight in his fingers and now just a boxful of broken glass, dribbling suds and amber stains over Gwen's polished linoleum.

He made one false attempt, then another, and finally managed to set the two cases down, handling even the broken one gently, as if he hoped it held something that might yet be salvaged. He fumbled his parka off, dropped it by the fridge, and finally sensing the chill from the open door, closed it hard by falling backwards against it.

"I said *hello*, Nanny!"

He rattled a chrome chair out from the table, arranged it with extraordinary precision, and then dropped into it, letting out one of the loudest belches Nanny had ever heard.

You wouldn't dare act like this if Gwen and Will were here. You're like every other drunk I've ever seen, with a kind of radar that lets you go on fooling certain people. All the rest, you don't want to fool. Them you want to impress with how nasty you can be. But I can see through you like a glass coffin lid, mister, see your grinning death's head face getting ready to pop out at me. Oh, I know you!

Nanny was feeling the heat of the stove now. She wanted to back away a little but was afraid to draw attention to herself.

If she could somehow remain inconspicuous for the next while, maybe Gwen and Will would come crunching in out of the snow, shaking off the night and filling the room with loud talk about the movie. As Gwen had promised earlier, everything would be all right.

Louie fumbled in his shirt for cigarettes. He didn't notice that he'd already put them on the table. He gave up with a flourish of disgust, leaned forward and hooked the undamaged beer case with his finger, dragged it to him across the floor. He popped the case open with one hand — even in his drunkenness it was a polished motion — opened a bottle, took a long sip, then groped again and finally found a cigarette.

He looked at Nanny.

"S'how the hell are ya?"

Nanny found herself wondering how she could appease the drunken man, knowing in her heart at the same time that appeasement was not possible. And even if it was, there was little she could do in her condition.

"Come here, Nanny, an' have a beer."

Her fingers fluttered at the controller. She was afraid to try it, afraid not to.

"Come *on*, Nanny!"

He swayed up out of his seat, leaning towards her with a list to one side. Then he was at the back of her chair, gripping the handles, pushing her up to the table. He was not gentle; he collided her with a table leg.

He giggled.

"Sorrysorrysorry! I'm sorry, Nanny. Don't tell Gwen on me, Nanny."

He sat down and faced her. She could smell the stink on him now, the acrid smokey bar, the heavy over-ripe scent of beer. He had mussed his hair somehow and it jutted from one side of his head like a wig that had slipped. He sucked on his bottle, then his cigarette, and put his head on one side, questioningly.

"You like tellin' Gwen things about me, don't you, Nanny? Why d'you do it? Ain't I always been friendly to you, Nanny? Don't I try to ch-cheer you up? Huh?"

He studied her down the length of his cigarette with his careful drunken eyes. She didn't like it. There was a menace in his tone, a hardening towards her with those last few words.

"Tellin' Gwen made-up stories about me. Not nice, Nanny, not nice."

And I'll have even more to tell her after tonight, you pig!

"You never liked me, Nanny.'

Darn right, I never liked you. I saw you for what you were the day Liz dragged you in here out of some barroom garbage can.

"You worked real hard, Nanny, turnin' Liz against me. Got what you wanted, too. Bust us up. Did a good job on us, Nanny, a real good wrecking job."

Not as good as I should have done. Or it'd be you out there in that freezer, and her in here talking to me.

Louie went to suck at his bottle, found it empty, and rapped it down hard on the table. He probed into the case at his feet and fished out two more bottles.

"Let's have a drink together, Nanny. An' a long talk. You an' me should've had a long talk years ago. Here, this is for you — you like beer, dontcha?"

He pushed the open bottle across the table. She wondered if in his drunkenness he had forgotten that she didn't have the use of her hands. He was watching her and smiling as if he were the most agreeable man God had ever put breath into. His head was propped up with the hand that held his cigarette clipped between two nicotine-stained fingers. He smoked steadily, taking a lungful, then regurgitating the smoke and dribbling it out of his mouth in curds of solid white, which he then swallowed up again. It was a wonder to Nanny that it didn't make him sick. Maybe it would yet.

"How come you doan like me, Nanny?"

Because you're evil.

"What's so wrong with me, anyway?"

You're a destroyer, a breaker-down of things, you're a killer!

"I tried t'make you like me, Nanny. Tried real hard for Liz. But you wouldn' let me, wouldn' give me a chance. An' Liz blamed *me* for that, Nanny. Me. S'at fair?"

Suddenly his heavy hand crashed down to make the table jump.

"You answer me!"

She flinched. He must have noticed.

Then he was calm again. Almost wheedling.

"Le's be friends, Nanny, okay? Le's be *good* friends. Bottoms up!" He drank, then watched her, waiting, blinking. He giggled. "Oops! Forgot, Nanny. Forgot your bum arm. Ole war wound, right? Here, lemme help you."

He picked up her bottle, loomed in at her, reaching, pressed it to her lips, tipped it forward. She took some of the bitter fluid into her mouth, gagged, and felt the rest of it splash down her chin, onto her blouse and her blanket.

Louie pulled the bottle away.

"Sorry, Nanny, sorrysorrysorry. *Sorry!* You doan drink fast, do you? You're a lady. A real lady." He frowned. "Liz was a real lady, too, jus' like her Nanny. Oh, I could have my pick of any girls, take 'em out anytime I want. But Liz was special. Better than the others. I loved her. Yup. You doan b'lieve that, do you?" His face clouded. "You never believe me, Nanny. Liz tole me once you said I was — a *LIAR!*"

Again he gave the table a heavy smack.

Nanny cringed inside at his Jekyll and Hyde transformations, from calm discussion to sudden rage. She found herself hating him with every atom of her being. She had always despised drunks, and she despised this one with a special passion. This was the drunk who had ruined the life of her granddaughter Liz. The drunk who had finally killed Liz in some intoxicated rage and sealed her up in a freezer. The hate made her paralysis even more intolerable. She wished she was once again a healthy woman who could leap up and strike at this disgusting brute; or a man, a strong man, who could take him by the neck and squeeze and squeeze . . . !

I hate you oh how I hate you, you drunken pig! I'd do any-thing to punish you for what you did to my Liz. I hope there's ghosts, and I hope I'm one real soon because even ghosts can do more in this world than a paralyzed old woman, and I'll come back to you then, cold and cadaverous and moldering, and I'll put my rotting hands on you and —

"Wanna see Liz, Nanny?"

She blinked.

He was gulping curds of smoke again and watching her with a brewing anticipation. She wondered if she had heard him right.

"Wanna see her, Nanny, or not?" He cackled. "You're pleased

t'hear that, arncha? I know what you been tellin' Gwen. Proves you were right, doan it? Proves they should've listened to you, Nanny. You knew best. You knew nobody could walk out on ole Louie." He emptied his beer down his throat, opened another one and scowled. "But later, Nanny. Yes, I think later. Then you can see her. Okay? Drink first. You'll need it. She ain't as pretty as she used to be!"

He laughed. Again he pushed the bottle at her, forcing open her mouth, pouring in the beer until she choked. He yanked it away so roughly this time that he pulled her false teeth askew. "Ooops," he said, giggling, "Sorry!" And stuck his fingers into her mouth to set them right again.

Nanny sat and glared at him. How terrible impotence was. It gripped you like a constricting snake and crushed the dignity out of you.

"You know," Louie said, "I was dancin' down at the Lantern tonight. I like dancin'. So did Liz. How 'bout you? Wanna dance, Nanny? Cut the old rug? Shake a tail feather?"

He was halfway to his feet when he fell back with a simpering grin.

"I fergot, Nanny. You doan dance so good now. Your legs doan work so hot." He took some beer, began laughing in the middle of a swallow, snorted it up his nose and coughed horribly.

He put his cigarette back in his mouth; it waggled as he spoke.

"An your arms too, huh, Nanny? An' your neck, an' your back, an' your feet, an' your hands — oh, you're in awful shape, aincha? Your whole damn bod is shot. If only you could wheel on down to the graveyard and dig yourself up a few spare parts, eh, Nanny?"

He collapsed in his chair, convulsed with laughter.

Go ahead. Laugh away. Laugh til you choke on your own rotten tongue. Then I'll do the laughing. In my mind. At your funeral while they're wheeling you down to the graveyard!

He tossed his head as if to shake the laughter away.

"I wanna dance. I'm a dancin' fool, Nanny! Me an' Liz use to dance alla time. You can do it, Nanny. I'll lead."

He pulled himself up by the edge of the table. Two bottles went crashing against the wall, scattering dark brown splinters of glass. He chortled. "Dead soldiers, Nanny." Then he had caught hold of the wheelchair from behind and was rolling her back and forth and around the room, and singing his own accompaniment.

It was a heavy chair, what with the battery and motor; he used it partly as a support for his lurching, unsteady body. Around and around he trundled her, hooting. She felt giddy. She closed her eyes; that was worse; she opened them again. The room ran liquidly around her in watercolors. The stove came and went, came and went. Louie howled in her ear. "ROUN' AN' ROUN' AN' ROUN' SHE GOES. WHERE SHE STOPS, NOBODY *KNOWS* . . . "

And he threw Nanny away.

The chair shot out and across, flying, soaring over the floor, through the room, and fetched slam-*bang!* into the stove.

The chimney pipes shuddered and dropped a dusting of soot. The stove jerked back three inches. Nanny felt herself lifted up, floating on and outward, the hot metal stove looming, halting, then receding again as she fell back into her chair, her nostrils filled with the stink of scorching steel.

She thanked God for Gwen's care in tucking her feet well back under the blanket. If not for that her toes would surely have been crushed.

She could not see Louie with her chair facing the stove. The heat beat against her face and trembled the little gray hairs that stuck out over her eyes. Behind her Louie groaned with laughter, creaked with it. In a moment or two his grunting subsided and she heard the snap of another beer being opened. The heat was terrible, she could scarcely breath. She yanked the chair control lever angrily back and, to her surprise, the chair responded instantly and rolled her backwards.

She stopped in the center of the room. She tried to get the chair to turn but the control lever had gone dead on her again. She sighed with frustration, and a nervous convulsion shook her violently.

She could only sit.

Hoping for Gwen.

Hating Louie.

Behind her, the sound of a cigarette pack being opened, the soft pop of the breaking seal, a crinkle of paper, a whisper of foil. The hiss and flare of a match.

"By God, you're a damn good dancer, Nanny."

Go to hell, Louie. Light another match. Set yourself on fire.

An acrid scent of sulfur reached her nose.

"A *damn* good dancer, Nanny. You mus've taught Liz every-thin' she knew. Oh, she was a dancer. We had a good time, Nanny, 'til you bust us up. Real mean of you. You turned her against me an' I never done nothin' to you. Mean. Mean as winter. Tha's you, Nanny. It's your fault me an' her had to go our ways."

Liz didn't go anywhere. You killed her.

"Now she's got nothin'. I got nothin . . . "

Oh yes you have. You've still got her. You've got her poor dead body out there in the back room, all frost and freezer burn and snowflakes on her eyes. Wrapped up in towels, maybe, or sheets. Like an Egyptian.

"You're hard, Nanny, hard."

Yes. I'm hard. I've had to be. But I'm not like you. Not a killer.

"You're like all those mean people I used to work for. You got no compassion for a man. You got a heart of . . . of ice. Black ice!"

Louie was beginning to wander in his thoughts. Beginning to mumble. Nanny was having trouble understanding him.

"You're old, Nanny. Used up. Got only dust in you, now. Dust and ice. Ever seen dust and ice mixed together, Nanny? Like a frozen chunk of midnight. Tha's what meanness looks like, Nanny. If we opened you up now with a knife an' looked inside you, tha's what we'd see. Old black ice." She heard him scraping at his cartons for more beer. A clink of glass. "Old things, Nanny, ought to be thrown away. Heaved down the basement an' tossed on a shelf to keep the dust off it. S'all you're good for now, Nanny. That an' breakin' up famblies."

There were more scuffling cardboard sounds, the chinking of tumbled glass.

Then a roar.

"NANNY!"

She shut her eyes. *Oh, God, what's got at him now, don't let him start flinging me round again, I'll throw up if he does, I'll faint, I'll die, oh please don't let him start in on me again!*

"NANNY, WHY'D YOU GO AN' BUST MY BEER?"

A chair crashed to the floor. Louie came around from the side into her view, breathing raggedly, and towered over her, enormous, dark, full of hurt and poison.

"WHY'D YOU DO IT, NANNY?"

I didn't break it, you stupid, stupid, stupid! Aren't I sitting paralyzed in a wheelchair? Didn't you drop it yourself when you came in? Think, you stupid, think, think!

He leaned even closer, wrinkling his face with disgust and hatred. He was only inches away now, as if he was trying to peer, not just into her eyes, but to something in behind them, her most secret thoughts.

He said, very coldly, his voice like a long sliver of ice that sank into her slowly, "I doan wanna drink with you no more, Nanny. No. I don't. You get mean when you drink, Nanny."

He pulled away then, trying to find his balance.

"An you're even meaner when you don't drink, Nanny."

Leave me alone. Get your horrid stinking face away from me. Don't you dare preach to me about meanness!

"I can be mean too, Nanny. Real mean. S'at what you want? S'at why you bust up me and Liz? To make me mean — like you?"

Go away!

"Why don't you say something, Nanny?"

BECAUSE I CAN'T! I CAN'T! I WANT TO, BUT I CAN'T!

He put on an expression of mock concern.

"Your eyes, Nanny. They're gettin' all red. You're cryin' inside of that old head, arncha Nanny? — just the way Liz used to cry after you'd tell her some mean thing about me. Show me some tears now, Nanny. Show me some tears for what you done to me an' Liz."

Leave me alone! Oh, please, please, Gwen, come home and help me now . . . !

I'll get tears out of you, Nanny. Tears for me and Liz." He straightened up, overbalanced and staggered to one side a step. "Soon as I find somethin' in this house to drink." He tottered away, opening drawers, cabinets, peering into corners bleary-eyed. "Muss be somethin' here. Will, he'll unnerstand when I tell him how you broke my beer. Cause of your meanness." He chortled. "I'm gonna have one more drink an' then I'm gonna *fix* you, Nanny."

You can't drink anything more. You mustn't. Oh dear God in heaven, don't let him find anything more to drink!

He swung her chair rudely to face the wall.

"Doan peek, Nanny."

Nanny looked down at her body, inert and immovable, something separate from herself, remote as a carving. Oh! The things this same body had done years before: like winning the sack race at the Sunday School picnic; and out-climbing the boys on the tree behind Mason's store. And even now she felt the tremendous churning life within it, the rushing and the hurrying of blood in her veins, the quivering nerves that screamed at her run, run, run, the terrors exploding in her brain like flash cards, visions of Louie beating her, holding lit cigarettes against her flesh, tipping her out of her chair —

Falling!

Oh, that was the worst!

The falling dream come to life. Full color and immediate. The floor starting toward her slowly, now lifting, now rising, faster, faster, now speeding, hurtling, rocketing at her while her arms planed useless at her sides.

Bang!

It was Louie slamming a cupboard door. He'd found something. A bottle. A quick new thrust of fear stabbed through her.

"Gin, Nanny. Only gin. I hate gin, Nanny, but it's better'n aftershave — better'n Aqua Velva." He cackled at his own wit like some evil warlock she heard him guzzle a large gulp of gin straight from the bottle, then cough. "And now I'm gonna fix you up a surprise."

Nanny closed her eyes, squeezed them lock-shut tight against the world. The worst had happened. She had prayed he would not find anything to drink, not find anything more to fuel the hatred and violence in him. Gin — straight gin. It was like dashing raw alcohol over naked flame. Surely God had deserted her.

There were muffled thumps behind her, and the creaking of floor-boards. She heard him grunt, than let out a long low chortle of wicked mirth.

"Just goin' to the sandbox Nanny. Doan go away."

He shambled away down the hall, past the living room, to the back of the house. A pause. Silence followed by a harsh scrape.

A door opening, closing. The flush of the toilet. Then footsteps returning.

He was coming back towards her, staggering. She kept her eyes screwed shut. He was coming, he was here! He turned her chair out into the room so that she could see what he was doing. He winked, then moved off again in his uneven drunken tread. She peeked out of herself to see what he was about.

He had crossed the kitchen towards the backroom doorway, the entrance to the room where he kept his freezer locked tight. But he didn't enter. He stopped. He bent over, down on one knee, reaching.

What in heaven's name — ?

He was lifting the cellar trapdoor. He was throwing back the lid. It yawned like a mouth.

Now he was up and teetering over the black maw in the floor, swaying dangerously, doing a breath-catching float out over the opening, then lurching safely back to Nanny's side, fumbling in his pocket, clutching, withdrawing.

He dropped a flat steel key into her lap.

"You been wantin' a look into my freezer, Nanny. Well, there it is, waitin'. All you got to do is get to it." He laughed. "Course, I din want to make it too easy. No fun then, Nanny. So all you got to do is get over to that trap an' drop it down somehow an' roll on in there an' have yourself a look. Simple." He bent crookedly like a kindly uncle offering a gift, and gusted his sour breath into her face. "If you make it past the trap," he whispered, "I'll even help you with the padlock."

He giggled away, pleased with himself, and fell into a chair.

The cellar trap opened sideways and to the right, like the cover of an enormous book. A chain held it upright, almost vertical. It only needed a nudge to send it crashing shut again. She wanted so bad to look into that freezer, already Nanny found herself wondering if there wasn't some way she could manage it. And there was! The way she closed her own bedroom door. She could hook one front wheel behind the door, and turn sharp left to bring the door slamming down. It was dangerous. She could easily fall — fall into the cellar! But here was the freezer key, here, right in her lap. And out there was the freezer, with Liz beckoning, Liz waiting, Liz calling silently out to her. . . . She had to try!

She thrust out her fingers to tilt the control switch to roll her forward. Nothing. She flicked at the switch again and again. Dead.

Louie cackled. He drank some more gin.

"S'matter? Outta gas? Dead batt'ry?" He squeaked with laughter, then arched his eyebrows. "Wanna boost?"

That sent a chill of terror through her. The idea of this stumbling drunk wheeling her toward that hole in the floor was too horrifying to imagine. Her fingers danced at the switch. She had to move. Had to —

The motor whirred, rolling her forward.

Louie, already halfway to his feet, collapsed again. He clapped his hands. "Go, Nanny, go! Yee-hah!"

The chair hummed Nanny across the kitchen, toward the yawning gulf in the floor. Three feet from the edge of the hole it stopped. Without even wanting to she had let got of the switch. Her nerve had given out. She wanted to continue, wanted to get out to the back room and see her Liz, her Liz, her lonely Liz, but she was brought up sharp by her own fear. Her fear of falling. That fear kept her from Liz as surely as Louie's padlock had done before. In her mind, she wept.

"Nanny! What's wrong now? Damn batt'ry again? I'll help you, Nanny, I'll help . . . "

He was standing now, grinning broadly, holding the gin bottle, swaying forward, catching himself, leaning back again, like a monstrous puppet worked by an uncertain hand on loose strings. A puppet baby taking its first steps. Look, Ma, no hands!

Stay away, Nanny screamed in her mind, *stay away from me! Don't touch me, don't push me into that hole. Oh, Gwen, come home! Come home!*

Louie took a step towards her, then another, and another.

Gwen, HELP ME!

Louie stretched out his hand for her, and stretching, lost his balance completely, tried to correct for it, leaned back, twirled around and crashed to the floor on his skinny rear end. He sat there a moment, looking back at her stunned. *Maybe he won't get up. Maybe he —*

But he was getting up, struggling to his feet and laughing, holding out the gin bottle. "I d'in' break it, Nanny. I d'in break it!"

He began rolling her forward.

"Here we go loop-de-loop, Nanny, here we go loop-de-lie . . ."

The cellar door gaped under her wheels like a hungry maw. Two more feet, one . . .

Over the edge!

She closed her eyes. She was falling. It was just the way it had been in her dream. A slow, haunting terrifying plunge into a black nothingness. A long trip through forever before the final stunning blow. An age. . . .

Nothing.

She opened her eyes.

Louie was reeling around the room like an airplane out of control, laughing fit to bust. The chair was grounded above the hole. Her right front wheel was dangling magically over the abyss. Her left front wheel was caught on the side lip of the hole! If she trembled, breathed, anything, she was going to fall straight in.

"Whooo!" Louie crowed, staggering, going down, kneeling, the bottle swinging out in his hand, catching and reflecting the light. "Whooo!" Then he caught himself up, gasped, and hooted. "Nanny. What happened? Got a flat? Wanna shove?" He came at her again, this time on his knees, his face beet-red with the humor of it all.

NO! Nanny shrieked silently, GET BACK! STAY — AWAY — FROM — ME!

She willed him to stop, flung all the strength of her mind at him. And it worked.

He did stop.

And then he fell.

He didn't have far to go, being on his knees already, and he passed out cleanly as he came knee-boning up to her, his face diving by her in a perfect blurred pink arc, his head booming off the sheet metal corner of the stove and hitting the floor with a dull vegetable sound.

This time he didn't move.

First, Nanny told herself, *got to get away from this hole.*

She feathered the control switch timidly, trembling it back and to the left. Once, three times, five times. Then it caught. The motor hummed. It reversed her clear of the hole.

Louie lay still, his head projecting out past the stove.

His thrusting Adam's apple only a foot from her rear wheel.

A surge of triumph flashed through Nanny and carried her away. Here was her enemy at her mercy! *Not so helpless now, am I?* she gloated. She touched the control switch. The motor hummed. She stopped, and from the corner of her eye she saw Louie's neck under her big rear wheel, his larynx bulging like a rope, his throat pulsing with each surge of his heart. All she had to do now was. . . . She hesitated. It was too easy. He was so vulnerable lying there.

But what about Liz? Didn't my Liz have a right to enjoy her life too? It hadn't been too difficult to kill her, had it? Not for a big, strong man like you. Hadn't she been vulnerable? And an execution was something different from a murder, oh yes something quite different.

Her fingers toyed with the control lever. She watched them in amazement. Her right hand, the only part of her body she'd had any real control over in months, now seemed to have taken on a will of its own. Like a spectator, she watched, as if from a great distance, the fingers having their own way, tightening, tightening. . . .

Then Louie's hand closed powerfully on the spokes of her wheel, his one eye flew open, and he grinned.

"Boo!" he said.

She shrieked in silent terror.

Louie clambered to his feet, kicked the trapdoor shut with a crash and a musty wind, and rolled her into the back room. Softly cackling he undid the lock, then paused with his hand on the lid of the freezer. He whispered:

"You ready for this, Nanny? Hope so! It's a horrible sight. A killer."

The lid flew back.

Nanny looked in.

Gentle vapors. Icy crusts. The freezer was empty.

The room spun crazily around her, grew larger, shrank away, went black, then blindingly bright. Louie went tramping away, whooping laughter, panting and wheezing with it, crashing into things. He dragged his parka around his shoulders, fumbled at the doorknob and staggered out into the night. She heard his car start, the crunch of tires on snow as he rolled away.

When Will and Gwen got home, they found Nanny parked inches away from the old stove, which was roaring away against the gale that had got its start at the North Pole, gathered power and speed on a journey to bring it leaping in at Nanny through the door Louie hadn't bothered to close. They shut the door with a huge slam, stood for a moment blinking stupidly at the broken glass, spilled beer, overturned chairs, stove knocked askew on its fire-proof pad. Will ran his fingers through his hair; his face was the color of ashes. Then Gwen was at Nanny's side in a rush, kneeling, clasping Nanny's hand, fussing and full of quick, questioning words, gripping Nanny's fingers tight, her gaze darting from Nanny to the mess in the room and back again.

"Oh, I'm so sorry, so sorry, Nanny, I'll never go off and leave you like that again, never." She looked at Will toeing a sodden beer case with the tip of his shoe. It was Louie, wasn't it? Oh, God! And he promised he'd take care of you." Her voice went suddenly vicious. "I'll never let him set foot in this house again! I won't! I'll throw him out — Will, *you'll* throw him out!" She was starting to cry. "Nanny, I don't know what to say, I'm just —"

She stopped. Swallowed. Stared.

Will was mumbling away to himself: "Must've been in one of his moods. Nothing *she* could do. She must've just sat here, scared out of her wits. . . ."

But Gwen stared past him. Stared into the back room with a feeling of numb bewilderment. Will turned to gaze with her into the back room shadows, at the long white waiting freezer with its lid thrown back. They then went slowly together to stand with linked hands and peer into the frosted emptiness. They turned then and looked at Nanny. Put their heads together, buzzed.

Gwen said sternly, "This freezer is empty, Nanny!"

Will stooped over her.

"Nanny, tell the truth, did you start in on him? That's it, isn't it? You made him understand your . . . your accusations. He got angry and raged around. Broke things. Then he gave you what you wanted — let you see into the freezer. That's what happened, isn't it, Nanny?" His voice was as firm and stern as his face. "I guess when he cools down and comes back, you'll owe him an apology, won't you?"

Gwen was glancing around the room, eyes angry with tears. "Oh, this *mess!* This awful *mess!* "

Gwen and Will both shook their heads. They'd had enough.

And so had Nanny. Her trembling fingers clutched at her control lever, and the chair obediently responded, whispered her off to her room with a silk swiftness of rubber tires on linoleum. She whirred past the living room where the shadows sat slumped in the chairs, along the twilite hall to the back of the house, turned into her room, spun expertly and caught the door with her right footrest to send it slamming shut.

The drapes were still undrawn, the night pushing in through the glass and filling the room with itself. An otherwise empty room. Like Nanny's heart. Empty yet tidy, with all the emptiness in its place.

You're too old. Too old and too foolish. A stupid. There's no place for you here anymore. You caused trouble tonight. You drove Louie and Liz apart with your whisperings. You're a misery, you leave trails of miserableness behind you, it rubs off you onto other people. . . .

You're responsible for everything that's happened between those two young people.

Gwen came into the room so briskly, the edge of the door clunked into Nanny's chair. She swooped in on a flood of dim electric light from the hall. She put firm hands on Nanny, hands that Nanny knew had been cleaning up the mess, impatient, sudden hands. Hands that said by their movements that they'd be better occupied somewhere else. Gwen lifted Nanny in a brisk Victorian Nurse dead lift, stretched her on the bed, tumbled her quickly out of her clothes and into her nighty, rolled her under the quilt, kissed her with hard, dry lips.

"Now you just go right to sleep. We'll have a good talk about this in the morning." She paused at the door. "I hope you're satisfied. I don't know *how* I'm going to deal with Will and Louie after this!"

The door closed.

All right, then. Be in a snit. Don't even ask me if I have to go to the bathroom. Blame me for everything. I don't mind. I know it's my fault. You can punish me, dump me into this old cold bed.

And it was a cold bed. Colder than it ought to be . . .

That's what guilt does to a person. Stops their circulation. Bed, get colder. I deserve it.

And it did. A numbing cold was creeping out of the bedding in waves. Also a frosty, cloying damp which gradually became a long slim bulk under the quilt only inches away. And then she knew she was not alone in her bed.

Not alone at all.

She remembered those few moments earlier when she had sat in the corner and listened to Louie's heavy footsteps in the hall.

There was, after all, something much worse than falling.

She began her silent screams.

1989 WINNER

JAS. R. PETRIN
"Killer in the House"
Alfred Hitchcock Mystery Magazine

Nominees:

WILLIAM BANKIER
"One Day at a Time"
Ellery Queen Mystery Magazine

JAMES POWELL
"Still Life with Orioles"
Ellery Queen Mystery Magazine

Humbug

The lieutenant earnestly hoped that his daughter's affair with the American would soon culminate in a wedding, and he had good grounds for such hope. But then Mack had an accident that excluded him from normal life for fourteen months, and the affair dragged on for another two years. What happened was that Mack got in the way of a bullet fired from a machine gun mounted on a tank. He was fortunate the bullet only damaged his thighbone, for another shot from the same gun in the same general direction struck one of his fellow students in the head as she was holding up a picture of First Secretary Dubcek for the benefit of the soldiers on the tanks. At least she was spared a lot of unpleasantness at school; the cadre personnel in charge of establishing each student's political behavior during the days of brotherly help did not bother with the childless dead. Mack himself did have difficulties, but his professor, a specialist in mesozoic turtles, displayed almost super-human heroism and a keen understanding of political tactics. With the help of a statement Mack's father had once made to the press to get out of military service in Korea, the professor managed to persuade the cadre people not to expel the wounded foreign student from the Department of Palaeontology.

❖

Lieutenant Boruvka survived all the upsets and reversals of that unsettled time after the Soviet invasion with his credentials intact. But his conscience, which gnawed at him during the best of times, was transformed into a toothy, piscatory fossil that his future son-in-law compared to those fish in the Paraná River that are capable of rapidly stripping the flesh off anyone unfortunate enough to fall in. The lieutenant, crushed by the events and once more mindful of his family's welfare, filled out the required questionnaires almost truthfully—except for the section labeled Origin, where he neglected to mention (as his father had neglected to mention in 1939, after a somewhat similar invasion) the fact that his otherwise demonstrably Catholic great-grandmother had had the suspicious maiden name of Silberstein. Guided by hints from politically adaptable colleagues, and using the language of the leading daily newspaper, he confessed that at the time of the Entry of the Fraternal Armies (this was what the press was now calling the invasion) he had been misled by revisionist propaganda and had succumbed to an emotional attitude to the events, but that he had been assailed by growing doubts until finally he had thrown off his emotional attitude and fully identified with the politics of the Party and the government. Sergeant Malek manufactured a model reply upon these lines for the entire Criminal Investigation Division, and all the officers used it on their questionnaires and ratified their admissions of error with their own signatures.

Thus the lieutenant navigated safely through dangerous waters — at the minor expense of a perjured declaration — and they even promoted him to first lieutenant for good behavior. Malek was made a lieutenant and the two filled out new questionnaires concerning their opinions on Vietnam, Korea, and the first and second world wars (all of them bourgeois-imperialist conflicts except for the Great Patriotic War of Russia against Hitlerite Germany), the Arab-Israeli conflict (Zionist aggression), Franz Kafka (totally alien to the socialist reader), Mao Tse Tung (head of the Chinese revisionist clique), pacifism (cosmopolitan idealistic trick to weaken the Peace Camp of Socialism), the assassination of Reinhard Heydrich (the politically irresponsible act of traitorous bourgeois émigrés), and many other items of ideological importance.

To the lieutenant's surprise, Major Kautsky, the division's former head, turned out to be a diehard revisionist. Instead of using Malek's model answer on his questionnaire he wrote, in the language of the leading newspaper, that he did not agree with the Entry of the Fraternal Armies. To make matters worse, he continued his hostile fraternization with the Dubcekist former minister of the Interior, Pavel, who had fought in Spain. In addition he formed a friendship with an expelled member of the Central Committee of the Party, Kriegl — who was a Jew, refused to sign the Moscow agreement about the temporary stationing of the Russian army on Czechoslovak territory, and as a young man had fought with Mao Tse Tung in China. Finally, along with his son and daughter, Major Kautsky was arrested for distributing leaflets reminding people of their constitutional right not to vote in the forthcoming elections (the government nevertheless received a mandate of 99.99½ percent).

The division gained a new chief, Major Tlama, and a new sergeant, Vladimir Pudil.

The first case that gave the lieutenant an opportunity to appreciate the expertise of his new subordinate officer was the murder of Ondrej Krasa, who drove a delivery truck for the Candy and Sweets Communal Enterprises. Krasa's body was found by a pair of lovers in a Prague park. It was lying on a pathway beneath a blood red moon. He had a fractured skull; someone had struck him from behind, probably with a heavy tool like a hammer or a wrench. He was still fairly young, thirty-five according to his ID booklet. Sergeant Pudil, the new acquisition of the Homicide Division and chairman of the criminal division's Soviet Socialist Youth, called the Ministry of the Interior from a phone booth in the park. A firm suspicion had formed in his mind that there was a class motivation for the crime since the murdered man not only was a worker, according to his ID booklet, but had a letter in his pocket revealing, that he had recently been given a bonus for exemplary work. To be completely certain, Pudil wanted the dead man's political profile.

In all his years of service Lieutenant Boruvka had never once resorted to Secret Police files for information, and when they got back to the division he looked into the criminal records. With a feeling of satisfaction (of which he immediately felt ashamed, for it was a malicious feeling) he informed his new sergeant that the exemplary worker had had a criminal record. Krasa had once studied economics, but in 1965 he had been arrested for failing to report a crime — intent to leave the country without permission —

and had been sentenced to six years in prison. The married couple who had tried unsuccessfully to escape had panicked and told police things they might have kept silent about with impunity, and so it came out that Ondrej Krasa had originally intended to go with them. In the end he hadn't because his girlfriend, Lida Oharikova, who was not yet seventeen at the time, didn't want to leave her widowed mother behind alone. Krasa denied (rather illogically) that Oharikova knew anything about the intended crime and told the court he had decided not to go because he couldn't bring himself to part with his young girlfriend. Eventually the public prosecutor decided not to press charges against Oharikova, but he made a great deal of some other circumstances revealed by the terrified couple. Krasa, they confessed, had provided them with a military map of the border region in the Sumava forest; he had stolen the map during army maneuvers in the region, and the public prosecutor characterized this as a betrayal of military secrets. He asked that Krasa be given six years and the judge brought his gavel down on it.

Krasa dutifully served his time. His girlfriend got married four years after his arrest, and as soon as he got out Krasa married someone else, but within a year they were divorced. When Sergeant Pudil came to Boruvka with his report, the lieutenant could not resist being sarcastic. "You needn't have bothered the comrades, comrade. I don't suppose they told you we have something called criminal records right here in the division."

But Pudil had some surprising information which the criminal records had not yielded.

"They did tell me, comrade lieutenant. But our records aren't as complete as the ones they have at Interior. Did you know, for example, that Krasa was a Zionist?"

"No, I didn't. Why would someone called Krasa —"

"Because his name isn't Krasa, that's why. It's Schoenfeld. You see how unreliable our records are, leaving out important information like that? And in 1968, Schoenfeld had a meeting with someone called Cohen," said the sergeant, pronouncing the name phonetically as Tsohen, "in the lobby of the Alcron Hotel. And this Cohen," he declared importantly, "is a member of the Zionist organization American Express Inc. — and what's more, his name isn't Cohen at all, it's Kohn. What do you think of that, comrade?"

"Cohen is the American form of our Kohn," said the lieutenant drily. That much he knew from his future son-in-law.

"That's beside the point," the sergeant shot back. "The important thing is that it's an alias. The two of them got together in the Terezin ghetto when they were kids, and Cohen is in fact from Breclav. Are you aware, comrade, of what a perfect combination that is for subversive activity? Since we're not equipped to handle stuff like this in Homicide, I recommend that we investigate only the basic facts and then turn the whole thing over, lock, stock, and barrel, to the comrades in Counter-Espionage."

Silence followed. Malek looked uncertainly at his superior officer. Recently, Boruvka felt, Malek had somehow lost his former impetuosity and élan; despite his promotion he was now displaying a respect for the new sergeant that belied the differences in their ranks and professional qualifications. So he replied, "Our job is to track down the murderer. What the comrades in Interior do with the culprit is, shall we say, their own business — perhaps. It's not our job to pass judgement on what is or is not our political jurisdiction. In every murder case we have full authority to ensure that justice takes its course."

"On the one hand you're quite right, comrade," said Pudil. "But on the other hand, everything has to be approached from the political angle — especially now, when the main task our society faces is to eliminate political deformations caused by Dubcek and his revisionist clique."

And indeed the Party and the government, along with undeformed citizens, were hard at work, vigilantly eliminating deformations — as the lieutenant discovered for himself that very evening.

Coming home after a full day of investigation, he found himself in a vale of tears. Mrs. Boruvka was lying on the couch with a cold compress on her forehead. In place of their usual coal-black outlines, Zuzana's eyes were rimmed with a red that was entirely natural. Mack was gloomily pacing up and down, strumming his guitar, but he stopped when the lieutenant stepped into the room. Mr. and Mrs. McLaughlin were sitting at the kitchen table. The lieutenant's heart stopped beating for a moment. He was anticipating the worst.

"They've banished us from the republic," declared Mr. McLaughlin in a sepulchral voice. "For serving as English announcers on those radio stations that went underground during the Soviet invasion."

The lieutenant had been afraid this would come back to haunt them one day. Mr. McLaughlin's voice, heavy with the unmistakable accent of his native Tennessee, had been recorded not only by monitors in the West but also by the pro-Soviet radio stations located in East Germany at the time, though pretending to broadcast from "somewhere in Bohemia." But two years had gone by, Mr. McLaughlin was still playing trumpet in the Lucerna Bar, and Lieutenant Boruvka had begun to hope that the whole thing might have been forgotten in high places.

They gave us twenty-four hours," said Mr. McLaughlin, "and when I asked whether Mack could remain behind because he wants to marry a Czech girl —"

Wants to marry. The lieutenant hardly expected that his innermost hopes concerning Mack and his daughter would be fulfilled under such bad, if not tragic, circumstances. But in spite of the circumstances, a wave of warmth filled his paternal heart. Then he realized that his future brother-in-law was addressing a question to him:

"When I asked, do you know what that weasel of a policeman said?"

The lieutenant shook his head but a dark premonition began to overshadow the warm feeling in his heart.

"He said, 'We don't believe in breaking up families,'" Mack interjected bitterly. "So I'm getting turfed out with my parents. And the cop told me that even if I did marry Zuzana, I couldn't expect to get permission to stay."

The lieutenant stopped feeling well, but he overcame the pain that now gripped his heart and said bravely, "Well then, I suppose Zuzana will have to go to America with you. We'll miss her but — but — a woman's place is with her husband."

"Guess again, Father," Zuzana interrupted. "The cop also told Mack that just because he's going to marry me he shouldn't expect they'll let me go with him, because I've got Lucy and Mack's not her father."

"He said what?" shouted the lieutenant, and the blood

rose to his head. "That — that —"

"We'll get married first thing in the morning," said Mack. "And we'll think of something. Maybe I could get my cousin Laureen in Memphis to help. She'd come here, you could paste Zuzana's picture in her passport —" the lieutenant leaped for the telephone and took it off the hook — Zuzana could fly out, Laureen could claim she'd lost her passport, and the American embassy would give her a new one. She's an American citizen so they can't do anything to her." The lieutenant had the receiver up to his ear but he could hear nothing, and he hoped that no one else could either.

He watched his daughter trying valiantly to hold back her tears, and succumbed to one of his many fits of paternal love. Then he got his feelings under control again and began unscrewing the receiver, just to make sure.

"You'll get married, no question," he said decisively, "but forget about that idea with your cousin, Mack. You're still young and you can stick it out for a year or two. Meanwhile I'll do what I can."

He realized what this could mean for a man in his position, what secret obligations he might be exposed to. Even blackmail. But he also knew that he would go through anything for Zuzana and Mack, even if those little fish picked the last ounce of flesh from his bones. "Things will have to ease up here again," he said uncertainly, and then added, "and I think that right now a lot of people can be — ahem —" turning to the telephone, he unscrewed the mouthpiece and disconnected the bell "— bribed. I'll find a way, don't worry."

"But what if they won't let me out even then, Mack?" said Zuzana desperately. "You're not going to — you can't always —"

"I'll get you out of here," said Mack resolutely.

"But I don't want you to feel — just because of those idiots —" Zuzana swallowed the terrible word. "I'll marry you, Mack —" and the lieutenant saw that the natural pluck of his athletic daughter fading "— but if they still haven't let me go after two —" and she stopped and sobbed — or five years at the most, then promise — promise me you'll get a divorce —" The pivotwoman who had once made the national basketball team as a spare collapsed on the table and began to weep uncontrollably.

The lieutenant clenched his fists. Suddenly he was overcome

by a feeling he had never known before. It wasn't just hatred. It was beyond that. It was a kind of feeling he had only heard about in political courses. Could this, he caught himself wondering, be class hatred?

There was nothing either glorious or gay about the wedding, but it was fast and, because several officials had to be bribed (the normal waiting period was three months), it was expensive as well. The only thing suggesting a traditional wedding was the bridesmaid, who wore white. Four-year-old Lucy had, with great weeping, refused to give up her promised function, even in these exceptional circumstances, and so behind Mack in his Sunday best and Zuzana in her suit for the theater stood a little girl in a white lace dress. Instead of the promised train she held a piece of pink ribbon which they had fastened, for that purpose, around the bride's waist. It was a civil ceremony, and in promising to honor and obey the republic and its socialist system the newlyweds may well have sworn a false oath. Indeed, Mack, with his pending expulsion, was committing what amounted to perjury. The lieutenant's mind was so distracted by the multiple ironies of the ceremony that he forgot to tip the officiator; although the man had already been abundantly bribed, habit got the better of him and he deliberately burned a hole in the marriage certificate with his cigarette.

The McLaughlins almost missed the Pan American flight out of Prague. Barely an hour after the wedding the bride was standing on the windswept observation deck, deafened by the roar of four jet engines and watching the plane carry her husband into the leaden clouds hanging low over the airport. Driving home in a taxi, the lieutenant was overwhelmed by a hatred he now definitely identified as the feeling described in textbooks on Marxism-Leninism — a feeling he had once regarded as purely theoretical.

The essential facts of the murder — the only ones Sergeant Pudil was prepared to go into before handing the case over to the more appropriate police force — were easy enough to ascertain. Not long before he was found dead on the pathway of the Nusle

Gardens by the lovers, Ondrej Krasa had been drinking beer in the Mermaid Tavern in Podoli with two of his co-workers, Svata Kudelka and Jindra Nebesky. According to the testimony of his pals, he had made a telephone call just before setting out on his fateful journey home. Neither Kudelka nor Nebesky knew whom he had talked to.

The lieutenant's group of detectives questioned Krasa's co-workers in the garage belonging to the Candy and Sweets Communal Enterprises, but Sergeant Pudil played first violin all the way. Boruvka realized that he had somehow lost interest in his work, and even Malek was more reticent than usual. But the chairman of the Soviet Socialist Youth (known popularly as the SS Youth) completely made up for their lack of zeal.

"What kind of man was this Schoenfeld, comrades?" he asked the circle of drivers sitting on the workbenches or leaning against the walls of the garage.

After a long pause, Jindra Nebesky said, "Schoenfeld?"

"You didn't know his real name was Schoenfeld?" asked the sergeant in mock surprise. "I suppose that's natural. He'd have kept it a secret. I'm talking about Krasa."

"Oh, him. A great guy," said Nebesky with feeling.

That's a fact," said another driver with a shock of blond hair. "Never a party-pooper. Always stuck by the group."

"Did you know he'd been in jail for a political crime?"

"Oh, that. Sure, I knew he'd done something dumb once," admitted Nebesky.

"But he was only twenty when he did it. Not even that — nineteen at the most," interjected a driver with a classic Czech button nose. His name was Cespiva. "And he did it for his friends. That's an extenuating circumstance."

"There are no circumstances in the world," Pudil reminded him severely, "that can extenuate betraying the republic."

"But he did his time," said Svata Kudelka, who was also a driver.

"And for as long as he was with us, he worked like the devil. Just ask the boss."

"That doesn't surprise me. Elements like him are good at masking their true feelings. Did he have any contact with other Zionists?"

The drivers looked at each other uncomfortably.

"As far as I know, anyway, there aren't any of that sort around here," said Cespiva.

"What about the assistant manager?" asked Pudil triumphantly.

"Comrade Roth? He certainly wasn't buddies with Krasa." Cespiva shook his head. "And besides, Comrade Roth is not — what d'you call them — Zionist. He's a Communist. Chairman of the Party organization. As far as we know, Ondra only hung around with us. Ever since he got divorced he was kind of a loner. But, like I say, he was a great guy."

"Did any foreigners ever come to see him?"

Once more the drivers looked at each other. Then Kudelka said, "Never heard of any foreigners. Do you guys know of any foreigners?"

All the drivers shook their heads in unison. It occurred to the lieutenant that their collective evidence was adding up to the portrait of a quasi-saint. Perhaps these simple men were keeping silent about something — not Pudil's fantastic connections, which, the old detective's experience told him, were unlikely to exist outside the political pages of the Party daily — but something that might have blemished Krasa's image. After all, people have some deep-rooted taboos, one of which is against speaking ill of the dead. The lieutenant himself honored such traditions. But only off duty.

Malek may possibly have been thinking along the same lines, for he plucked up his courage and said, "You guys are making him out to be some kind of angel. Didn't he even pick his nose?"

The group of drivers again exchanged uneasy glances. Then Cespiva spoke. "I'm telling you, comrade, he was a great guy, honest. Except for beer he never drank, and he didn't even smoke."

I'll bet he wore a halo too, eh?"

"Pretty near," retorted Cespiva. "He only had one weakness and he couldn't help that."

"Women?"

"A woman. One woman," said Cespiva. "The bitch who couldn't wait for him to get out. Lida Oharikova. She was the reason his marriage bust up too."

And anyways, he only married someone else because he was pissed off at her," said Kudelka. "At least, that's what he said."

Aha," said Malek. "So he picked up where he'd left off six years before?"

Once more the drivers paused for a moment of silent consultation. Then Nebesky spoke. "No sense in trying to hush it up. You'll find out anyway," he said. "He was seeing her. And once he told Svata here that he was going to marry her one day, and that she was hardly sleeping with her old man any more, anyway."

"Enough of this false solidarity, comrades!" Pudil piped up. "What about foreign women?"

We'll look into that later," the lieutenant interrupted quickly.

They were the only words he had uttered during the entire interrogation.

An hour later he was looking at the walls of a room in a co-op flat. They were hung with paintings depicting a variety of setting suns, Prague's skyline with Hradcany Castle, and cows grazing against a background of white birch. He looked at the cheap furniture of no definable style, and at the young woman in a cluster, whose eyes were large, black, and — as Zuzana's had been not long ago — ringed with red circles.

"I did wait for him. Almost five years. But you know, I was very young and silly. I'll never forgive myself as long as I live. Any woman would count herself lucky if she had a man like — like Ondra."

"I understand. Your husband's a metalworker, is that right?" asked Malek.

"Yes. In the CKD plant."

"That him?" Malek pointed to a photograph of a mustached muscleman in a wrestler's leotard covered with more medals than the average Soviet general.

"Yes, that's Sucharipa. Franta. He's on the Hercules team in Nusle."

Malek looked significantly at the lieutenant, but when he found no sign of comprehension he turned towards Pudil. The sergeant, however, was studying the young woman's physiognomy closely. She had black hair, black eyes, a rather large and somewhat angular nose, and full red lips. The sergeant, unaware that Malek was looking at him, asked with characteristic directness,

"What are your origins, comrade?"

She looked startled. "Working class," she said, "except one grandfather who was a private cobbler. But he employed only members of his own family."

"That's not what I mean. I was thinking of your —"

"You were saying," the lieutenant broke in, "that Mr. Krasa was a good man and that you regret not having waited for him. It is possible that recently you may have come to some kind of an — ah — understanding?"

The young woman turned pink. The lieutenant could tell a good deal from the expression of her eyes. He knew very well that the sergeant suspected her of having origins he would refer to as 'racial' — but the sergeant was unaware of the connotations that word had for the lieutenant, who, twice already in his lifetime, had had to keep silent about the maiden name of one of his grand-mothers. But, the old detective thought, perhaps he just doesn't know any better — he was born after the war. Still, they shouldn't — "We've ascertained," he said quietly, "that you were seeing Mr. Krasa. Is that how it was?"

The woman looked at him. She was the color of a peony.

"Yes. I wanted a divorce. We met every Wednesday. I usually go to see my mother that day, so my husband never suspected — at least —" She stopped.

"Well, did he or didn't he?" asked Malek sharply.

"I mean he didn't know we were meeting on Wednesdays because Mother covered up for us. She's never liked Franta, she says he's a crude bully. She says all wrestlers are bullies."

"And is he?" asked Malek.

The black eyes looked down.

"Has he ever beaten you?"

The woman nodded. "Someone told him about Ondra and me. An anonymous phone call. So Franta wanted me to tell him if it was true or not."

She was silent again. Malek said, "And he beat you, is that it?"

The woman lifted her eyes and looked at the lieutenant. "Yes. But I told him straight to his face that I was going to divorce him and marry Ondra. And then he went out looking for Ondra —"

"So he roughed up your sweetheart too, is that it?" asked Malek.

Unexpectedly, the woman answered with a tone of pride in her voice.

"Not at all. Ondra beat him up. Sucharipa had to go to the hospital and they gave him seven stitches, here." She pointed to her forehead.

Malek looked at Pudil, but the SS Youth chairman was still scrutinizing the woman's suspicious-looking nose from behind halfclosed blond eyelashes. So Malek turned to the lieutenant and whistled softly. This time the lieutenant reacted. "But you said your husband was a wrestler."

"He's a heavyweight, but I don't know if you could really call him a wrestler. He usually just stands with his feet planted apart; his opponents pull and push, but he weighs 148 kilos and they never manage to budge him. Most of his matches end in a draw. That's why they keep him on at the club — he guarantees them at least a point in any competition. Once in a blue moon the other fellow loses his balance and Franta falls on him and pins him for two points." She spoke with deep disgust. "But basically he's a clumsy coward. And Ondra knew how to box. Before they locked — before he was sentenced, he boxed in tournaments. First he closed Franta's eyes so badly they swelled up like onions. And then, because Ondra was wearing a kind of — well, a kind of ring —"

"Was that from you?" Malek interrupted.

"Well — yes, from me. Anyway, then Ondra knocked him out — he hit him on the head so hard they had to put seven stitches into him," said the wrestler's wife, almost proudly.

"Obvious, isn't it?" deduced Malek when they were back in the car. "A wrestler, 148 kilos. Krasa was a shrimp, weighed only 67 kilos when he died, and he knocks him out and gives him an inferiority complex. And on top of that he's crawling into bed with the guy's old lady. According to the coroner's report, Krasa was killed with a blunt instrument, probably a hammer or wrench. So there you are — let's go wrap him up."

The lieutenant nodded gloomily, but before he could say anything the sergeant spoke up. "Did you look at that woman? A hook nose, dark as a crow, Hapsburg lips, a narrow face —"

"So what?" asked Malek uneasily.

"And Krasa was a boxer!" The sergeant raised his eyebrows dramatically. "Have you ever heard of a boxer punching someone in the forehead?"

"It wasn't exactly a regulation match."

"It makes no sense for a boxer to hit anyone in the forehead. But they train them that way," said Pudil mysteriously. "In karate. See what I'm getting at? It's a kind of South Korean fighting technique used for killing your opponent."

"In the West, maybe," said the lieutenant. "But Krasa was never in the West."

"Ah, but he was," said the sergeant triumphantly. "Right after the entry of the fraternal armies. Schoenfeld spent a week in Vienna."

The lieutenant couldn't resist loading his response with irony. "A week? And they taught him karate? Is that what you're saying?"

"A crash course," said the sergeant eagerly — himself a product of a crash course in criminology. "They have their methods."

"I doubt it," said the lieutenant. Although Pudil should have praised Boruvka's skeptical assessment of Western spy centers, he argued.

"I wouldn't underestimate them, comrade. Zionist circles have been stepping up their efforts recently. Look at how they're stirring up trouble in the Soviet Union: they all want to emigrate to Israel, which is out-and-out provocation. We weren't born yesterday."

"Well, that's very — interesting," said Malek, "but I don't see what it has to do with —"

They're so goddamn full of themselves!" shouted the SS chairman, beginning to lose his temper. They want to turn the wheel of history back! They call themselves the chosen people! But the historical role of the working class —"

All the way to the CKD factory to see the 148-kilo giant, Pudil tried to enlighten his superior officers on the Zionist conspiracy against peace, about which they displayed miserably little knowledge. When they found Sucharipa in the plant, the sergeant regarded him with undisguised sympathy. Also, he was working on the low turret of a tank into which some others were installing a naval cannon, and this sent Pudil into such transports of enthusiasm that he let Boruvka ask all the questions.

"That wasn't fair," said the giant, pointing to a flaming red scar on his forehead. "I'll bet he was wearing a set of knucks."

"Apparently he closed both your eyes," said the lieutenant. "Was that with brass knuckles too?"

That wasn't fair either. A boxer always has the advantage over a Graeco-Roman wrestler, and he fought dirty. He landed a one-two punch to my brows and blew out both my lights and then, when I couldn't see for the blood, that's when he probably slipped on the knucks."

"And you haven't seen him since he assaulted you, comrade?" asked the sergeant at last, having managed to overcome his fascination with the flattened gun turret.

"No. But he had the nerve to call me."

"When was that?" asked the detective.

"Same night he croaked. Could have been after ten. I was just watching the news."

What did he want?"

"Not me, that's for sure. The stupid bastard wanted to speak to Lida."

The lieutenant looked up. He suddenly remembered that he had forgotten to ask the giant's wife why she wasn't with her lover that night. After all, it had been a Wednesday. He said, "Did you call her to the phone?"

"Are you kidding?" growled the giant. "Of course not. I told him that if he tried phoning once more, I'd bust his jaw. Besides, Lida wasn't home anyway. She goes to see her mother every Wednesday."

"You believe that, do you?" said Malek.

The giant turned to him, a look of surprised suspicion growing in his eyes. "Her mother says so."

"She does, does she?" Malek pressed. "We've ascertained that your wife met Krasa every Wednesday evening. And your mother-in-law covered for them." Then he suddenly shouted, "And don't try to tell us you didn't know anything about it. Where were you Wednesday evening?"

But Malek's shout was drowned out by the wrestler's own

outburst. "That fucking witch? And I fucking believed her! I'll — I'll —"

"Just relax, comrade," said Malek, taken aback. "Relax —"

"He doesn't look much like a killer to me," admitted Malek when they were back in the squad car. "More like a chump. On the other hand, he was out to get him. And he had two good reasons. Plus he's got no alibi."

"What do you mean, no alibi?" Pudil retorted. "He was watching the news on TV."

"By himself," said Malek. "He'd have to have a witness."

"He remembered what the news was. Not in much detail, but he knew they showed a delegation and a blast furnace. And a speech by some comrade, either in a collective farm or in the mines. It's just that he couldn't recall whether the comrade was Comrade Bilak or Indra or someone else. And besides that, he remembered the weather. Not what they said, but that there was a weather report." Pudil's voice trailed off.

The lieutenant reflected that listening to TV news alone was perhaps the easiest available alibi in Czechoslovakia. Unless a Kennedy was assassinated that day —

Malek came to the sergeant's aid. "If we can prove that Krasa really did call him —"

"That's it, comrade! The telephone call. We can check that at the exchange —"

There's no way of tracing a local call," said the lieutenant, and couldn't resist another sarcastic comment. That is, not unless the comrades from the Interior were tapping Sucharipa's line."

"Hardly." Pudil shook his head. "Sucharipa's a reliable comrade. There'd be no reason to plant a bug."

"But we can try asking at the Mermaid," said the old detective.

"I couldn't say for sure, gentlemen." The pub-keeper shook his head. "He may have made a call. He was one of the regulars — when they call, they just toss the money into a box by the phone. They never ask me first. As far as I know, no one's ever cheated."

The pub-keeper looked around nervously. It was early afternoon on a weekday and the pub was humming with activity. A waitress with two fists full of half-liter glass mugs was hurrying among the tables, and a waiter in a spattered white shirt was distributing bowls of tripe soup and plates of sausages and onions. The Vltava River was sparkling in the sun outside the window. The lieutenant couldn't concentrate for the life of him.

"Far as I know, only Nebesky called," said the pub-keeper. "I remember him standing by the telephone. But you know, things aren't as slow at night as they are this time of the day."

What time did you see him call?"

"Oh, it must have been just before Krasa paid up and got ready to leave."

"Did you hear what Nebesky said? Or do you know who he called?"

"Are you kidding? In this racket?"

What about the fellows Krasa was drinking with? What were they doing? Playing cards?"

"No, just drinking. And they were arguing about something."

"About what?"

"No idea. Evenings, I don't know where my own head is. We've got our hands full here, not like now. There's no time to sit and talk with the customers."

The harried waitress rushed by with twenty brimming beer mugs. Malek said, "But they were arguing?"

"I'm sure of that. Krasa finally lost his temper — at least, that's the impression I got. Then he left. He usually stayed longer."

"Well, well," remarked Malek when they were back in the car. "So our angel got into an argument."

"Speak no ill of the dead," said the sergeant. "That's why the comrades kept up that false front of solidarity. Of course, I criticized them for it. In Schoenfeld's case their solidarity was definitely out of place."

The question did not embarrass the wrestler's wife. We'd arranged not to meet that evening. I'd promised my mother I'd go with her to visit my aunt. She's sick and alone at home."

"Naturally your mother and aunt will confirm that?" asked the sergeant.

"Why, certainly." The young woman looked surprised, and the sergeant squinted significantly at Boruvka and then at Malek. He met with two sphinx-like expressions and scowled.

"Did Schoenfeld — I mean Krasa — ever complain about conditions at work?"

Lida hesitated. "Well — the fact of the matter is, he wasn't too happy working at Humbug."

Where?"

"I mean at Candy and Sweets. He called it Humbug. Ondra had a . . . sense of humor —" The young woman had to stop to fend off tears once more.

"What didn't he like about it?" asked Lieutenant Boruvka.

Lida was struggling with her emotions and didn't answer right away. The sergeant spoke instead: "The work was too tough for him, eh? It's no bed of roses, loading and unloading all day, dragging those boxes around to the stores. The comrade drivers told me what hard work it is."

"No, he never complained about that part of it," said Lida quickly. "He was used to hard work."

"He also got a bonus recently. Two hundred crowns, for being an exemplary worker," Malek put in bravely.

"That wasn't the first time," said the young woman. "But it was something else. He said the group he was working with wasn't — well, they weren't a good group, if you know what I mean."

An almost sardonic smile appeared on the face of the chairman of the SS Youth. Malek said quickly, "But his buddies told us he always stuck by the group."

"Well, that's —" The young woman swallowed. "He had, you know, very high standards — I mean, of honor and things like that. It came from spending so many years in —" and she looked uneasily at the grinning sergeant — in that correctional institution. He said they all stuck together there."

"And here the comrades don't stick together, is that what you're trying to say?"

"I don't know. I only — I had the impression Ondra wasn't very fond of — the other drivers."

Maybe they weren't too fond of him either, eh?" said the sergeant.

"I don't know. He never told me much. He just used to say that if it weren't for the fact that you were in prison, doing time was better than working for Humbug."

"Why the hell should they be fond of him?" said Pudil angrily in the squad car. "They're all real workers, not the proletarized bourgeoisie that came out of the class struggle of the fifties, like him. And a Zionist to boot! Of course he fit in badly with the group."

They claim differently."

"They're too polite. They lack Lenin's toughness. There are still leftovers from the past, even among workers. 'Speak no ill of the dead.' But when the dead man is someone like Schoenfeld, 'nothing ill' means either a lie or a pipe dream. Naturally he was an exemplary worker. How else could he penetrate their collective? That's the only way the enemy can worm their way in!"

And after all," said the lieutenant, "the whole collective is exemplary. We found out they all get bonuses. Why should Krasa be unpopular with them for being an exemplary worker as well?"

The sergeant shot an offended glance at the lieutenant. "You don't understand, comrade?"

The lieutenant only shrugged his shoulders.

"It was most likely something else about him that spoiled their relationship. Probably something to do with his world view, if you ask me."

The old detective thought for a minute, then said quietly, "You may be right, comrade."

"An argument? With Ondra?" Jindra Nebesky was flabbergasted.

"That's what the pub-keeper says."

Why should we argue? We were the best of friends. Anyway, Ondra was as mild as a lamb."

"The pub-keeper says Krasa left the pub early because of an argument with you two."

What can I say?" Nebesky shook his head.

Suddenly Kudelka whispered, "Jindra —" He seemed nervous

to the lieutenant. In the few minutes they had been standing there in the garage with a small group of drivers, Kudelka had smoked two cigarettes and was working on his third. "Unless it was about —"

"About what?" asked the detective.

"About — you know — Lida." The lieutenant's experienced ears recognized clearly the voice of a prompter. But for a long time Nebesky said nothing and the old detective made no attempt to break the silence. Finally the driver said, "Oh, that!"

What?" barked Malek.

"It was nothing," said Kudelka. We just made fun of him. But in a friendly way. We weren't nasty about it."

"But he got mad anyway?"

Well — sort of mad. We were ribbing him because — like, we didn't know he'd be coming to the pub that night — that is, we weren't expecting him."

"Why not?" asked the lieutenant.

"Because he used to see her every Wednesday night. Lida, I mean."

"Then what was he doing in the pub that particular Wednesday?"

The question seemed to bring Nebesky to life again. "We asked him the same thing. He said Lida was off visiting a sick aunt. So I says, 'How do you know it's not a sick uncle and how do you know the uncle's not in the pink and are you sure it's just an uncle?' Dumb stuff like that. And he got sore."

"Was that all there was to it?'

"Well, I guess we did lay it on a little thick. You know, told him to ditch her, that kind of thing. We said she didn't wait for him last time and she'd dump him again when they got married, stuff like that. Stupid ribbing, I admit it. Poor bugger, we made his last night miserable."

"It's not your fault, comrades," said the sergeant. "He had it coming to him, seducing another comrade's wife."

"By the way," the lieutenant interrupted, turning to Nebesky, "who did you call just before Krasa left the pub?"

The driver obviously didn't expect the question. He coughed, then cleared his throat.

"I called Olda," he said and cleared his throat again. "I

— wanted him to — to bring his — set of wrenches to work the next day."

"Olda?"

"That's me." A fellow with a pale face got up from the work-bench. "Olda Huml. But I wasn't home."

Malek looked around sharply and then turned to Nebesky. "So you haven't got a witness to that telephone call?" Then, As you were!" he shouted at himself, "Yes he does, he's got the pub-keeper." He spun to face Huml instead. "But you," he roared, you don't have an alibi!"

"My father was home," said Huml. "He told Nebesky I was at Karel Bousek's place. So Jindra called me there."

"And what were you doing at Bousek's?" asked Malek, sheepish at his outburst.

"We were playing cards with Zbynek — I mean Cespiva," Huml replied, looking around the garage. "Karel's not here yet, but you can ask him. He lives in that highrise on Lookout Hill."

"Is that a co-op building?" asked the lieutenant.

For a moment there was silence. Then Nebesky said, "No, those are the new flats they've put straight onto the private mar-ket. Karel has a three-bedroom —" Nebesky's voice trailed off and there was silence once more.

"Who does Krasa's route now?" asked the lieutenant. "Me," said Kudelka.

At the office of Candy and Sweets the lieutenant asked for a list of the stores the dead driver had delivered to. He was given several lists — obviously Krasa had frequently been transferred from route to route. Perhaps because he was such an exemplary work-er. Perhaps because he wanted to penetrate the collective.

The old detective wondered.

Hell, I really put my foot in it over those telephone calls," lament-ed Malek in the squad car. "I knew the pub-keeper had seen him and I go asking him for witnesses — and Huml's not even under suspicion. He's got no motive and I —"

"You didn't put your foot in it at all, Pavel," said the lieutenant.

"You were right to ask. There are too many of those phone calls and they've got too many witnesses and they're all too dependable."

"What do you mean by that, comrade first lieutenant?" asked Pudil, annoyed. "Are you suggesting workers would lie?"

"People do lie," said the lieutenant gloomily. "After all, you don't consider Lida Sucharipa's mother and sick aunt as dependable witnesses."

"But that's something else altogether. We know the mother was part of the conspiracy —"

"What did you say, comrade?" asked the old detective with interest. "Conspiracy?"

Well, okay, maybe it's not the right word. What I mean is, she aided and abetted their screwing around."

"But maybe it is the right word," said the lieutenant. Malek looked at him in surprise.

"Though probably not for the activities that make for a divorce action," added the lieutenant.

That night, as usual in the past few years, the old detective had trouble getting to sleep. Through the open bedroom window the smell of flowers drifted in from Mala Strana, and also the faint strains of Eine kleine Nachtmusik, played by a string orchestra in the Ledeburske Gardens. But over the melody of the violins he could hear something else — an oft-played record coming from Zuzana's room. The sound was muffled but clear enough to the lieutenant's attentive ear:

Help me, Information,
Get in touch with my Marie;
She's the only one who'd phone me here
From Memphis, Tennessee. . . .

The lieutenant couldn't sleep. In his mind he saw the lanky young man in his blue jeans, now his son-in-law, in a clty he had never seen and would never in his life see, a city that bore the name of a famous brand of prewar cigarettes. Once, in a fit of holy indignation, the venerable Father Meloun had confiscated a packet of them from him. And then the usual ghostly procession of cases passed through the old detective's troubled mind — all solved yet unresolved, thanks to the vagaries of Justice. Or rather, class justice. The procession was led by a chalk-white dancer, followed by a skull with several teeth missing, then by female legs and arms in an almost aesthetic ornament. . . . The lieutenant was suddenly afraid he would go mad and do something that . . .

> Marie, she's so very young,
> So Information, please,
> Try to put me through to her
> In Memphis, Tennessee. . . .

Lieutenant Boruvka's heart almost stopped beating under its terrible burden of sadness.

"I'd like a hundred grams of Italian Mix," he said next morning to the white-haired lady behind the counter in a fussy little sweet-shop in Mala Strana. It was 8:30 and he was the first customer.

"A hundred grams of Italian Mix coming up, sir," sang the old lady in an unsteady voice, ladling up the candies from a bin with a chrome-plated scoop. She sifted them out into a paper bag on the scales and then, with her little finger — on which the lieutenant noticed a blackened fingernail — she pushed small pieces of chocolate from the scoop into the bag until the needle came to rest at a hundred grams.

She made sure it was the full hundred, perhaps because the customer was watching her so intently.

That will be three-ninety, please." She smiled at the old detective.

The lieutenant didn't return her smile. He reached into his pocket and, instead of money, pulled out a hundred-gram weight. He lifted the bag off the scales and replaced it with the weight.

"Sir, what are you —" The old lady made a feeble protest but her guilty conscience was too obvious. The detective gently pushed the wrinkled hand reaching for the weight. The needle of the scales came to rest at 120 grams and the old lady turned white.

The lieutenant looked at her reproachfully. He pulled his

badge out of his pocket and held it so that she could see it. Instead her eyes closed, and he just managed to catch her before she hit the floor. Then he carried her into the storage space behind the shop and put her in a chair until she regained consciousness.

"Whenever they come," she said, "they always say, 'I'm in a terrible hurry today, ma'am. I've got ten more stores to do before closing!' And then they start heaving the boxes into the storeroom and I haven't got time to count them and then they give me the invoice to sign and say, 'Come on, lady, don't give us a hard time, count them later. If there's anything missing, just let me know next week.' And there's always something missing."

The old lady began to cry.

"And do you tell them?"

"Yes, of course. And they just laugh at me. They say I'm an old woman and my eyes are bad. One time they counted the boxes as they unloaded them and the count was right. But then I weighed the boxes and they were all short."

"Why don't you report this to the head office?"

"I do, but they always brush me off and tell me I'll have to prove the delivery men are responsible. Once I told them to send someone to check and, wouldn't you know it, the very next day they sent a comrade from head office who hid out in front when they came, and that day everything was right."

The lieutenant nodded sadly. "So you started to steal from the customers."

"Oh, my God, sir, I had to. I've got to hand over all our cash received and it has to be correct, right down to the last heller. Anything short comes off my wages — and with what I'm getting, it would take half my pay just to make up the difference."

She was overwhelmed by a new fit of sobbing.

What about Mr. Krasa — did you complain to him too?"

The old lady wiped her eyes and looked into the lieutenant's moon-shaped face. "I told him about it, yes. Because after he started making deliveries, it all stopped. He seemed like a decent young man, so I told him what had been going on and he promised to look into it. And about a week after that they transferred him to another route and it started all over again. Maybe he was just talking, or maybe there was nothing he could do. It's not easy standing up to those crooks —"

"So you doctored the scales and started cheating again?"

"Please, sir, don't report me. I'll try and make it up to the customers, even if I have to die of starvation. I know almost all my customers, in person."

"There's no need to be upset," said the lieutenant. "I guarantee you that matters will soon be put right." He hesitated, then added, "There's more at stake than a few grams of Italian Mix."

From the division, he called the State Office of Inspection and gave them several clear instructions. Next he ordered Malek and Pudil to go to the Price Inspection Bureau and personally ensure that his orders were properly carried out. Then he went to the police garage, signed out an unmarked Skoda MB, and drove into the city.

On the seat beside him was the map of another route, which he had obtained in the Candy and Sweets office the day before. He looked at his watch, then drove to the candy shop in Konev Street and parked a short distance away. About a quarter of an hour later the delivery truck pulled up to the shop. On the sides of the truck were crude paintings of ice-cream bars, chocolates, and cakes. A wiry driver jumped out, opened the doors at the back of the truck, picked up an armful of boxes, and disappeared into the store. When he walked back through the shop to the truck, the lieutenant was standing at the counter ordering a hundred grams of humbugs. He looked grimly at the driver and the man recognized him immediately.

"Oh, morning, lieutenant," he said, turning slightly pale. Then he added conventionally — although it didn't sound like a convention — "How are things going?"

"All right," said the lieutenant gloomily.

"Well, I — excuse me, lieutenant, but I'm in a terrible rush. I've got eight more stores to do today," said an embarrassed Svata Kudelka, and rushed for the exit.

"Don't let me keep you," said the lieutenant, glowering like a thundercloud.

Then he paid for the humbugs, got into the Skoda MB, consulted the map on the seat beside him, and drove, at the greatest possible legal speed, to Zukov Street.

When Svata Kudelka saw the lieutenant in the Zukov Street shop, somberly watching the attendant weigh out a hundred grams of humbugs, he turned white.

"What a coincidence — isn't it?" he said.

"It is," agreed the detective. "Better get a move on so you can make it to those other stores — how many are left, seven?"

Kudelka tried to respond but finally said nothing. He left the store like a walking ghost.

In the shop on Tolbuchin Street the driver reeled, leaned against the counter, and stared at the lieutenant without even making an effort to say anything. So it was Boruvka who spoke first.

"Shall we go?" he asked. He paid for his hundred grams of humbugs and led the driver, now dripping with sweat, to the Skoda MB. They left the delivery van parked in the street. The lieutenant noticed that under the crudely drawn ice-cream bar someone had chalked in a faded word: HUMBUG.

It was like an epitaph.

"He simply gave them an ultimatum," Boruvka said that evening to Malek and Pudil. "He had served his term with criminals and murderers. As you know, in our correctional institutions we don't separate Krasa's kind from the hardened criminals." The sergeant was evidently getting ready to respond, so the detective hurried to finish what he wanted to say. "Perhaps it's democratic, but it gave Krasa a hatred — or rather, a need to have nothing more to do with such people. And then he got his job with Humbug and realized his co-workers were exactly the sort of people he'd learned to loathe in jail. According to Kudelka, when old Mrs. Souckova complained to him he went to the other drivers with an ultimatum. He said, 'If you were stealing from the state, maybe I'd keep quiet. But you're stealing from old women —'"

"There, you see, comrade lieutenant? Stealing from the state, which means from all of us — that wouldn't have bothered him."

"Yes," admitted the lieutenant, ideologically that was hardly the correct attitude. But after all, he was a proletarized bourgeois, as you know. Anyway, he gave them an ultimatum. They tried to bribe him but he refused."

"Because he was afraid!" burst out Pudil. "Not because he was such a holier-than-thou angel! He knew that our correctional institutions are no holiday camps!"

"Subjective motivation — as you'll certainly agree, comrade — does not count," said the lieutenant. What counts is what a man does."

Pudil snorted, but his Marxism failed him.

"The other drivers even invited him to join their —" he hesitated, then said it — their gang. A number of shop managers were members — these managers received the goods stolen from the other stores. Then they split the profits." He paused and then, against his will, added, "In America they call it racketeering."

He paused, waiting for Pudil's reaction, but the SS chairman only scowled.

"Anyway, he gave them this ultimatum," continued Lieutenant Boruvka, "and they decided to get rid of him. Bousek did the job. By the way, that was what put me on the right track: a delivery boy who can afford to buy a flat on the free market? And a three-bedroom one, yet? An apartment like that costs as least a hundred thousand. Probably more."

Why shouldn't a driver be able to buy a flat?" growled Pudil. "We're certainly not putting them up for the bourgeoisie."

"Could you afford it, man?" Malek blurted with unusual bitterness. He, like so many others, hadn't had the lieutenant's luck; he was on the wrong end of a long waiting list for a flat in the housing co-operative. "Or me?" he said. "And I'm not a bourgeois either. My father was a shoemaker who got ruined in the Depression by competition from the Bata company."

The SS chairman was silent. He was a graduate of several courses, but they had all been crash courses, and the case, from a class point of view, was obviously too complicated for him. The lieutenant went on.

"They knew that every Wednesday Krasa walked Lida home before eleven o'clock. Bousek was going to wait for him near where the Sucharipas lived. They were supposed to be playing cards — to give Bousek an alibi — at Huml's place, but Huml's father unexpectedly showed up on a visit. So they got up and went to Bousek's place, but they didn't have time to get word to the other two who were establishing their alibis in the Mermaid. Then a second thing happened that they weren't prepared for: Krasa showed up at the Mermaid at eight o'clock. That's why Nebesky called — first to Huml's place and then, when Huml's father told him where they were, to Bousek's. They made a quick change of plan and one of them drove to the street where Sucharipa lives to pick up the waiting Bousek. He took him to Nusle Gardens because that's the way Krasa had to walk back from the pub."

The lieutenant lit a cigar. There was still no reaction from Pudil.

"So it wasn't Lida they were arguing about," said the detective. "It was Krasa's ultimatum. And it wasn't Krasa who called Sucharipa, it was Nebesky. All he had to do was disguise his voice a little. Sucharipa was not what you'd call bright. But they had to make sure Lida wasn't already home, because they had an idea. They knew that Sucharipa was jealous of Krasa and that Krasa had beaten him up. It worked right into their plan: Sucharipa would have no alibi, being at home alone, but he had a motive and he's a metal-worker. And they planned to kill Krasa with a hammer."

The hour of five struck from a nearby church tower. The lieutenant looked out the window. In a nest above a little-known saint, two young pigeons were getting ready to make their first flight.

"Very well," said Pudil in an annoyed tone. "They're a bunch of chumps and an embarrassment to the working class. And they have to be justly but harshly punished.

The lieutenant looked at the small, scowling face of the confused idealist.

"If it makes you feel any better, comrade," he said, "stealing from old lady shopkeepers was just a sideline. The real operation was a big one. The company director himself was involved. And even —" he glanced at Pudil out of the corner of his eye and almost felt sorry for him, so he decided to buck him up — "even Comrade Roth, the Party secretary. For example, a whole wagonload of cocoa got lost —"

The sergeant suddenly went red in the face and was gripped

by a fierce outburst of hatred, undoubtedly of the class variety. "What a bloody mess!" he shouted. They made a real pigsty out of the country in just nine months, those filthy Dubcekists. Revisionists, all of them! It's going to take years to set things right again!"

This time the little fish from the Paraná River were satisfied; the lieutenant's conscience remained calm and no one else joined the pale procession in his night dreams. Yet still he had trouble sleeping. Into the August night of his inner hearing (or was it from his daughter's room?) he heard a young man in blue jeans calling across the distances from a city whose name smelled of those cigarettes confiscated ages ago by the venerable Father Meloun. . . .

Help me, Information
Can't ask for more, but please!
You don't know how I miss her
In Memphis, Tennessee. . . .

The old detective had a miserable feeling that the young man was calling out in vain.

1990 WINNER

JOSEF SKVORECKY
"Humbug"
The End of Lieutenant Boruvka

Nominees:

WILLIAM BANKIER
"One Day at a Time"
Cold Blood II

ELAINE MITCHELL MATLOW
"Safe as Houses"
Cold Blood II

JAMES POWELL
"Burning Bridges"
Ellery Queen Mystery Magazine

ERIC WRIGHT
"Kaput"
Mistletoe Mysteries

Innocence

F rancis must be late, surely, Reed thought as he stood waiting on the bridge by the railway station. He was beginning to feel restless and uncomfortable; the handles of his holdall bit into his palm, and he noticed that the rain promised in the forecast that morning was already starting to fall.

Wonderful! Here he was, over two hundred miles away from home, and Francis hadn't turned up. But Reed couldn't be sure about that. Perhaps he was early. They had made the same arrangement three or four times over the past five years, but for the life of him, Reed couldn't remember the exact time they'd met.

Reed turned and noticed a plump woman in a threadbare blue overcoat come struggling against the wind over the bridge towards him. She pushed a large pram, in which two infants fought and squealed.

"Excuse me," he called out as she neared him, "could you tell me what time school gets out?"

The woman gave him a funny look — either puzzlement or irritation, he couldn't decide which — and answered in the clipped, nasal accent peculiar to the Midlands: "Half past three." Then she hurried by, giving Reed a wide berth.

He was wrong. For some reason, he had got it into his mind that Francis finished teaching at three o'clock. It was only twenty-five past now, so there would be at least another fifteen minutes to wait before the familiar red Escort came into sight.

The rain was getting heavier and the wind lashed it hard against Reed's face. A few yards up the road from the bridge was the bus station, which was attached to a large modern shopping center, all glass and escalators. Reed could stand in the entrance there, just beyond the doors where it was warm and dry, and still watch for Francis.

At about twenty-five to four, the first schoolchildren came dashing over the bridge and into the bus station, satchels swinging, voices shrill and loud with freedom. The rain didn't seem to bother them, Reed noticed: hair lay plastered to skulls; beads of rain hung on the tips of noses. Most of the boys' ties were askew, their socks hung loose around their ankles, and their shoelaces snaked along the ground. It was a wonder they didn't trip over themselves. Reed smiled, remembering his own schooldays.

And how alluring the girls looked as they ran smiling and laughing out of the rain into the shelter of the mall. Not the really young ones, the unformed ones, but the older, long-limbed girls, newly aware of their breasts and the swelling of their hips. They wore their clothes carelessly: blouses hanging out, black woolly tights twisted or torn at the knees. To Reed, there was something wanton in their disarray.

These days, of course, they probably all knew what was what, but Reed couldn't help but feel that there was also a certain innocence about them: a naive, carefree grace in the way they moved, and a casual freedom in their laughter and gestures. Life hadn't got to them yet; they hadn't felt its weight and seen the darkness at its core.

Mustn't get carried away, Reed told himself, with a smile. It was all very well to joke with Bill in the office about how sexy the schoolgirls who passed the window each day were, but it was positively unhealthy to mean it, or (God forbid!) attempt to do anything about it. He couldn't be turning into a dirty old man at thirty-five, could he? Sometimes the power and violence of his fantasies worried him, but perhaps everyone else had them too. It wasn't something you could talk about at work. He didn't really think he was abnormal; after all, he hadn't acted them out, and you couldn't be arrested for your fantasies, could you?

Where the hell was Francis? Reed peered out through the glass. Wind-blown rain lashed across the huge plate windows and distorted the outside world. The scene looked like an Impressionist painting. All detail was obliterated in favor of the overall mood: gray-glum and dream-like.

Reed glanced at his watch again. After four o'clock. The only schoolchildren left now were the stragglers, the ones who lived nearby and didn't have to hurry for a bus. They sauntered over the bridge, shoving each other, playing tag, hopping and skipping over the cracks in the pavement, oblivious to the rain and the wind that drove it.

Francis ought to be here by now. Worried, Reed went over the arrangements again in his mind. He knew that he'd got the date right because he'd written it down in his appointment book. Reed had tried to call the previous evening to confirm, but no-one had answered. If Francis had been trying to get in touch with him at work or at home, he would have been out of luck. Reed had been visiting another old friend — this one in Exeter — and Elsie, the office receptionist, could hardly be trusted to get her own name right.

When five o'clock came and there was still no sign of Francis, Reed picked up his holdall again and walked back down to the station. It was still raining, but not so fast, and the wind had dropped. The only train back home that night left Birmingham at nine-forty and didn't get to Carlisle until well after midnight. By then the local buses would have stopped running and he would have to get a taxi. Was it worth it?

There wasn't much alternative, really. A hotel would be too expensive. Still, the idea had its appeal: a warm room with a soft bed, shower, color television, and maybe even a bar downstairs where he might meet a girl. He would just have to decide later. Anyway, if he did want to catch the train, he would have to take the eight-fifty from Redditch to get to Birmingham in time. That left three hours and fifty minutes to kill.

As he walked over the bridge and up towards the town center in the darkening evening, Reed noticed two schoolgirls walking in front of him. They must have been kept in detention, he thought, or perhaps they'd just finished games practice. No doubt they had to do that, even in the rain. One looked dumpy from behind, but her friend was a dream: long wavy hair tumbling messily over her shoulders; short skirt flicking over her long, slim thighs; white socks fallen around her ankles, leaving her shapely calves bare. Reed watched the tendons at the back of her knees flex and loosen as she walked and thought of her struggling beneath him, his hands on her soft throat. They turned down a side street and Reed carried on ahead, shaking off his fantasy.

Could Francis have got lumbered with taking detention or games? he wondered. Or perhaps he had passed by without even noticing Reed sheltering from the rain. He didn't know where Francis's school was, or even what it was called. Somehow, the subject had just never come up. Also, the village where Francis lived was about eight miles away from Redditch, and the local bus service was terrible. Still, he could phone. If Francis were home, he'd come out again and pick Reed up.

After phoning and getting no answer, Reed walked around town for a long time looking in shop windows and wondering about how to get out of the mess he was in. His holdall weighed heavy in his hand. Finally, he got hungry and ducked out of the light rain into the Tandoori Palace. It was still early, just after six, and the place was empty apart from a young couple absorbed in one another in a dim corner. Reed had the waiter's undivided attention. He ordered pakoras, tandoori and dhal. The food was very good, and Reed ate it too fast.

After the spiced tea, he took out his wallet to pay. He had some cash, but he had decided to have pint or two, and he might have to take a taxi home from the station. Best hang onto the paper money. The waiter didn't seem to mind taking plastic, even for so small a sum, and Reed rewarded him with a generous tip.

Next he tried Francis again, but the phone just rang and rang. Why didn't the bugger invest in an answering machine? Reed cursed. Then he realized he didn't even have one himself, hated the things. Francis no doubt felt the same way. If you were out, tough tittie; you were out, and that was that.

Outside, the street-lights reflected in oily puddles on the roads and pavements. After walking off his heartburn for half an hour, thoroughly soaked and out of breath, Reed ducked into the first pub he saw. The locals eyed him suspiciously at first, then ignored him and went back to their drinks.

"Pint of bitter, please," Reed said, rubbing his hands together. "In a sleeve glass, if you've got one."

"Sorry, sir," the landlord said, reaching for a mug. "The locals bring their own."

"Oh, very well."

"Nasty night."

"Yes," said Reed. "Very."

"From these parts?"

"No. Just passing through."

"Ah." The landlord passed over a brimming pint mug, took Reed's money, and went back to the conversation he'd been having with a round-faced man in a pin-stripe suit. Reed took his drink over to a table and sat down.

Over the next hour and a half, he phoned Francis four more times, but still got no reply. He also changed pubs after each pint, but got very little in the way of a friendly greeting. Finally, at about twenty to nine, knowing he couldn't bear to wake up in such a miserable town even if he could afford a hotel, he went back to the station and took the train home.

Because of his intended visit to Francis, Reed hadn't planned anything for the weekend at home. The weather was miserable, anyway, so he spent most of his time indoors reading and watching television, or down at the local. He tried Francis's number a few more times, but still got no reply. He also phoned Camille, hoping that her warm, lithe body and her fondness for experiment might brighten up his Saturday night and Sunday morning, but all he got was her answering machine.

On Monday evening, just as he was about to go to bed after a long day catching up on boring paperwork, the phone rang. Grouchily, he picked up the receiver: "Yes?"

"Terry?"

"Yes."

"This is Francis."

"Where the hell —"

"Did you come all the way down on Friday?"

"Of course I bloody well did. I thought we had an —"

"Oh God. Look, I'm sorry, mate, really I am. I tried to call. That woman at work — what's her name?"

"Elsie?"

"That's the one. She said she'd give you a message. I must admit she didn't sound as if she quite had her wits about her, but I'd no choice."

Reed softened a little. "What happened?"

"My mother. You know she's been ill for a long time?"

"Yes."

"Well, she died last Wednesday. I had to rush off back to Manchester. Look, I really am sorry, but you can see I couldn't do anything about it, can't you?"

"It's me who should be sorry," Reed said. "To hear about your mother, I mean."

"Yes, well, at least there'll be no more suffering for her. Maybe we could get together in a few weeks?"

"Sure. Just let me know when."

"All right. I've still got stuff to do, you know, things to organize. How about if I call you back in a couple of weeks?"

"Great, I'll look forward to it. Bye."

"Bye. And I'm sorry, Terry, really."

Reed put the phone down and went to bed. So that was it — the mystery solved.

The following evening, just after he'd arrived home from work, Reed heard a loud knock at his door. When he opened it, he saw two strangers standing there. At first he thought they were Jehovah's Witnesses — who else came to the door in pairs, wearing suits? — but these two didn't quite look the part. True, one did look a bit like a Bible salesman — chubby, with a cheerful, earnest expression on a face fringed by a neatly-trimmed dark beard — but the other, painfully thin, with a long, pock-marked face, looked more like an undertaker, except for the way his sharp blue eyes glittered with intelligent suspicion.

"Mr Reed? Mr Terence J. Reed?" the cadaverous one said, in a deep, quiet voice, just like the way Reed imagined a real undertaker would speak. And wasn't there a hint of the Midlands nasal quality in the way he slurred the vowels?

"Yes, I'm Terry Reed. What is it? What do you want?" Reed could already see, over their shoulders, his neighbors spying from their windows: little corners of white net-curtain twitched aside to give a clear view.

"We're police officers, sir. Mind if we come in for a moment?" They flashed their identity cards but put them away before Reed had time to see what was written there. He backed into the hallway, and they took their opportunity to enter. As soon as they had closed the door behind them, Reed noticed the one with the beard start glancing around him, taking everything in, while the other continued to hold Reed's gaze. Finally, Reed turned and led them into the living-room. He felt some kind of signal pass between them behind his back.

"Nice place you've got," the thin one said, while the other prowled the room, picking up vases and looking inside, opening drawers an inch or two, then closing them again.

"Look, what is this?" Reed said. "Is he supposed to be poking through my things? I mean, do you have a search warrant or something?"

"Oh, don't mind him," the tall one said. "He's just like that. Insatiable curiosity. By the way, my name's Bentley, Detective Superintendent Bentley. My colleague over there goes by the name of Inspector Rodmoor. We're from the Midlands Regional Crime Squad." He looked to see Reed's reactions as he said this, but Reed tried to show no emotion at all.

"I still don't see what you want with me," he said.

"Just routine," said Bentley. "Mind if I sit down?"

"Be my guest."

Bentley sat in the rocker by the fireplace, and Reed sat opposite on the sofa. A mug of half-finished coffee stood between them on the glass-topped table, beside a couple of unpaid bills and the latest Radio Times.

"Would you like something to drink?" Reed offered.

Bentley shook his head.

"What about him?" Reed glanced over nervously towards Inspector Rodmoor, who was looking through his bookcase, pulling out volumes that caught his fancy and flipping through them.

Bentley folded his hands on his lap: "Just try to forget he's here."

But Reed couldn't. He kept flicking his eyes edgily from one to the other, always anxious about what Rodmoor was getting into next.

"Mr Reed," Bentley went on, "were you in Redditch on the evening of November 9? Last Friday, that was."

Reed put his hand to his brow, which was damp with sweat. "Let me think now. . . . Yes, yes, I believe I was."

"Why?"

"What? Sorry. . .?"

"I asked why. Why were you in Redditch? What was the purpose of your visit?"

He sounded like an immigration control officer at the airport, Reed thought. "I was there to meet an old university friend," he answered. "I've been going down for a weekend once a year or so ever since he moved there."

"And did you meet him?"

"As a matter of fact, no, I didn't." Reed explained the communications breakdown with Francis.

Bentley raised an eyebrow. Rodmoor rifled through the magazine rack by the fireplace.

"But you still went there?" Bentley persisted.

"Yes. I told you, I didn't know he'd be away. Look, do you mind telling me what this is about? I think I have a right to know."

Rodmoor fished a copy of Mayfair out of the magazine rack and held it up for Bentley to see. Bentley frowned and reached over for it. The cover showed a shapely blonde in skimpy pink lace panties and camisole, stockings and a suspender belt. She was on her knees on a sofa, and her round behind faced the viewer. Her face was also turned towards the camera, and she looked as if she'd just been licking her glossy red lips. The thin strap of the camisole had slipped over her upper arm.

"Nice," Bentley said. "Looks a bit young, though, don't you think?"

Reed shrugged. He felt embarrassed and didn't know what to say.

Bentley flipped through the rest of the magazine, pausing over the color spreads of naked women in fetching poses.

"It's not illegal you know," Reed burst out. "You can buy it in any newsagent's shop. It's not pornography."

"That's a matter of opinion, isn't it, sir?" said Inspector Rodmoor, taking the magazine back from his boss and replacing it.

Bentley smiled. "Don't mind him, lad," he said. "He's a Methodist. Now where were we?"

Reed shook his head.

"Do you own a car?" Bentley asked.

"No."

"Do you live here by yourself?"

"Yes."

"Ever been married?"

"No."

"Girlfriends?"

"Some."

"But not to live with?"

"No."

"Magazines enough for you, eh?"

"Now just a minute —"

"Sorry," Bentley said, holding up his skeletal hand. "Pretty tasteless of me, that was. Out of line."

Why couldn't Reed quite believe the apology? He sensed very strongly that Bentley had made the remark on purpose to see how he would react. He hoped he'd passed the test. "You were going to tell me what all this was about . . ."

"Was I? Why don't you tell me about what you did in Redditch last Friday evening first. Inspector Rodmoor will join us here by the table and take notes. No hurry. Take your time."

And slowly, trying to remember all the details of that miserable, washed-out evening five days ago, Reed told them. At one point, Bentley asked him what he'd been wearing, and Inspector Rodmoor asked if they might have a look at his raincoat and holdall. When Reed finished, the heavy silence stretched on for seconds. What were they thinking about? he wondered. Were they trying to make up their minds about him? What was he supposed to have done?

Finally, after they had asked him to go over one or two random points, Rodmoor closed his notebook and Bentley got to his feet: "That'll be all for now, sir."

"For now?"

"We might want to talk to you again. Don't know. Have to check up on a few points first. We'll just take the coat and the holdall with us, if you don't mind, sir. Inspector Rodmoor will give you a receipt. Be available, will you?"

In his confusion, Reed accepted the slip of paper from Rodmoor and did nothing to stop them taking his things. "I'm not planning on going anywhere, if that's what you mean."

Bentley smiled. He looked like an undertaker consoling the bereaved. "Good. Well, we'll be off then." And they walked towards the door.

"Aren't you going to tell me what it's all about?" Reed asked again as he opened the door for them. They walked out onto the path, and it was Inspector Rodmoor who turned and frowned. "That's the funny thing about it, sir," he said, "that you don't seem to know."

"Believe me, I don't."

Rodmoor shook his head slowly. "Anybody would think you don't read your papers." And they walked down the path to their Rover.

Reed stood for a few moments watching the curtains opposite twitch and wondering what on earth Rodmoor meant. Then he realized that the newspapers had been delivered as usual the past few days, so they must have been in with magazines in the rack, but he had been too disinterested, too tired, or too busy to read any of them. He often felt like that. News was, more often than not, depressing, the last thing one needed on a wet weekend in Carlisle. Quickly, he shut the door on the gawping neighbors and hurried towards the magazine rack.

He didn't have far to look. The item was on the front page of yesterday's paper, under the headline, MIDLANDS MURDER SHOCK. It read,

The quiet Midlands town of Redditch is still in shock today over the brutal slaying of schoolgirl Debbie Harrison. Debbie, 15, failed to arrive home after a late hockey practice on Friday evening. Police found her partially-clad body in an abandoned warehouse close to the town centre early Saturday morning. Detective Superintendent Bentley, in charge of the investigation, told our reporter that police are pursuing some positive leads. They would particularly like to talk to anyone who was in the area of the bus station and noticed a strange man hanging around the vicinity late that afternoon. Descriptions are vague so far, but the man was wearing a light tan raincoat and carrying a blue holdall.

He read and reread the article in horror, but what was even worse than the words was the photograph that accompanied it. He couldn't be certain because it was a poor shot, but he thought it was the schoolgirl with the long wavy hair and the socks around her ankles, the one who had walked in front of him with her dumpy friend.

The most acceptable explanation of the police visit would be that they needed him as a possible witness, but the truth was that the "strange man hanging around the vicinity" wearing "a light tan raincoat" and carrying a "blue holdall" was none other than himself, Terence J. Reed. But how did they know he'd been there?

The second time the police called, Reed was at work. They marched right into the office, brazen as brass, and asked him if he could spare some time to talk to them down at the station. Bill only looked on curiously, but Frank, the boss, was hardly able to hide his irritation. Reed wasn't his favorite employee, anyway; he hadn't been turning enough profit lately.

Nobody spoke during the journey, and when they got to the station, one of the local policemen pointed Bentley towards a free interview room. It was a bare place: gray metal desk, ashtray, three chairs. Bentley sat opposite Reed, and Inspector Rodmoor sat in a corner, out of his line of vision.

Bentley placed the buff folder he'd been carrying on the desk and smiled his funeral director's smile. "Just a few further points, Terry. Hope I don't have to keep you long."

"So do I," Reed said. "Look, I don't know what's going on, but shouldn't I call my lawyer or something?"

"Oh, I don't think so. It isn't as if we've charged you or anything. You're simply helping us with our enquiries, aren't you? Besides, do you actually have a solicitor? Most people don't."

Come to think of it, Reed didn't have one. He knew one, though. Another old university friend had gone into law and practised nearby. Reed couldn't remember what he specialized in.

"Let me lay my cards on the table, as it were," Bentley said, spreading his hands on the desk. "You admit you were in Redditch last Friday evening to visit your friend. We've been in touch with him, by the way, and he verifies your story. What puzzles us is what you did between, say, four and eight-thirty. A number of people saw you at various times, but there's at least an hour or more here and there that we can't account for."

"I've already told you what I did."

Bentley consulted the file he had set on the desk. "You ate at roughly six o'clock, is that right?"

"About then, yes."

"So you walked around Redditch in the rain between five and six, and between six-thirty and seven? Hardly a pleasant aesthetic experience, I'd imagine."

"I told you, I was thinking things out. I looked in shops, got lost a couple of times. . . ."

"Did you happen to get lost in the vicinity of Simmons Street?"

"I don't know the street names."

"Of course. Not much of a street, really, more an alley. It runs by a number of disused warehouses —"

"Now wait a minute! If you're trying to tie me in to that girl's murder, then you're way off beam. Perhaps I had better call a solicitor, after all."

"Ah!" said Bentley, glancing over at Rodmoor. "So you do read the papers?"

"I did. After you left. Of course I did."

"But not before?"

"I'd have known what you were on about, then, wouldn't I? And while we're on the subject, how the hell did you find out I was in Redditch that evening?"

"You used your credit card in the Tandoori Palace," Bentley said. "The waiter remembered you and looked up his records."

Reed slapped the desk. "There! That proves it. If I'd done what you seem to be accusing me of, I'd hardly have been as daft as to leave my calling card, would I?"

Bentley shrugged. "Criminals make mistakes, just like everybody else. Otherwise we'd never catch any. And I'm not accusing you of anything at the moment. You can see our problem, though, can't you? Your story sounds thin, very thin."

"I can't help that. It's the truth."

"What state would you say you were in when you went into the Tandoori Palace?"

"State?"

"Yes. Your condition."

Reed shrugged. "I was wet, I suppose. A bit fed up. I hadn't been able to get in touch with Francis. Hungry, too."

"Would you say you appeared agitated?"

"Not really, no."

"But someone who didn't know you might just assume that you were?"

"I don't know. Maybe. I was out of breath."

"Oh? Why?"

"Well I'd been walking around for a long time carrying my holdall. It was quite heavy."

"Yes, of course. So you were wet and breathless when you ate in the restaurant. What about the pub you went into just after seven o'clock?"

"What about it?"

"Did you remain seated long?"

"I don't know what you mean."

"Did you just sit and sip your drink, have a nice rest after a heavy meal and a long walk?"

"Well, I had to go to the toilet, of course. And I tried phoning Francis a few more times."

"So you were up and down, a bit like a yo-yo, eh?"

"But I had good reason! I was stranded. I desperately wanted to get in touch with my friend."

"Yes, of course. Cast your mind back a bit earlier in the afternoon. At about twenty past three, you asked a woman what time the schools came out."

"Yes. I . . . I couldn't remember. Francis is a teacher, so naturally I wanted to know if I was early or late. It was starting to rain."

"But you'd visited him there before. You said so. He'd picked you up at the same place several times."

"I know. I just couldn't remember if it was three o'clock or four. I know it sounds silly, but it's true. Don't you ever forget little things like that?"

"So you asked the woman on the bridge? That was you?"

"Yes. Look, I'd hardly have done that, would I, if . . . I mean . . . like with the credit card. I'd hardly have advertised my intentions if I was going to . . . you know. . . ."

Bentley raised a beetle-black eyebrow. "Going to what, Terry?"

Reed ran his hands through his hair and rested his elbows on the desk. "It doesn't matter. This is absurd. I've done nothing. I'm innocent."

"Don't you find schoolgirls attractive?" Bentley went on in a soft voice. "After all, it would only be natural, wouldn't it? They can be real beauties at fifteen or sixteen, can't they? Proper little temptresses, some of them, I'll bet. Right prick-teasers. Just think about it — short skirts, bare legs, firm young tits. Doesn't it excite you, Terry? Don't you get hard just thinking about it?"

"No, it doesn't," Reed said tightly. "I'm not a pervert."

Bentley laughed. "Nobody's suggesting you are. It gets me going, I don't mind admitting. Perfectly normal, I'd say, to find a fifteen-year old schoolgirl sexy. My Methodist Inspector might not agree, but you and I know different, Terry, don't we? All that sweet innocence wrapped up in a soft, desirable young body. Doesn't it just make your blood sing? And wouldn't it be easy to get a bit carried away if she resisted, put your hands around her throat...?"

"No!" Reed said again, aware of his cheeks burning.

"What about those women in the magazine, Terry? The one we found at your house?"

"That's different."

"Don't tell me you buy it just for the stories."

"I didn't say that. I'm normal. I like looking at naked women, just like any other man."

"Some of them seemed very young to me."

"For Christ's sake, they're models. They get paid for posing like that. I told you before, that magazine's freely available. There's nothing illegal about it." Reed glanced over his shoulder at Rodmoor, who kept his head bent impassively over his notebook.

"And you like videos, too, don't you? We've had a little talk with Mr Hakim in your corner shop. He told us about one video in particular you've rented lately. Soft porn, I suppose you'd call it. Nothing illegal, true, at least not yet, but a bit dodgy. I'd wonder about a bloke who watches stuff like that."

"It's free country. I'm a normal single male. I have a right to watch whatever kind of videos I want."

"*School's Out*," Bentley said quietly. "A bit over the top, wouldn't you say?"

"But they weren't real schoolgirls. The lead was thirty if she was a day. Besides, I only rented it out of curiosity. I thought it might be a bit of a laugh."

"And was it?"

"I can't remember."

"But you see what I mean, don't you? It looks bad: the subject-matter, the image. It all looks a bit odd. Fishy."

"Well it's not. I'm perfectly innocent, and that's the truth."

Bentley stood up abruptly and Rodmoor slipped out of the room. "You can go now," the superintendent said. "It's been nice to have a little chat."

"That's it?"

"For the moment, yes."

"But don't leave town?"

Bentley laughed. "You really must give up those American cop shows. Though it's a wonder you find time to watch them with all those naughty videos you rent. They warp your sense of reality — cop shows and sex films. Life isn't like that at all."

"Thank you. I'll bear that in mind," Reed said. "I take it I am free to go?"

"Of course." Bentley gestured towards the door.

Reed left. He was shaking when he got out onto the wet, chilly street. Thank God the pubs were still open. He went into the first one he came to and ordered a double Scotch. Usually, he wasn't much of a spirits drinker, but these, he reminded himself as the fiery liquor warmed his belly, were unusual circumstances. He knew he should go back to work, but he couldn't face it: Bill's questions, Frank's obvious disapproval. No. He ordered another double, and after he'd finished that, he went home for the afternoon. The first thing he did when he got into the house was tear up the copy of Mayfair and burn the pieces in the fireplace one by one. After that, he tore up his Video Club membership card and burned that too. Damn Hakim!

"Terence J. Reed, it is my duty to arrest you for the murder of Deborah Susan Harrison. . . ."

Reed couldn't believe this was happening. Not to him. The world began to shimmer and fade before his eyes, and the next thing he knew Rodmoor was bent over him offering a glass of water, a benevolent smile on his Bible salesman's face.

The next few days were a nightmare. Reed was charged and held until his trial date could be set. There was no chance of bail, given the seriousness of his alleged crime. He had no money anyway, and no close family to support him. He had never felt so alone in his life as he did those long dark nights in the cell. Nothing terrible happened. None of the things he'd heard about in films and documentaries: he wasn't sodomized; nor was he forced to perform fellatio at knife-point; he wasn't even beaten up. Mostly he was left alone in the dark with his fears. He felt all the certainties of his life slip away from him, almost to the point where he wasn't even sure of the truth any more: guilty or innocent? The more he proclaimed his innocence, the less people seemed to believe him. Had he done it? He might have done.

He felt like an inflatable doll, full of nothing but air, manoeuvred into awkward positions by forces he could do nothing about. He had no control over his life anymore. Not only couldn't he come and go as he pleased, he couldn't even think for himself any more. Solicitors and barristers and policemen did that for him. And in the cell, in the dark, everything seemed to close in on him and some nights he had to struggle for breath.

When the trial date finally arrived, Reed felt relief. At least he could breathe in the large, airy courtroom, and soon it would be all over, one way or another.

In the crowded court, Reed sat still as stone in the dock, steadily chewing the edges of his newly grown beard. He heard the evidence against him — all circumstantial, all convincing.

If the police surgeon had found traces of semen in the victim, an expert explained, then they could have tried for a genetic match with the defendant's DNA, and that would have settled Reed's guilt or innocence once and for all. But in this case it wasn't so easy: there had been no seminal fluid found in the dead girl. The forensics people speculated, from the state of her body, that the killer had tried to rape her, found he was impotent, and strangled her in his ensuing rage.

A woman called Maggie, with whom Reed had had a brief fling a year or so ago, was brought onto the stand. The defendant had been impotent with her, it was established, on several occasions towards the end of their relationship, and he had become angry about it more than once, using more and more violent means to achieve sexual satisfaction. Once he had gone so far as to put his hands around her throat.

Well, yes he had. He'd been worried. During the time with Maggie, he had been under a lot of stress at work, drinking too much as well, and he hadn't been able to get it up. So what? Happens to everyone. And she'd wanted it like that, too, the rough way. Putting his hands around her throat had been her idea, something she'd got from a kinky book she'd read, and he'd gone along with her because she told him it might cure his impotence. Now she made the whole sordid episode sound much worse than it had been. She also admitted she had been just eighteen at the time, as well, and, as he remembered, she'd said she was twenty-three.

Besides, he had been impotent and violent only with Maggie. They could have brought on any number of other women to testify to his gentleness and virility, though no doubt if they did, he thought, his promiscuity would count just as much against him. What did he have to do to appear as normal as he needed to be, as he had once thought he was?

The witnesses for the prosecution all arose to testify against Reed like the spirits from Virgil's world of the dead. Though they were still alive, they seemed more like spirits to him: insubstantial, unreal. The woman from the bridge identified him as the shifty-looking person who had asked her what time the schools came out; the Indian waiter and the landlord of the pub told how agitated Reed had looked and acted that evening; other people had spotted him in the street, apparently following the murdered girl and her friend. Mr Hakim was there to tell the court what kind of videos Reed had rented lately — including *School's Out* — and even Bill told how his colleague used to make remarks about the schoolgirls passing by: "You know, he'd get all excited about glimpsing a bit of black knicker when the wind blew their skirts up. It just seemed like a bit of a lark. I thought nothing of it at the time." Then he shrugged and gave Reed a pitying look. And as if all that weren't enough, there was Maggie, a shabby Dido, refusing to look at him as she told the court of the way he had abused and abandoned her.

Towards the end of the prosecution case, even Reed's barrister was beginning to look depressed. He did his best in cross-examination, but the damnedest thing was that they were all telling the truth, or their versions of it. Yes, Mr Hakim admitted, other people had rented the same videos. Yes, he might have even watched some of them himself. But the fact remained that the man on trial was Terence J. Reed, and Reed had recently rented a video called *School's Out*, the kind of thing, ladies and gentlemen of the jury, that you wouldn't want to find your husbands or sons watching.

Reed could understand members of the victim's community appearing against him, and he could even comprehend Maggie's hurt pride. But why Hakim and Bill? What had he ever done to them? Had they never really liked him? It went on and on, a nightmare of distorted truth. Reed felt as if he had been set up in front of a funfair mirror, and all the jurors could see was his warped and twisted reflection. I'm innocent, he kept telling himself as he gripped the rail, but his knuckles turned whiter and whiter and his voice grew fainter and fainter.

Hadn't Bill joined in the remarks about schoolgirls? Wasn't it all in the spirit of fun? Yes, of course. But Bill wasn't in the dock. It was Terence J. Reed who stood accused of killing an innocent fifteen-year-old schoolgirl. He had been in the right place at the right time, and he had passed remarks on the budding breasts and milky thighs of the girls who had crossed the road in front of their office every day.

Then, the morning before the defence case was about to open — Reed himself was set to go on the dock, and not at all sure by now what the truth was — a strange thing happened.

Bentley and Rodmoor came softly into the courtroom, tiptoed up to the judge and began to whisper. Then the judge appeared to ask them questions. They nodded. Rodmoor looked in Reed's direction. After a few minutes of this, the two men took seats and the judge made a motion for the dismissal of all charges against the accused. Pandemonium broke out in court: reporters dashed for phones and the spectators' gallery buzzed with speculation. Amidst it all, Terry Reed got to his feet, realized what had happened, if not how, and promptly collapsed.

Nervous exhaustion, the doctor said, and not surprising after the ordeal Reed had been through. Complete rest was the only cure.

When Reed felt well enough, a few days after the trial had ended in uproar, his solicitor dropped by to tell him what had happened. Apparently, another schoolgirl had been assaulted in the same area, only this one had proved more than a match for her attacker. She had fought tooth and nail to hang onto her life, and in doing so had managed to pick up a half brick and crack the man's skull with it. He hadn't been seriously injured, but he'd been unconscious long enough for the girl to get help. When he was arrested, the man had confessed to the murder of Debbie Harrison. He had known details not revealed in the papers. After a night-long interrogation, police officers had no doubt whatsoever that he was telling the truth. Which meant Reed couldn't possibly be guilty. Hence, motion for dismissal, end of trial. Reed was a free man again.

He stayed home for three weeks, hardly venturing out of the house except for food, and even then he always went further afield for it than Hakim's. His neighbors watched him walk by, their faces pinched with disapproval, as if he were some kind of monster in their midst. He almost expected them to get up a petition to force him out of his home.

During that time he heard not one word of apology from the undertaker and the Bible salesman; Francis still had "stuff to do . . . things to organize"; and Camille's answering machine seemed permanently switched on.

At night, Reed suffered claustrophobic nightmares of prison. He couldn't sleep well, and even the mild sleeping pills the doctor gave him didn't really help. The bags grew heavier and darker under his eyes. Some days he wandered the city in a dream, not knowing where he was going, or, when he got there, how he had arrived.

The only thing that sustained him, the only pure, innocent, untarnished thing in his entire life, was when Debbie Harrison visited him in his dreams. She was alive then, just as she had been when he saw her for the first and only time, and he felt no desire to rob her of her innocence, only to partake of it himself. She smelled of apples in autumn, and everything they saw and did together became a source of pure wonder. When she smiled, his heart almost broke with joy.

At the end of the third week, Reed trimmed his beard, got out his suit, and went in to work. In the office, he was met with an embarrassed silence from Bill and a redundancy cheque from Frank, who thrust it at him without a word of explanation. Reed shrugged, pocketed the cheque and left.

Every time he went in town, strangers stared at him in the street and whispered about him in pubs. Mothers held more tightly onto their daughters' hands when he passed them by in the shopping centres. He seemed to have become quite a celebrity in his home-town. At first, he couldn't think why, then one day he plucked up the courage to visit the library and look up the newspapers that had been published during his trial.

What he found was total character annihilation, nothing less. When the headline about the capture of the real killer came out, it could have made no difference at all; the damage had already been done to Reed's reputation, and it was permanent. He might have been found innocent of the girl's murder, but he had been found guilty too, guilty of being a sick consumer of pornography, of being obsessed with young girls, unable to get it up without the aid of a struggle on the part of the female. None of it was true, of course, but somehow that didn't matter. It had been made so. As it is written, so let it be. And to cap it all, his photograph had appeared almost every day, both with and without the beard. There could be very few people in England who would fail to recognize him in the street.

Reed stumbled outside into the hazy afternoon. It was warming up towards spring, but the air was moist and grey with rain so fine it was closer to mist. The pubs were still open, so he dropped by the nearest one and ordered a double Scotch. The other customers looked at him suspiciously as he sat hunched in his corner, eyes bloodshot and puffy from lack of sleep, gaze directed sharply inwards.

Standing on the bridge in the misty rain an hour later, Reed couldn't remember making the actual decision to throw himself over the side, but he knew that was what he had to do. He couldn't even remember how he had ended up on this particular bridge, or the route he'd taken from the pub. He had thought, drinking his third double Scotch, that maybe he should go away and rebuild his life, perhaps abroad. But that didn't ring true as a solution. Life is what you have to live with, what you are, and now his life was what it had become, or what it had been turned into. It was what being in the wrong place at the wrong time had made it, and that was what he had to live with. The problem was, he couldn't live with it; therefore, he had to die.

He couldn't actually see the river below — everything was grey — but he knew it was there. The River Eden, it was called. Reed laughed harshly to himself. It wasn't his fault that the river that runs through Carlisle is called the Eden, he thought; it was just one of life's little ironies.

Twenty-five to four on a wet Wednesday afternoon. Nobody about. Now was as good a time as any.

Just as he was about to climb onto the parapet, a figure emerged from the mist. It was the first girl on her way home from school. Her gray pleated skirt swished around her long, slim legs, and her socks hung over her ankles. Under her green blazer, the misty rain had wet the top of her white blouse so much that it stuck to her chest. Reed gazed at her in awe. Her long blonde hair had darkened and curled in the rain, sticking in strands over her cheek. There were tears in his eyes. He moved away from the parapet.

As she neared him, she smiled shyly.

Innocence.

Reed stood before her in the mist and held his hands out, crying like a baby.

"Hello," he said.

1991 WINNER

PETER ROBINSON
"Innocence"
Cold Blood III

Nominees:

JOHN NORTH
"Out of Bounds"
Cold Blood III

JAS. R. PETRIN
"Man on the Roof"
Cold Blood III

SARA PLEWS
"Blind Date"
Cold Blood III

JAMES POWELL
"The Tamerlane Crutch"
Cold Blood III

Two in the Bush

From the day The Boozer became my cell mate and first told me about Clyde Parker, it took us nearly a year to set him up. In the end, though, the long delay turned out to be for the best because when we did catch up with him, the timing, Christmas Eve, was perfect.

Clyde Parker was the owner of a pub on King Street East. The Old Bush was a beer parlor, not a "men only" parlor but not the kind of place that ladies felt comfortable in either, and as the man said, those that came in left, or they did not remain ladies very long. It had graduated from being one of the worst holes in the east end of the city to being quaint, one of the last unrenovated survivors of the days when drink was as feared as polyunsaturated fat is now. The Old Bush was such a relic that it was discovered a few years ago by a wine columnist who wrote an article about it which brought in a few people who were looking for an authentic experience, but they didn't come back once they'd got it. The regular patrons stared at them. If there was only one or two of these tourists they'd leave them alone, but if six or eight of them came in, someone would give a signal and the pub would go quiet as the regular patrons stared at them. They didn't like that. A lot of old-timers used the place, and you could generally count on finding a few rounders there on a weeknight.

It was The Boozer who put us on to the fact that Clyde Parker, the owner, might be whispering into the ear of the coppers. I say "might" because we weren't sure for a long time, which was why we didn't go for Parker in a heavy way as soon as Boozer had tipped us. We had to give him the benefit of the doubt.

The Boozer had just done a nice little job over in Rosedale. At the time he was paying a window cleaner to let him know of any empties he came across, and one day he reported that the inhabitants of a certain house on Crescent Road had gone on vacation, and access was relatively simple. The Boozer duly dropped by at 3 a.m. with a few copies of *The Globe and Mail* in case anyone was about, let himself in the back door, and helped himself to a sackful of small stuff — silver, jewelry, and such, including a real piece of luck, a twenty-ounce gold bar he found in a desk drawer. The Boozer claimed it was about the cleanest little job he'd ever done. He worked with Toothy Maclean on lookout. Utterly reliable, Toothy was. So when they came for The Boozer, three days later, he had a long think and the only one he could see shopping him was Clyde Parker.

See, the night after the job, The Boozer had called in at the Bush for a few draft ales, and to pay for his beer he off-loaded a few trinkets, cuff links and such, on Old Perry. Old Perry paid him about a tenth of what they were worth, which in itself was about a tenth of what you'd have to pay in a store, but The Boozer was thirsty and he had plenty of goods left. Old Perry made his living by having the money in his pocket when you were thirsty, and we'd all dealt with him. We'd have known years ago if he was a narc. The other alternative, Toothy Maclean, was unthinkable. Then The Boozer remembered that Clyde Parker had been hovering round when he passed the stuff over to Old Perry, so he began to wonder. He confided in me and the two of us did some asking around and we came up with three others who'd been fingered not long after they'd brushed up against Parker. So that's how it was; we didn't have any proof, but we were pretty sure.

The Boozer wanted to send a message to the outside to have Parker done, but I talked him out of it. Not too heavy, I told him, because we might be wrong, and anyway, let's do it ourselves, let's be there when it happens. I was beginning to get an idea; though, when The Boozer asked, I said I didn't know yet. We had plenty of time to think about it. I got The Boozer calmed down, but he said if I didn't get a good idea, then he'd torch the Bush as soon as he got out.

I wanted something a bit subtler than that. I wanted to hurt Parker in his pride and his wallet at the same time, I wanted to cost him money and make him look foolish, and, if possible, I wanted him to know who'd done it without him being able to do anything about it. It wouldn't be easy getting past all those pugs that Parker used as waiters to look out for him.

About three-quarters of the way through our term — me and The Boozer had both of us still a couple of months to do — I got an idea. Or rather, I got the last piece of an idea I'd been putting together for a few months. Ideas are like that with me.

The first part of the idea came from a cell mate I'd had at the beginning of my stretch. He'd got ninety days for impersonating a Salvation Army man. You know, going door to door, soliciting contributions and giving you a blessing with the receipt. What he'd done, he'd got a Salvation Army cap one night from the hostel when no one was watching, and another night he got a pad of receipts off the desk in the office, and with a black raincoat and a shirt and tie he looked the part perfectly. He said he picked up five hundred a night, easy, in a district like Deer Park. A lot of people gave him checks, of course, which he threw away, but he didn't count on them calling the office when the checks didn't go through. (A lot of people deserve to be inside.) Two months later the coppers were waiting for him. He should have worked it for a week, then stayed off the streets for at least six months, as a Sally Ann collector, I mean. There's plenty of other things he could have been doing. But he got greedy and silly and they caught up with him taking up a collection round the Bunch of Grapes on Kingston Road. So that's where I got a bit of an idea.

I got the second part of my idea at a prison concert. You had to attend, and there was this citizen on the bill, singing a lot of old-fashioned songs. "Sons of Toil and Sorrow" was one. "A Bachelor Gay Am I" was another. In prison, I ask you. Some of the younger cons thought he'd made the songs up himself. And it wasn't just the choice of song. He couldn't sing. He was terrible — loud and embarrassing, hooting and hollering away, the veins sticking out all over his neck as he tried to get near the notes. The others nick-named him Danny Boy, which he said was his signature tune. I thought, you should stick to hymns, buddy, because he reminded me exactly of a carol singer who used to sing with a Salvation Army band when I was a kid.

Then I realized that I had it.

All I needed was a trumpet player and someone on the accordion, and we were all set.

Me and The Boozer were both sprung in October and we moved in together. My wife had visited me once to tell me not to try going home again, ever, and Boozer had no home, so we found this little apartment on Queen Street near the bail and parole unit where we had to appear from time to time.

We were both on welfare, of course, at first; then we both found jobs of the kind that offered no temptation, and that no one else wanted. The Boozer got taken on at a car wash, and I found a situation in a coal-andwood yard, filling fifty-pound sacks with coal. Neither of us needed the work. Boozer had gone down protesting his innocence, so he still had his loot stashed away, but he couldn't touch it for a few months because they were watching him. As for me, I was always the saving kind.

Did I tell you what I got shipped for? I sell hot merchandise on the streets. You've seen me, or someone like me, if you've ever gone shopping along the Danforth. I'm the one who jumps out of a car and opens a suitcase full of Ralph Lauren sweatshirts that I am prepared to let go for a third of the price, quick, before the cops come. You buy them because you think they're stolen, which is the impression I'm trying to create, but in point of fact I buy them off a Pakistani jobber on Spadina for five dollars each. I'd pay ten if they weren't seconds and the polo player looked a bit more authentic. I've sold them all — fake Chanel Number 5, fake Gucci, Roots, the lot. Anything to appeal to the crook in you. Sometimes the odd case of warmish goods does come my way, but I prefer to deal in legit rubbish if I can get it.

So there I was, unloading a suitcaseful of shirts that had withstood a warehouse fire, good shirts if a bit smoky, and the fuzz nabbed me for being an accomplice to a dip.

I was working the dim-sum crowd on the corner of Spadina and Dundas on a Sunday morning and I was just heading for my car to load up again, when someone shouted his wallet was gone, and then another shouted, and then another. Before you knew it, two martial-arts experts grabbed me and the cops were called and I got twelve months. I never even saw the dip.

But to get back to my story. First I had to get a couple of musicians. That wasn't easy until I bumped into one in the lineup at the bail and parole unit, a guy I'd known inside, who played in the prison band. He played trumpet, or cornet really, when he wasn't doing time for stealing car radios. He found me a trombone player. Then I had a real piece of luck because right after that I ran into the original authentic terrible hymn singer from the prison concert.

At first he wouldn't hear of it, but I went to work on him and he saw the virtue in what we were planning and promised to think it over. The next time we met, he agreed. I should have known.

We decided we could manage without an accordion player.

Now we had to get some uniforms. All we really needed were the caps. The trumpet player used to be a legit chauffeur and he still had his old black jacket, and he thought he could put his hand on some others. The owner of the limousine fleet kept a bundle of uniforms in his garage storeroom, and Digger Ray assured us that getting access to them would not be a problem. Digger Ray was the trombone player. He was Australian and his specialty was playing the fake sucker in crooked card games, but he'd done a few B and E jobs. Toothy Maclean lifted the caps for us while The Boozer created a disturbance during prayers at the Salvation Army shelter. (He started crying and repenting right in the middle of a prayer and Toothy got all the caps from the office while they were comforting him.)

Now The Boozer had to line up three or four cooperating citizens who would be unknown to Clyde Parker, fellas who didn't use the Old Bush. It wasn't easy, but Boozer came up with three guys who hardly ever drank — not too common among his acquaintance, I can tell you — and once they heard about it they were keen to be included. So we were set. Now I had to go to work. I had the trickiest job of all.

I was the obvious person to approach Clyde Parker because I'd only been in the Bush once, years ago. I hate the place, always have. It's the kind of beer parlor where there's a civil war being fought at every table and the waiters are hired to break up fights, and if you stay until midnight someone will throw up all over your shoes. I like a nice pub, myself.

So Parker didn't know me and when I approached him he was very wary, at first. I went in two or three times until I was sure who he was, then I got talking to him. Had he heard, I asked, of this fake Salvation Army band that was going around the pubs collecting? He hadn't, but if they came near the Old Bush, he'd be ready, he said. He nodded to indicate a couple of his waiters who were lounging against the wall, waiting for orders. I don't know where he finds them, but they look as if he has to chain them up when the pub is closed. No, no, I said, there's a better way than that, and then I told him.

People like Parker are born suspicious, but they are also born greedy and very conceited. They think they are smart. So the plan was designed to make Parker feel smart, which it did, and to make him some money, and when he saw the point, he was in.

It was a lovely night, Christmas Eve. About ten o'clock the sky was black and clear with thousands of stars winking away. It must have been like that the night one of them started to move. I'd've followed it.

Danny Boy had the car and we were to meet at my place. I drove after that. We reached the street behind the Bush at ten-fifteen. Zero hour was ten-thirty. We figured four carols, about fifteen minutes, then the collection during one more, and out of there by eleven.

They waited in the car while I slipped across to the pub and made sure Hooligan was in place. Didn't I mention Hooligan? His real name was Halligan, and renaming him Hooligan tells you something about the level of wit in the Don Jail. He was our ace in the hole, the one Parker didn't know about. Because of him we had to steal another cap, and this time I couldn't get to one nohow. Then Toothy remembered that a buddy of his had a dog that his kids had trained to catch Frisbees. It got very good at picking them out of the air, but the trouble was that when there were no Frisbees to chase, he filled in the time chasing kids and snatching their hats off. He was harmless, but parents complained, and they had to keep him locked up. The kids could get him to snatch anyone's hat by pointing to it and whispering. As I say, Herman never hurt anyone. He could take off your hat from behind clean as a whistle without touching you, just one leap. So we borrowed Herman one night and waited near the Salvation Army shelter and pretty soon out came an officer and set off down Sherbourne Street. A few minutes later Herman lifted his hat. It fit Hooligan pretty good, too.

I checked that Hooligan was in place, and in we went. Parker had arranged a little clear space by the door, though he pretended to be surprised when we walked in. I approached him, very formal-like, and asked his permission to play some carols and pass round the collection plate. He acted up a bit by shaking his head, then be seemed to change his mind. "All right," he said. "Four carols." I looked grateful and swung my arm the way conductors do, and off they went.

A trumpet and a trombone wouldn't amount to much, you would think, but these fellas made them seem just made for the job. Very simple, just the notes, no twiddly bits. They were good. And of course, there was Danny Boy. He was as good as another trumpet. He didn't wait for a cue. Just started right in, head back, veins sticking out. He could be heard right in the back of the room, right in the corners. They started with "O Come, All Ye Faithful," which Danny Boy gave a verse in Latin of, then "Good King Wenceslas" and "We Three Kings," and finally, one of Danny's shut-eyed ones, "O Holy Night." By then we had them. Danny was terrible, of course, but he was very sincere and you could recognize the tunes. I wouldn't say anyone was crying — this was the Old Bush, after all — but they were quiet. So now we went into "O Little Town of Bethlehem," very soft, "piano" they call it, and Toothy and I began the rounds with the money bags.

This was Parker's signal. We was getting something from nearly everyone, a dollar here, two there, a five, then another. There's a psychology to these things. As soon as someone puts in five dollars, that becomes standard, like the ante in a poker game. People stop fingering their change and open their wallets. After four tables, five was normal. Then Parker spoke. "Gents," he said. "Gents, this is Christmas Eve." He paused, looking sincere. "I want to announce that I will match all contributions made tonight toward this good cause."

"And a free beer all around," someone shouted.

One of the waiters moved to throw him out, but Parker only hesitated for a second. "Never mind the free beer tonight, of all nights," he said, implying that free beer was standard on other nights at the Bush. "Tonight is for the others out there." He waved at the door. "The ones with no beer," he said.

The arrangement was, of course, that Parker would get half,

three-quarters, really, including his own money, but free beer could never be recovered.

The next voice, though, nearly took him off balance, I reached a table where The Boozer had planted one of his cronies, and Boozer gave him a wink from the back of the room, and he jumps up and shouts, "Then here's fifty dollars."

Parker looked a bit greasy for a minute, but he caught himself in time to shout, "Good for you."

Then the fever took hold. The biggest single contribution we got was a hundred dollars, but no one gave less than twenty, and every time I came to one of The Boozer's cronies he would whip up the excitement with a fresh fifty. We went round the room with Danny Boy crooning away in the background, and when we were done we went back to the counter and emptied the bags onto the bar. Digger Ray and one of the bartenders counted it and Digger made the announcement. "Two thousand three hundred and twenty-seven." Someone shouted, "Your turn now, Parker."

Parker turned to the barman and held out his hand and received a wad of money which he handed over to Digger. Digger held it up to show it was a lot of money, no need to count it on Christmas Eve, and he swept all the money back into one of the bags and we were ready to go. There was still three minutes on my watch, so I made a little speech, and then, right on time, Hooligan made his entrance.

He was got up like the rest of us — Salvation Army gear, and a little collection box.

We'd rehearsed the next bit carefully.

"Merry Christmas all, and God bless you," Hooligan says, while the crowd started to look a bit puzzled.

Parker looked at me in a panic. The smell of something fishy was now reaching into the farthest corners of the room and I would have given the patrons about ten more seconds. "Holy Jesus," I said to Parker. "It's a real one. What'll we do now? There'll be a riot if they find out."

The two musicians and Danny Boy slid out the door and one of the patrons said, "What the hell's going on?"

Give him the money," I said. "For God's sake, give him the money."

Parker couldn't speak, but he nodded, and I stepped forward.

"Coals to Newcastle," I said very loud and heartily. "Coals to Newcastle, sending two groups to the same place. But you're just in time, Captain. Here." I handed him the sack of money.

Hooligan's eyes rolled up in holy wonder. "Bless you, gentlemen," he said. "Bless you."

I was praying he wouldn't do anything silly like make the sign of the cross over the room, and I signaled to Toothy that we should be on our way. Then I heard a sound that made my blood run cold. Someone opened the door and "Joy to the World" came flooding through, played by all fifteen members of the Salvation Army's silver band.

Parker, of course, was not surprised. Hooligan was his surprise, and he assumed that the band was backup for him.

Now there was just me and Toothy — Hooligan could look after himself — so I put my hand on Toothy's shoulder in a brotherly way and we almost got through the door before we were stopped by Sister Anna herself. She looked at Hooligan, puzzled. Hooligan looked at me. Parker looked at us both, and I did the only thing I could. I took the money off Hooligan, put it in the sister's hands, said, "Merry Christmas, Sister," and took Toothy and Hooligan with me through the door.

The car was gone, of course — the motto with us, if a job goes wrong, is "Pull the ladder up, Jack. I'm in." But no one was chasing us, so we threw our caps away and hailed a cab.

We waited until after New Year's, then we got an educated friend of Toothy's to pretend to be a reporter for a news station doing a story on Christmas giving, and the Salvation Army commander told him what had happened. "Someone phoned us, here at the shelter," the commander said. "They told us if we would come to the Old Bush and play a few carols, we would get a major contribution. We gathered it was some kind of surprise, arranged by the proprietor."

We never knew for a long time who had done it; then, about six months after, The Boozer and I were stopped dead in Nathan Phillips Square by the sight of Danny Boy, eyes closed, head back, in the middle of "Abide With Me." He was in full uniform. Behind him was the Salvation Army silver band.

We waited for him to come round with the collecting box. We kept our heads down, and when he drew level I looked up sharply.

"Hello, Danny Boy," I said. "How long you been with this mob?"

He looked surprised, but not for long. "I saw the light last Christmas," he said. "Brother." And he moved away, shaking his box. The Salvation Army were just being charitable, of course, welcoming the backslider, never mind that his singing hadn't improved a bit, not to sinners' ears, anyway. You could say that what mattered was that he was in tune with God.

The Boozer wanted to do him right then and there, but I held him off. As I pointed out, it had cost us nothing, but Parker was out a couple of thousand, and the boys in the Old Bush (to whom we'd slipped the story) were still laughing.

Even on a good day, you can't win every race.

1992 WINNER

ERIC WRIGHT
"Two in the Bush"
Christmas Stalkings

Nominees:

GAIL HELGASON
"Wild Stock"
Great Canadian Murder and Mystery Stories

JAMES POWELL
"Santa's Way"
Ellery Queen Mystery Magazine

JAMES POWELL
"Winter Hiatus"
Ellery Queen Mystery Magazine

PETER SELLERS
"This One's Trouble"
Alfred Hitchcock Mystery Magazine

Mantrap

"Women don't know anything about Mantraps!" Johnson declared. He wore the embittered expression of an ex-cop, an expression that reminded me of my ex-husband. Without waiting for my response, he limped away. I followed him through Level 1 of the Natural History Museum.

I'd just settled on a pithy reply when Johnson, a huge man, graceful despite the bad leg, stopped abruptly and fired at me, "Been in security long, Margaret?"

"It's Maggie, and I worked part-time at a condo for a year."

He snorted, an old war-horse not about to approve of mares on the battlefield. "Gonna meet Bill Warren soon. Forewarned's forearmed. Do unto him before he gets a chance to do you."

"Pardon?" But Johnson ignored me. He headed for double doors in the south wall. They looked the same as dozens of other "No Admittance" double doors throughout the museum.

"Never stops John Q. Public," he complained, punching the crash bar. "Once you're through, these lock automatically. Key-man, that's me today, has the key." He shook a ring of dozens of keys in my face and turned and hobbled down the steps.

"Where do they go?" I nodded at the stairs leading up.

"Invertebrate Level 2. Early Man Level 3. Big brass above it all." He unlocked the doors on Level B-1. They opened onto a large and people-free gallery of mannequins wearing Native Canadian traditional dress and positioned in "realistic" situations. I scanned the room, peering at bone-handled hunting knives, bows and arrows, lances and tomahawks, all dangerous weapons in the wrong hands. Outside the gallery was a corridor

I recognized. It led to the Control Room and the Supervisor's office, where I came in.

I followed Johnson back into the stairwell and down the last two flights. As we descended, the air warmed considerably.

"Level-1 North come in." Ann Macintosh's sultry voice wafted out of my walkie-talkie, static-riddled.

"Go ahead."

"Instead of your 11:30 break, proceed directly to Level-2 North. Got that?"

"Roger."

"You handle that like a pro," Johnson commented.

I slipped the walkie-talkie back into the case slung across my body. "I'm electronically inclined."

He checked his watch. "Eleven seven. Let's go."

We went through the lowest set of doors and entered a long and wide, gray-concrete corridor, our soles and Johnson's wheeze faintly echoing in the hollowness. The air was hotter and thinner. We trudged along to a fork.

"Mantrap 14's to the right." Johnson, gasping and trying to hide it, pointed to the tunnel with the best lighting. "This way," he started limping down the dimly lit tunnel, "leads to M-15. Both exit the south side of the building."

The fire tunnel narrowed and curved. Bad lighting and sweltering heat produced claustrophobia, accompanied by blind faith. I'd been phobia-free since my divorce. Maybe it was being alone with a dense male in a cramped space.

"Don't come down here alone," he warned gruffly, as though I was hell-bent on the idea. "Tunnels are long. Some maniac could be waiting with an axe. Besides, if you're trapped you could be here a while before anybody finds you. If you don't have the keys you can't get out. Happened once. New guard wandered down by mistake. Time we found him he was screaming."

Johnson looked at me like a teller of ghost tales who'd just delivered the scariest line.

I waved my radio rebelliously.

He snorted. "That call you got was in the stairwell. Tunnel's different. Weak batteries, you can't transmit."

Finally, we came to the end of the tunnel and yet another set of double doors.

"This is Mantrap 15. In here's a space and a door to the street. Open these doors and the one to the street automatically dead bolts. An alarm goes off in Control that automatically locks the first set of doors too. Whoever's in here's trapped."

"How do they get out?"

"In a real fire, Control can release all the locks. Otherwise they send down the Key-man to check the individual violation."

"But if an alarm goes off every stairwell door you open, Control would know about the violation long before the intruder got this far."

"If the alarms go off. Problem is, all stairwells and Mantraps are on the same panel. Two triggered at once, both could fail to signal. Overloads happen all the time because the doors are opened all the time. That's electronics. Give me manpower any day."

Johnson called Control for permission to enter Mantrap 15. A faint voice from the radio said 'roger'.

I pressed the push-bar but the door only opened twelve inches. A dead body blocked the way.

The following morning I sat with Lucy Stone Martin in herm spacious office on Level B-I. "No thanks," I said again. The Chief of Security was a stylish woman with flecks of steel in her hair and in her tone. She'd hired me the week before to investigate death threats she'd received that seemed related to the escalating ugliness between management and security guards. "You've got a real mess here," I repeated, trying to stick to the subject. "Lots of hostility on all sides. But nobody's talking shop now."

"Further reason to expand your investigation to include this, this distasteful. . ."

"Murder?"

"As I'd already suggested, Bill Warren was probably responsible for those vicious phone calls I received."

"Which means he wasn't one of your favorite people."

She looked non-plussed. "My likes and dislikes have little bearing on this matter. He was an inciter who contributed, both alive and now in death, to an already tense situation. That tension is my priority."

I would have suggested that a murderer on the loose in the museum created more serious problems than labor tension, but she seemed like a woman who didn't alter her views easily. I reminded her, "Detective Beltrano told me what he told you: The deceased's skull was crushed by a sharp blow on the top of the head at the back, indicating a tall killer or a long weapon. The murder weapon hasn't been found. No prints in and around the Mantrap that can't be accounted for. Ms. Martin, I excel at bad marriages and corporate intrigue. You've got more homicide detectives in the museum than paying public."

"Ms. Marshall. May I call you Margaret?"

"I prefer Maggie." My ex called me Margaret. Still does, or tries to before I hang up on him.

"Maggie, Detective Beltrano has no suspects. I believe a private investigator of your caliber can speed up the conclusion of this unfortunate business."

Since my marriage, I've become immune to flattery. But apparently Martin was sharper than I gave her credit for. She sat back in her chair and transmitted one of her heavy-metal looks. "I'm prepared to triple your usual fee."

Money sweet-talks better than words.

After I left Martin, I popped around the corner into the cramped supervisor's office across from the glass-walled Control Room. Nattie, a Jamaican, one of five security supervisors, was grimly bowed over a cluttered desk, juggling the upcoming week's schedule.

"How's it going?" I asked.

"With this bad business, nobody wants overtime. How about you?"

"Put me down for Tuesday night." That barely dented his mood. "I only met Bill yesterday, but he seemed nice enough."

Nattie's eyebrows shot up.

Just then blond, drop-dead-handsome Randy Owen walked out of the Control Room across the hall and stuck his head in the door. About five years younger than me, maybe thirty, Randy had worked in movies from both the acting and technical end. I'd found that out as the ambulance attendants carted away Bill Warren's remains. Randy and I'd had a long, one-sided chat. The museum was strictly cash, bareable because he got himself assigned regularly to the Costume Gallery. "What's up?"

"We were talking about Bill Warren," I said. "Seemed like a good guy."

"Warren? Our own Saddam Hussein?" Randy gave Nattie, who dropped his eyes to his paperwork, a peculiar look. "For one thing, he was a first-class butt ache. The guy vented his sadism on all life forms."

"And another thing?"

"He'd use any excuse to threaten a strike. I don't know the details, but Johnson fell down one of the stairwells recently and hurt his leg. Warren was there. He tried to convince the union to call a work-to-rule, claiming the building's unsafe. Then there's lower management."

Nattie shifted.

"Hell," Randy said, "the guy wouldn't do his job without citing some section of the contract. Nattie, you had a push-and-shove with him Sunday didn't you, and Bill threatened to get you axed."

"Isn't it time you were both back on the floor?" Nattie said tightly.

"Listen, sweetie, I'm on break." Randy responded in a flawless mimic of Bea Arthur.

"Then break somewhere else."

At lunch in the cafeteria, I took my bowl of soup and sat next to James Macintosh. The lean ash-haired Scot had been at the museum for two decades and, I suspected, had seen most of the closets and quite a few of the skeletons. He was also a shop steward, as Warren had been.

"Good soup?" he asked.

I swallowed a spoonful and grimaced. "If you like lentils. James, I know I'm new, but I've got a couple of gripes. How do I join the union?"

"You'll have to wait three months." He stirred his coffee with one hand and reached into his uniform pocket with the other. "In the meantime, read this."

He handed me a small booklet of union information. His name was on the cover. Above Bill Warren's.

"I guess a lot more work will fall on your shoulders now that Bill's gone."

James shrugged. "Not more, less."

"Oh?" I shoved the soup away and studied a saltine.

"I don't like speaking ill of the departed, but between you, me, and the mummies, he didn't do the union much good. An advocate for the devil, pittin' one against another to suit his whims."

"My toes are on fire!" Ann Macintosh, James' wife, sat down. Gorgeous enough to be in the movies, she was a petite, flirty girl who must have been a toddler when her husband started at the museum. "Shouldn't have taken Bill's shift today. I'm so used to sitting I can't walk the galleries anymore." She giggled and raked well-manicured nails through her shimmering black hair.

James gazed at her with sympathy and adoration.

"So, what'd they say?" Ann asked.

"They know a load when they smell one," he told her.

She nodded at her Caesar salad.

James looked at me. "Well, it's out in the open now. Bill hauled me up before a disciplinary committee Sunday morning. Tried to get me dismissed on the grounds my wife's workin' here and she's just been promoted to the Control Room. She's still on probation."

"I don't follow," I said.

"Ann's the first woman assigned to Control. She's got the most seniority. Still, there was trouble — her bein' bumped over the heads of guys here years, Warren being one — but that wasn't my doing. We had to fight for it. The museum had the employment equity people badgering 'em to give women and minorities a break."

"He was a filthy pit bull." Ann gnashed a crouton. "He couldn't see a woman in security, let alone Control, but he damn well didn't have trouble seeing them in bed."

"That one's better off where he is." James's voice was hard, his face a stone mask.

"Weren't you in the Control Room when Bill was murdered?" I asked Ann.

She raised a pair of jade eyes, "All morning. I was so busy I didn't get a break. God, that murder's all anybody talks about."

She smiled up at Randy, who joined us.

"Maggie M., you still playing V.I. Warshawski?" he grinned at me, sounding like Kathleen Turner.

"And Randy was in the Costume Gallery. And James in Dinosaurs. Until I went to lunch at noon, anyway," Ann volunteered. She held a cigarette to her lips that James lit, inhaled and blew smoke in my direction. I tried not to take it personally.

"How come you're so sure?"

"I talked to them both by radio. Several times. Can't we bury this topic? Murder's so grisly."

"Murder can be like that," I muttered.

Tuesday, before my overnight shift, Lucy Stone Martin gave me an access card to her office where I found the information I'd asked her to gather. The overnight is a skeleton crew — five guards, no supervisor. I had ample hours for research.

Sunday's work schedule revealed that three quarters of the museum staff was off. Besides the security department, only cashiers for the entrance, shop, checkroom and cafe punched in. And the three well-heeled matrons who regularly volunteered as guides. And the Curator of Egyptology, a dried-out myopic who apparently stalked the halls at all hours. I listed this lot under Possibles-but-not-Probables.

There had been twenty-five security guards and one supervisor, Nattie, in the building at 9:30 Sunday morning. Most recalled seeing Bill Warren at the check-in. Each had made a statement to police as to their whereabouts. I eliminated the five guards from the night shift — they'd all checked out by 9:45. With the exception of two isolated galleries — Costumes on Level B-l and Dinosaurs on Level 2 — guards vouched for seeing one another at intervals of approximately five minutes throughout the morning. Still, I examined all security guard and supervisor employee records and resumes anyway.

Bill Warren, assigned Break Relief, had carried a ring of keys identical to those of the Key-man. At 10:30 he relieved Johnson who, after his fifteen minute break, met me for the rookie tour. Warren was supposed to stay in Johnson's gallery until he returned, then relieve the other guards, including me at 11:30. Rigor mortis had not set in and the coroner estimated T.O.D. at between 10:30 and 11:00.

Before checking in for the morning shift, I viewed the video tape recorded outside M-15. Warren answered a Mantrap violation. The film showed him from the back walking down the corridor, peering into the empty Mantrap, radioing in the clear and walking back up the corridor.

The police found hairs matching those on Warren's head along the corridor floor; he'd been dragged back down the tunnel and shoved into the Mantrap. The tape showed none of that.

There was a printout from the Control Room computer. It recorded an M-15 violation at 10:40 — the one Warren answered — and another at 11:15 — when Johnson and I found the corpse. On record was only one other violation — the stairwell on the north side of the building at 10:50, approximately the same time as the murder was taking place. The logbook noted that because Warren was busy with the M-15 violation, Control radioed the guards in the north galleries to just look into the stairwell on their floor. Funny, I was in a north gallery, but I hadn't been radioed.

What was missing was glaring — no record of the M-15 violation when Warren's body was shoved through the door. If Johnson was right about overloads, two alarms ringing close together might have jammed the system temporarily. But why didn't the video show the murder? It was likely hooked up to the alarm but it should have operated independently as well.

I made a quick call to the union office, punched out at 9:25 and punched right back in again for my regular shift. I was tired and cranky and when Nattie designated me Key-man, the easiest job, I was grateful. I picked up my walkie-talkie and keys from Ann in Control and headed to Dinosaurs to relieve Robertson, who'd also done an overnight. Looking at skulls smaller than my own helped me think.

There were obvious suspects.

Ann Macintosh. Working the Control Room on Level B-1 the entire morning, she'd know if anybody else had been in that tunnel, and who wasn't accounted for. And why I hadn't been radioed to check the north stairwell violation.

Johnson. As Key-man he could have snuck into the tunnels, killed Warren and met me by ten to eleven.

James. He was assigned to the Dinosaur Gallery, an isolated gallery on Level 2, and nobody could vouch for his whereabouts. When he checked the north stairwell, he could have slipped down a floor or two, crossed to the south stairwell that led to M-15 and killed Warren. With a wife in Control, obtaining a master key would have been easy.

Nattie. He claimed to be alone in a small room outside the Dinosaur Gallery testing the alarm panel protecting specific exhibits. Nobody saw him. He had a complete set of keys.

Randy. He had been in the isolated Costume Gallery on Level B-1, the gallery closest to the murder.

Lucy Stone Martin. She had logged in on Sunday morning, ostensibly to draft a report to the Board about the death threats. She was alone in her office, also on Level B-1. She had keys to everything.

None of them loved Warren. Any of them could have killed him.

"Key-man come in. This is Control. Over."

I hoisted my radio to my mouth, "Go ahead."

An unidentifiable female voice said, "M-15 has been violated."

My first thought was, I'm being set up. My second? Only Martin knows I'm a P.I. "Roger. Checking M-15."

I headed to the south stairwell, down two flights, passing the doors that led to the Costume Gallery. In the lowest basement I went through the doors to the tunnel. "Key-man to Control. Come in." The radio blasted me with static.

At the fork I turned left. I was already sweating. Thin hot air and fear caused me to inhale shallowly. The tunnel snaked, narrowing into a concrete birth canal. Overhead fading yellow bulbs cast too many shadows, but nobody was directly ahead or behind me. I just hoped that the other tunnel, leading to M-14, was as barren.

As I rounded the final curve, M-15 lay in darkness. Bulbs near it had blown. Or been blown. I glanced back at the camera, a silent, apathetic sentry.

I approached the Mantrap cautiously, wishing for more than a one pound walkie-talkie for protection, and listened. Except for my pulse thudding in my ears, there was nothing. Behind me the tunnel to the curve was still empty. I stepped into the gloom.

The bar on the door felt icy, despite the heat. I grabbed it and pressed hard, pushing inward. The Mantrap was empty.

I let myself quiver enough to shake off the tension then pulled the door shut and started back up the tunnel. At the fork, the brighter tunnel to M-14 was clear, as far as I could see. Finally I reached the double doors to the stairwell.

The master key was one of the big ones, which eliminated the small keys on the ring. But I tried all sizes. Twice. I had been set up. Trapped in hot hell, for God knows how long, waiting for God-knows-what.

"Control, dammit, can you read me?" I changed radio frequencies. The red light flickered, telling me plainly the state of the batteries. Batteries that were supposed to have been recharged overnight.

There was no getting around it. I had to violate Mantrap 14. On the positive side, the alarm might sound. Help might arrive. Unless, as I'd been warned, the signals crossed, then I could be stuck here a long time. If my cup was half empty, the murderer would be in there. Unless the murderer was on his or her way to the tunnels. The heat and lack of good air were wearing; I decided I'd better see if I had company while I was still in shape to greet them accordingly.

I entered the M-14 tunnel. It was just as curved as M-15, but shorter, and the lighting was better. Best of all, it was empty. So was the Mantrap. As I headed back to the double doors, I wondered how long the air could sustain life.

Initially, static regularly belched from my radio, but it didn't take long for the batteries to expire. That didn't bother me, though. I dismantled the walkie-talkie and stripped the wires, twisting them around each other until they were strong and the right shape to function like a key.

At the end of the second hour I was slumped against the last double doors, dizzy, sweaty, hyperventilating, picking that lock. When the doors opened, I collapsed into the Costume Gallery. The air felt like a plunge in the lake in mid-July.

"Good God, girl! Have you been in there all this time?" James helped me up. "Nattie found your keys and radio on his desk. It looked like you'd walked off the job."

The noise of a screaming mother and squalling kid cleared my head. I told James he'd better come with me to the Control Room.

"Maggie M! What happened to you?" Randy swivelled from the VDT. He watched me rip the printout from the printer. No M-15 violation was recorded. Nor my violation of M-14.

"How long have you been here?" I snapped.

"I'm relieving Ann, why?"

"Press the alarm that hooks up with police emergency."

"I can't just call the cops. A supervisor has to order it. You have to tell me why. . ."

I reached around him and jabbed the green button. A crowd had begun gathering in the Control Room. All of the suspects had joined the party, including Lucy Stone Martin, who demanded, "What's going on here?"

"I know who murdered Bill Warren," I said.

"Could have been anybody," Johnson snorted.

"Including you."

Johnson grunted and eyed me as though I'd turned into the idiot he'd thought I was.

"None of you cried over Warren. There are only six people whose whereabouts couldn't be corroborated. I eliminated you first," I told Ms. Martin, "not because you hired me to investigate but because you can't even say the word murder."

"I'm grateful," she said dryly.

"So I'm a suspect." Johnson gave out another of his famous snorts.

"You hated him enough. If the truth be known, I think Warren had something to do with your injury. But you were with me from ten-fifty on. You'd have had to get to the tunnel, kill Warren and wash your hands in twenty minutes. Not impossible. But given your difficulty walking, not probable either. At the very least, you'd have been red-faced when you met me, and you weren't."

He nodded approval which, for Johnson, was the same as awarding a badge of competence. "Who else is on your list?"

"Nattie claimed to be outside the Dinosaur Gallery, but James, working that gallery, couldn't vouch for him. No one could vouch for James, either. Or Ann, assigned to Control. And you, Randy, in Costumes."

I walked to the door and closed it; no use letting the murderer just wander off. "But Nattie, you were working on the exhibit alarm panel. James didn't see you, but Robinson in the gallery across the hallway did, about quarter to eleven. He only mentioned it today when I asked specifically about seeing a supervisor, rather than a guard."

I turned to James. He looked startled. "Whoever did it needed someone in Control to rig the alarms. I assumed you met the union's disciplinary committee inside the museum because your time card didn't show you punching out. But the union pamphlet said union business is considered part of working time. At nine this morning I called the union's head office; they confirmed you had a twenty minute meeting in a nearby cafe until eleven. You couldn't find Nattie when you left and anyway didn't want to mention the complaint until it was settled. Only Ann knew where you'd gone. You couldn't have gotten a call to check the north stairwell because you weren't here. That was a double lie — Ann protecting you protecting Ann."

He looked shaken.

"Which leaves Ann or Randy as the killer."

"Me?" Ann said. "You've gotta be kidding. I was in here all Sunday morning."

"Except for your break."

"I told you, I didn't get a break."

"You didn't get a recorded break. But you got a break, just like you got one today."

"Randy's on the schedule to relieve me today. Bill was on Break Relief Sunday. He never showed up."

"But Randy relieved you on Sunday morning, isn't that true?"

"I don't know what you're talking about. I was alone. . ."

"Isn't it Randy?"

He shook his head.

"Maggie, you'd best be certain of these accusations," Martin warned.

"They're lovers."

"That's ridiculous!" Ann shouted. Scarlet flared in her cheeks as color drained from the faces of James and Randy.

"Warren caught you together. He threatened to get you both fired, or tell James, who would have been crushed and who would have withdrawn his support for you regarding the Control

Room job. Warren would have gained an additional advantage — discrediting James with the union."

"Speculation," Johnson said.

"But it fits. Randy always asked to be assigned to the Costume Gallery, the gallery closest to both Control and the stairwell to the M-14 and M-15 tunnels. With a duplicate master key from Ann, he could have snuck down to the tunnel, murdered Bill and been back before anybody missed him. At least two people knew he was not in the Costume Gallery."

"Us." Johnson turned to the others. "I showed Maggie the Gallery on the way to the Mantrap Sunday. No guard."

"Hey, I was probably in the bathroom," Randy said, his voice saturated with sincere terror.

"When I heard your imitations," I said, "I realized you could sound like anybody, especially over the radio. I was new, not on the schedule yet. Ann knew Nattie had put me in the Level 1 North gallery and she radioed me at 11:07. But you hadn't met me and consequently didn't call me at 10:50 to check the north stairwell violation. Your resumé boasts you not only excelled in acting classes but in technical subjects as well. Computers, tape editing. You would have had a great career."

"He edited the tapes and jammed the alarms," Johnson said. "Must have been in the Control Room when Warren was murdered."

"You can't prove that," Ann said.

I turned to her. "You told me how busy you were Sunday morning. But the only activity the printout showed was three Mantrap violations in four hours, two about the same time.

"It got crazy when you guys requested an ambulance," she said tightly.

"That was around 11:30. You had lunch at noon. While Warren checked M-15, you were hiding in the M-14 tunnel. On his way out, at the fork, you hit him from behind. Of the two Mantraps, M-14 is triggered more often —"

"Because it's better-lit. Anybody gets that far heads down that tunnel," Johnson supplied. "She didn't think the body'd be found for a while."

Ann shook her head and crossed her arms over her chest. "This is such bullshit."

"Today you handed me a radio with dying batteries and a key ring without the master."

"I got them from Nattie."

"You planted another radio and spare set of keys to make it look like I'd quit. I was asking too many questions. You had to shut me up."

"Ridiculous," she said again. "Bill Warren was six inches taller than me. I couldn't have hit him on the top of the head."

"Unless you had the right weapon."

"Which is?" Johnson asked.

"Maybe," I turned to Randy, "you'd like to discuss the props."

"Don't play into this," Ann warned.

Randy, terrified, looked from her to me. In the end, when illicit lovers are caught, they usually save their own skin first. At least that's what my ex did.

"Improv," he said. "She used a tomahawk. From the Native Exhibit in the Costume Gallery."

Ann bolted before any of us could stop her. Through the glass wall I saw Sargeant Beltrano arrive in time to stop her. He'd find the weapon and on it traces of blood and hair matching that of Warren's. Ann had been pressed for time; Beltrano might even pick up a print or two.

James' eyes had dulled. "Bill hinted she was screwing around. I was afraid it was with him."

"Warren forced her to have sex," Randy blurted, which clarified for me how Ann persuaded him to help her commit murder.

Johnson snorted in disgust. "Men know a damn sight less than women about Mantraps."

1993 WINNER

NANCY KILPATRICK
"Mantrap"
Murder, Mayhem and Macabre

Nominees:

WILLIAM BANKIER
"Wade in the Balance"
Criminal Shorts

HOWARD ENGEL
"Custom Killing"
Criminal Shorts

GAIL HELGASON
"Fracture Patterns"
Grain

TED WOOD
"Murder at Louisburg"
Cold Blood IV

Just Like Old Times

The transference went smoothly, like a scalpel slicing into skin.

Cohen was simultaneously excited and disappointed. He was thrilled to be here — perhaps the judge was right, perhaps this was indeed where he really belonged. But the gleaming edge was taken off that thrill because it wasn't accompanied by the usual physiological signs of excitement: no sweaty palms, no racing heart, no rapid breathing. Oh, there was a heartbeat, to be sure, thundering in the background, but it wasn't Cohen's.

It was the dinosaur's.

Everything was the dinosaur's: Cohen saw the world now through tyrannosaur eyes.

The colors seemed all wrong. Surely plant leaves must be the same chlorophyll green here in the Mesozoic, but the dinosaur saw them as navy blue. The sky was lavender; the dirt underfoot ash gray.

Old bones had different cones, thought Cohen. Well, he could get used to it. After all, he had no choice. He would finish his life as an observer inside this tyrannosaur's mind. He'd see what the beast saw, hear what it heard, feel what it felt. He wouldn't be able to control its movements, they had said, but he would be able to experience every sensation.

The rex was marching forward.

Cohen hoped blood would still look red.

It wouldn't be the same if it wasn't red.

"And what, Ms. Cohen, did your husband say before he left your house on the night in question?"

"He said he was going out to hunt humans. But I thought he was making a joke."

"No interpretations, please, Ms. Cohen. Just repeat for the court as precisely as you remember it, exactly what your husband said."

"He said, 'I'm going out to hunt humans.'"

"Thank you, Ms. Cohen. That concludes the Crown's case, my lady."

The needlepoint on the wall of the Honourable Madam Justice Amanda Hoskins's chambers had been made for her by her husband. It was one of her favorite verses from The Mikado, and as she was preparing sentencing she would often look up and re-read the words:

> My object all sublime
> I shall achieve in time —
> To let the punishment fit the crime —
> The punishment fit the crime.

This was a difficult case, a horrible case. Judge Hoskins continued to think.

It wasn't just colors that were wrong. The view from inside the tyrannosaur's skull was different in other ways, too.

The tyrannosaur had only partial stereoscopic vision. There was an area in the center of Cohen's field of view that showed true depth perception. But because the beast was somewhat wall-eyed, it had a much wider panorama than normal for a human, a kind of saurian Cinemascope covering 270 degrees.

The wide-angle view panned back and forth as the tyrannosaur scanned along the horizon.

Scanning for prey.

Scanning for something to kill.

The Calgary Herald, Thursday, October 16, 2042, hardcopy edition: Serial killer Rudolph Cohen, 43, was sentenced to death yesterday.

Formerly a prominent member of the Alberta College of Physicians and Surgeons, Dr. Cohen was convicted in August of thirty-seven counts of first-degree murder.

In chilling testimony, Cohen had admitted, without any signs of remorse, to having terrorized each of his victims for hours before slitting their throats with surgical implements.

This is the first time in eighty years that the death penalty has been ordered in this country.

In passing sentence, Madam Justice Amanda Hoskins observed that Cohen was "the most cold-blooded and brutal killer to have stalked Canada's prairies since Tyrannosaurus rex. . . ."

From behind a stand of dawn redwoods about ten meters away, a second tyrannosaur appeared. Cohen suspected tyrannosaurs might be fiercely territorial, since each animal would require huge amounts of meat. He wondered if the beast he was in would attack the other individual.

His dinosaur tilted its head to look at the second rex, which was standing in profile. But as it did so, almost all of the dino's mental picture dissolved into a white void, as if when concentrating on details the beast's tiny brain simply lost track of the big picture.

At first Cohen thought his rex was looking at the other dinosaur's head, but soon the top of other's skull, the tip of its muzzle and the back of its powerful neck faded away into snowy nothingness. All that was left was a picture of the throat. Good, thought Cohen. One shearing bite there could kill the animal.

The skin of the other's throat appeared gray-green and the throat itself was smooth. Maddeningly, Cohen's rex did not attack. Rather, it simply swiveled its head and looked out at the horizon again.

In a flash of insight, Cohen realized what had happened. Other kids in his neighborhood had had pet dogs or cats. He'd had lizards and snakes — cold-blooded carnivores, a fact to which expert psychological witnesses had attached great weight. Some kinds of male lizards had dewlap sacks hanging from their necks. The rex he was in — a male, the Tyrrell paleontologists had believed — had looked at this other one and seen that she was smooth-throated and therefore a female. Something to be mated with, perhaps, rather than to attack.

Perhaps they would mate soon. Cohen had never orgasmed except during the act of killing. He wondered what it would feel like.

❖

"We spent a billion dollars developing time travel, and now you tell me the system is useless?"

"Well — "

"That is what you're saying, isn't it, professor? That chrono-transference has no practical applications?"

"Not exactly, Minister. The system does work. We can project a human being's consciousness back in time, superimposing his or her mind overtop of that of someone who lived in the past."

"With no way to sever the link. Wonderful."

"That's not true. The link severs automatically."

"Right. When the historical person you've transferred con-sciousness into dies, the link is broken."

"Precisely."

"And then the person from our time whose consciousness you've transferred back dies as well."

"I admit that's an unfortunate consequence of linking two brains so closely."

"So I'm right! This whole damn chronotransference thing is useless."

"Oh, not at all, Minister. In fact, I think I've got the perfect application for it."

❖

The rex marched along. Although Cohen's attention had first been arrested by the beast's vision, he slowly became aware of its other senses, too. He could hear the sounds of the rex's footfalls, of twigs and vegetation being crushed, of birds or pterosaurs singing, and, underneath it all, the relentless drone of insects. Still, all the sounds were dull and low; the rex's simple ears were incapable of picking up high-pitched noises, and what sounds they did detect were discerned without richness. Cohen knew the late Cretaceous must have been a symphony of varied tone, but it was as if he was listening to it through earmuffs.

The rex continued along, still searching. Cohen became aware of several more impressions of the world both inside and out, including hot afternoon sun beating down on him and a hungry gnawing in the beast's belly.

Food.

It was the closest thing to a coherent thought that he'd yet detected from the animal, a mental picture of bolts of meat going down its gullet.

Food.

The Social Services Preservation Act of 2022: Canada is built upon the principle of the Social Safety Net, a series of entitlements and programs designed to ensure a high standard of living for every citizen. However, ever-increasing life expectancies coupled with constant lowering of the mandatory retirement age have placed an untenable burden on our social- welfare system and, in particular, its cornerstone program of universal health care. With most taxpayers ceasing to work at the age of 45, and with average Canadians living to be 94 (males) or 97 (females), the system is in danger of complete collapse. Accordingly, all social programs will henceforth be available only to those below the age of 60, with one exception: all Canadians, regardless of age, may take advantage, at no charge to themselves, of government-sponsored euthanasia through chronotransference.

There! Up ahead! Something moving! Big, whatever it was: an indistinct outline only intermittently visible behind a small knot of fir trees.

A quadruped of some sort, its back to him/it/them.

Ah, there. Turning now. Peripheral vision dissolving into albino nothingness as the rex concentrated on the head.

Three horns.

Triceratops.

Glorious! Cohen had spent hours as a boy pouring over books about dinosaurs, looking for scenes of carnage. No battles were better than those in which Tyrannosaurus rex squared off against Triceratops, a four-footed Mesozoic tank with a trio of horns projecting from its face and a shield of bone rising from the back of its skull to protect the neck.

And yet, the rex marched on.

No, thought Cohen. Turn, damn you! Turn and attack!

Cohen remembered when it had all begun, that fateful day so many years ago, so many years from now. It should have been a routine operation. The patient had supposedly been prepped properly. Cohen brought his scalpel down toward the abdomen, then, with a steady hand, sliced into the skin. The patient gasped. It had been a wonderful sound, a beautiful sound.

Not enough gas. The anesthetist hurried to make an adjustment.

Cohen knew he had to hear that sound again. He had to.

The tyrannosaur continued forward. Cohen couldn't see its legs, but he could feel them moving. Left, right, up, down.

Attack, you bastard!

Left.

Attack!

Right.

Go after it!

Up.

Go after the Triceratops.

Dow —

The beast hesitated, its left leg still in the air, balancing briefly on one foot.

Attack!

Attack!

And then, at last, the rex changed course. The ceratopsian appeared in the three-dimensional central part of the tyrannosaur's field of view, like a target at the end of a gun sight.

"Welcome to the Chronotransference Institute. If I can just see your government benefits card, please? Yup, there's always a last time for everything, heh heh. Now, I'm sure you want an exciting death. The problem is finding somebody interesting who hasn't been used yet. See, we can only ever superimpose one mind onto a given historical personage. All the really obvious ones have been done already, I'm afraid. We still get about a dozen calls a week asking for Jack Kennedy, but he was one of the first to go, so to speak. If I may make a suggestion, though, we've got thousands of Roman legion officers cataloged. Those tend to be very satisfying deaths. How about a nice something from the Gallic Wars?"

The Triceratops looked up, its giant head lifting from the wide flat gunnera leaves it had been chewing on. Now that the rex had focussed on the plant-eater, it seemed to commit itself.

The tyrannosaur charged.

The hornface was sideways to the rex. It began to turn, to bring its armored head to bear.

The horizon bounced wildly as the rex ran. Cohen could hear the thing's heart thundering loudly, rapidly, a barrage of muscular gunfire.

The Triceratops, still completing its turn, opened its parrot-like beak, but no sound came out.

Giant strides closed the distance between the two animals. Cohen felt the rex's jaws opening wide, wider still, mandibles popping from their sockets.

The jaws slammed shut on the hornface's back, over the shoulders. Cohen saw two of the rex's own teeth fly into view, knocked out by the impact.

The taste of hot blood, surging out of the wound . . .

The rex pulled back for another bite.

The Triceratops finally got its head swung around. It surged forward, the long spear over its left eye piercing into the rex's leg . . .

Pain. Exquisite, beautiful pain.

The rex roared. Cohen heard it twice, once reverberating within the animal's own skull, a second time echoing back from distant hills. A flock of silver-furred pterosaurs took to the air. Cohen saw them fade from view as the dinosaur's simple mind shut them out of the display. Irrelevant distractions.

The Triceratops pulled back, the horn withdrawing from the rex's flesh.

Blood, Cohen was delighted to see, still looked red.

❖

"If Judge Hoskins had ordered the electric chair," said Axworthy, Cohen's lawyer, "we could have fought that on Charter grounds. Cruel and unusual punishment, and all that. But she's authorized full access to the chronotransference euthanasia program for you." Axworthy paused. "She said, bluntly, that she simply wants you dead."

"How thoughtful of her," said Cohen.

Axworthy ignored that. "I'm sure I can get you anything you want," he said. "Who would you like to be transferred into?"

"Not who," said Cohen. "What."

"I beg your pardon?"

"That damned judge said I was the most cold-blooded killer to stalk the Alberta landscape since Tyrannosaurus rex." Cohen shook his head. "The idiot. Doesn't she know dinosaurs were warm- blooded? Anyway, that's what I want. I want to be trans- ferred into a T. rex."

"You're kidding."

"Kidding is not my forte, John. Killing is. I want to know which was better at it, me or the rex."

"I don't even know if they can do that kind of thing," said Axworthy.

"Find out, damn you. What the hell am I paying you for?"

❖

The rex danced to the side, moving with surprising agility for a creature of its bulk, and once again it brought its terrible jaws down on the ceratopsian's shoulder. The plant-eater was hemor- rhaging at an incredible rate, as though a thousand sacrifices had been performed on the altar of its back.

The Triceratops tried to lunge forward, but it was weakening quickly. The tyrannosaur, crafty in its own way despite its trifling intellect, simply retreated a dozen giant paces. The hornface took one tentative step toward it, and then another, and, with great and ponderous effort, one more. But then the dinosaurian tank teetered and, eyelids slowly closing, collapsed on its side. Cohen was briefly startled, then thrilled, to hear it fall to the ground with a splash — he hadn't realized just how much blood had poured out of the great rent the rex had made in the beast's back.

The tyrannosaur moved in, lifting its left leg up and then smashing it down on the Triceratops's belly, the three sharp toe claws tearing open the thing's abdomen, entrails spilling out into the harsh sunlight. Cohen thought the rex would let out a victorious roar, but it didn't. It simply dipped its muzzle into the body cavity, and methodically began yanking out chunks of flesh.

Cohen was disappointed. The battle of the dinosaurs had been fun, the killing had been well engineered, and there had certainly been enough blood, but there was no terror. No sense that the Triceratops had been quivering with fear, no begging for mercy. No feeling of power, of control. Just dumb, mindless brutes moving in ways preprogrammed by their genes.

It wasn't enough. Not nearly enough.

Judge Hoskins looked across the desk in her chambers at the lawyer.

"A Tyrannosaurus, Mr. Axworthy? I was speaking figuratively."

"I understand that, my lady, but it was an appropriate observation, don't you think? I've contacted the Chronotransference people, who say they can do it, if they have a rex specimen to work from. They have to back-propagate from actual physical material in order to get a temporal fix."

Judge Hoskins was as unimpressed by scientific babble as she was by legal jargon. "Make your point, Mr. Axworthy."

"I called the Royal Tyrrell Museum of Paleontology in Drumheller and asked them about the Tyrannosaurus fossils available worldwide. Turns out there's only a handful of complete skeletons, but they were able to provide me with an annotated list, giving as much information as they could about the individual probable causes of death." He slid a thin plastic printout sheet across the judge's wide desk.

"Leave this with me, counsel. I'll get back to you."

Axworthy left, and Hoskins scanned the brief list. She then leaned back in her leather chair and began to read the needlepoint on her wall for the thousandth time:

My object all sublime
I shall achieve in time —

She read that line again, her lips moving slightly as she subvocalized the words: "I shall achieve in time . . . "

The judge turned back to the list of tyrannosaur finds. Ah, that one. Yes, that would be perfect. She pushed a button on her phone. "David, see if you can find Mr. Axworthy for me."

There had been a very unusual aspect to the Triceratops kill — an aspect that intrigued Cohen. Chronotransference had been performed countless times; it was one of the most popular forms of euthanasia. Sometimes the transferee's original body would give an ongoing commentary about what was going on, as if talking during sleep. It was clear from what they said that transferees couldn't exert any control over the bodies they were transferred into.

Indeed, the physicists had claimed any control was impossible. Chronotransference worked precisely because the transferee could exert no influence, and therefore was simply observing things that had already been observed. Since no new observations were being made, no quantum-mechanical distortions occurred. After all, said the physicists, if one could exert control, one could change the past. And that was impossible.

And yet, when Cohen had willed the rex to alter its course, it eventually had done so.

Could it be that the rex had so little brains that Cohen's thoughts could control the beast?

Madness. The ramifications were incredible.

Still. . . .

He had to know if it was true. The rex was torpid, flopped on its belly, gorged on ceratopsian meat. It seemed prepared to lie here for a long time to come, enjoying the early evening breeze.

Get up, thought Cohen. Get up, damn you!

Nothing. No response.

Get up!

The rex's lower jaw was resting on the ground. Its upper jaw was lifted high, its mouth wide open. Tiny pterosaurs were flitting in and out of the open maw, their long needle-like beaks apparently yanking gobbets of hornface flesh from between the rex's curved teeth.

Get up, thought Cohen again. Get up!

The rex stirred.

Up!

The tyrannosaur used its tiny forelimbs to keep its torso from sliding forward as it pushed with its powerful legs until it was standing.

Forward, thought Cohen. Forward!

The beast's body felt different. Its belly was full to bursting.

Forward!

With ponderous steps, the rex began to march.

It was wonderful. To be in control again! Cohen felt the old thrill of the hunt.

And he knew exactly what he was looking for.

"Judge Hoskins says okay," said Axworthy. "She's authorized for you to be transferred into that new T. rex they've got right here in Alberta at the Tyrrell. It's a young adult, they say. Judging by the way the skeleton was found, the rex died falling, probably into a fissure. Both legs and the back were broken, but the skeleton remained almost completely articulated, suggesting that scavengers couldn't get at it. Unfortunately, the chronotransference people say that back-propagating that far into the past they can only plug you in a few hours before the accident occurred. But you'll get your wish: you're going to die as a tyrannosaur. Oh, and here are the books you asked for: a complete library on Cretaceous flora and fauna. You should have time to get through it all; the chronotransference people will need a couple of weeks to set up."

As the prehistoric evening turned to night, Cohen found what he had been looking for, cowering in some underbrush: large brown eyes, long, drawn-out face, and a lithe body covered in fur that, to the tyrannosaur's eyes, looked blue-brown.

A mammal. But not just any mammal. Purgatorius, the very first primate, known from Montana and Alberta from right at the end of the Cretaceous. A little guy, only about ten centimeters long, excluding its ratlike tail. Rare creatures, these days. Only a precious few.

The little furball could run quickly for its size, but a single step by the tyrannosaur equaled more than a hundred of the mammal's. There was no way it could escape.

The rex leaned in close, and Cohen saw the furball's face, the nearest thing there would be to a human face for another sixty million years. The animal's eyes went wide in terror.

Naked, raw fear.

Mammalian fear.

Cohen saw the creature scream.

Heard it scream.

It was beautiful.

The rex moved its gaping jaws in toward the little mammal, drawing in breath with such force that it sucked the creature into its maw. Normally the rex would swallow its meals whole, but Cohen prevented the beast from doing that. Instead, he simply had it stand still, with the little primate running around, terrified, inside the great cavern of the dinosaur's mouth, banging into giant teeth and great fleshy walls, and skittering over the massive, dry tongue.

Cohen savored the terrified squealing. He wallowed in the sensation of the animal, mad with fear, moving inside that living prison.

And at last, with a great, glorious release, Cohen put the animal out of its misery, allowing the rex to swallow it, the furball tickling as it slid down the giant's throat.

It was just like old times.

Just like hunting humans.

And then a wonderful thought occurred to Cohen. Why, if he killed enough of these little screaming balls of fur, they wouldn't have any descendants. There wouldn't ever be any Homo sapiens. In a very real sense, Cohen realized he was hunting humans — every single human being who would ever exist.

Of course, a few hours wouldn't be enough time to kill many of them. Judge Hoskins no doubt thought it was wonderfully poetic justice, or she wouldn't have allowed the transfer: sending him back to fall into the pit, damned.

Stupid judge. Why, now that he could control the beast, there was no way he was going to let it die young. He'd just —

There it was. The fissure, a long gash in the earth, with a crumbling edge. Damn, it was hard to see. The shadows cast by neighboring trees made a confusing gridwork on the ground that obscured the ragged opening. No wonder the dull-witted rex had missed seeing it until it was too late.

But not this time.

Turn left, thought Cohen.

Left.

His rex obeyed.

He'd avoid this particular area in future, just to be on the safe side. Besides, there was plenty of territory to cover. Fortunately, this was a young rex — a juvenile. There would be decades in which to continue his very special hunt. Cohen was sure that Axworthy knew his stuff: once it became apparent that the link had lasted longer than a few hours, he'd keep any attempt to pull the plug tied up in the courts for years.

Cohen felt the old pressure building in himself, and in the rex. The tyrannosaur marched on.

This was better than old times, he thought. Much better.

Hunting all of humanity.

The release would be wonderful.

He watched intently for any sign of movement in the underbrush.

1994 WINNER

ROBERT J. SAWYER
"Just Like Old Times"
OnSpec

Nominees:

JAS. R. PETRIN
"East End Safe"
Alfred Hitchcock Mystery Magazine

JAMES POWELL
"The Fixer-Upper"
Ellery Queen Mystery Magazine

ERIC WRIGHT
"The Casebook of Dr. Billingsgate"
The New Mystery

ERIC WRIGHT
"The Duke"
2nd Culprit

ROSEMARY AUBERT

The Midnight Boat to Palermo

What I loved most about meeting the midnight boat was not the motion of the waves, though I often thought the movement of the sea made it easier to sleep than the stillness of my bed. Nor was it the moonlight that I loved, for I was afraid of moonlight and am to this day. Many of the women in our self-help group speak of their fear of moonlight. Sometimes they connect it to abusive fathers or to their general terror of night. I loved my father and he never abused me in the way some of these women have been abused. But, like them, talking now about my youth, I have stirred up a memory that I had buried long ago — forty years, in fact. I have suddenly understood that my father was murdered. I have suddenly remembered that I was there when he was killed. I have suddenly realized the name of his killer.

What I loved most about the midnight night boat to Palermo was the silence. For my world, both then and now, has been a very noisy one. When I first came to this country, though I could not speak the language, I knew already that I spoke too loudly. How else could it be? There were, after all, seven of us, and we lived in a tiny hut on the shore of the inlet. We didn't call it an inlet, of course. That's a word I learned much later — in a writing class sponsored by the government. But an inlet it was, a little indentation in the rocks of the shore of Sicily. And when you spoke, if you were to be heard at all, you had to shout not only above the sound of all the brothers and sisters, not only above the arguing of my parents, but above the sound of the sea. That's what we called it. Not an inlet, the sea.

Like most of the people of our village, we were not rich. But we had plenty to eat and good clothes to wear, even though the Second World War had been over for only a few years. Twice a year, my mother would go to Rome and buy me and my sisters dresses, blouses with lace, shoes to wear to church on Sunday. Looking back on it now, it amazes me that we never questioned such extravagance. Nor did I question my mother's attitude about these trips. For weeks before, she'd be so sweet to us, so kind. Instead of her usual severity, she'd be almost gay. Though she said she hated to leave us, it was hard to ignore her happiness, just as when she returned, it was hard to ignore how angry she seemed to be for weeks. My mother, I thought then, was an unpredictable woman. But now I see, after all these years, she was far more predictable than I could have imagined.

When my mother was home, which was most of the time, she was a good mother. She sewed, she cleaned, and she made a tomato sauce that was famous in our little village. To this day, I can see her standing at the stove preparing it. She would start by heating a huge black iron pan and carefully dripping onto its hot surface a thin dribble of the purest olive oil. Then she would take a bud of garlic and carefully separating out each clove, would peel it with her slow, strong hands. When the heated oil had turned the garlic as golden as itself, she would add pieces of beef. This meat, too, would soon turn a golden color, filling our little house with its aroma. When the meat was done, she would add the tomato paste. It has been more than forty years since I have seen these things, but I remember as if I were standing there now how she would go to a little pantry off our kitchen, a place that was always cold, no matter the time of year, and from one of its shelves, would take an earthenware crock of tomato paste. This paste had been dried in the sun by her own grandmother, and it was almost black. Of course, I used to think it looked like poison. Yet even then I understood that the tomato paste made the sauce rich and thick and gave it such a deep flavor that it seemed to have been cooked forever. However, when she added this ingredient, my mother had to be very careful. If she added too much, or if she didn't cook it until it, too, was almost golden, the sauce would be bitter — a failure. After the tomato paste, the only other ingredient she added was fresh tomatoes. And one other thing — the secret. When the sauce had cooked for two hours, my mother would add a little cupful of sugar. It was my job to bring her the sugar from a cupboard across the kitchen, and I would sneak a taste for myself before I got to her side. When, she caught me doing this, she would laugh.

Thursday was the day she made sauce. And Thursday was the night that it was my father's turn to meet the midnight boat to Palermo. I always thought that my father died on a Friday, but now I understand that was too simple a way to look at things. He was found dead on a Friday. He was killed on Thursday — the Thursday we, he and I, like always, were supposed to meet the Palermo boat but didn't.

My father, and all the other men in the village, worked in the sugar factory. Being only eight years old, I thought the factory had been there forever. Now I see that was wrong. It could only have been set up after the war, when I was two or three. When I was little, though, the sugar factory was one of the centers of my life. Though my own children seemed to spend all their time in school when they were eight years old, I certainly did not. There was only one teacher, an old woman whose son had gone away and never come back and who could speak of little else, even when she was supposed to be teaching us math or the history of the rulers of Sicily. It was easy to slip out of school — or not to go at all, which was what I often did. The minute I was free, I headed for the factory.

Now it is very important for me to explain that I did not go to the factory to eat the sugar. The mysterious thing about the factory was that nobody was ever allowed to eat the sugar there. Zi Antonio had forbidden it. Anyone who so much as tasted the tiniest bit would have to leave their work — forever. Zi Antonio was the mayor of our little village, though that word — mayor — is another that we never used, that I never even learned until I came here. My father told me that Zi Antonio said it was bad business to eat your own product, that that was how people lost money, that it showed a lack of respect.

I had another way of looking at it, and it was one of the

reasons that I visited the sugar factory so often. In order for this to make sense, I have to describe how the sugar factory looked. Though now that I finally know what I'm really describing, I must admit that this might not at all have been how the factory was — just how it looked to me when I was eight years old.

Unlike any other building in our village, the factory was built of some clean, smooth material — concrete, I'd say. And it had no windows. The only way you could see inside was if you stood by the wide rear door, which I often did.

The roof of the factory was covered in pipes, sticking up toward the sky. Sometimes steam shot up from them like a volcano. When this happened, it scared me and I ran away. But I always came back.

The only times I ever stayed away for long were the few times that Zi Antonio, himself, chased me. He hardly ever came to the sugar factory, though he seemed to be everywhere else in town, including our house. As I recall, the first time he caught me, I was merely wandering around the factory yard. Out there were piles and piles of barrels just like the ones we got when we met the Palermo boat. He caught me completely by surprise. I was leaning over a row of barrels, thumping them, the way I'd seen my mother thump an eggplant to see if it was ripe. I'd just about decided that the barrels were empty, when I heard a shout close behind me. I jumped a mile. Zi Antonio towered over me like the picture of the orge in the storybook my cousin Teresa had sent me from America. I started to cry.

Now I have to say about Zi Antonio that he always treated me and my brothers and sisters very well. "No, no, no," he said simply and shooed me away.

The second time he caught me, I was doing the same thing. The barrels seemed empty that time, too. The third time Zi Antonio said that if I continued to play there, my father would lose his job.

What I was really trying to figure out was whether the sugar in the factory was poison and whether something the men did to it made it not be poison any more, so that when it left the factory we could eat it.

Everybody knew that Zi Antonio was the boss of the factory. We knew also that he was a special friend of the old woman who was our teacher. We knew too, that Zi Antonio was somehow in charge of the parish church, though we assumed that must only be when the priest wasn't praying or doing holy things. Zi Antonio, for instance, was in charge of charity — being a very generous man. He was also always present at funerals, consoling the mother and the widow.

Zi Antonio was also a special friend of my mother. It was because of him, I always thought, that she took such care every Thursday when she made the sauce, for he was always our dinner guest on that night.

It was regular as the clock. All afternoon my mother would cook the sauce while my father worked at the factory. Zi Antonio would arrive. My father, being a quiet man, would say very little at the table, but Zi Antonio was funny, and his jokes kept us in stitches.

I ate faster than the others because I had to get ready to go with my father to meet the Palermo boat. I packed us a lunch. I got our sweaters and blankets. And I filled the lantern we needed to signal the big boat and let the sailors see what they were doing when they lowered the barrels into our boat.

Once in a while, a wind would arise, or the open boat would be slashed by rain, but my trust in my father was absolute. I see now that what I was doing with him was the most dangerous thing I've ever done, but I felt more safe then than I have ever felt since.

I would ask him to tell me his stories of the sea, and he always did. He knew about pirates, about explorers, about the sacred missionaries of the Church.

As we pulled away from the beach behind the sugar factory, the sun would be low over the water. I would lie against the pile of blankets as my father rowed slowly away from the village. As the last thing to fade from sight — the chimneys of the sugar factory — slipped away, the rocking of the boat would start to get to me. I would doze off. Often, the next thing I knew, I would be lying on the boat bottom staring straight up toward the stars.

Nothing in my life since has ever equalled the peace of those voyages. It seemed we drifted out there for hours. In the silence of the night, I asked my father what was in the barrels that we took from the Palermo ship into our own. He smiled and said that it was a syrup from far away, that was needed in order to make sugar. Sugar cane? I asked him. But his eyes were trained on the water and he didn't answer.

I also asked him why nobody at the sugar factory could eat the sugar. This was a trick question. I knew, as all children do, that sometimes if you ask a question over and over again, the answer that has always been the same answer, can slip into a different answer — the truth. But he said, as he always did, that it was bad business, that it showed a lack of respect and that all the sugar at the factory belonged to Zi Antonio.

He said that Zi Antonio was the boss of the sugar factory but that he, too, had his own bosses and no matter how you lived your life, there was always somebody who had the power to tell you what to do. I didn't know what he was talking about.

I asked him why we had to wait so long. This he had explained again and again. He said that the boat to Palermo had left a country called Turkey, that when a ship was at sea, the wind could speed it or slow it, that the waves could be so high that the boat had twice as far to go — up one side, down the other. I laughed at this joke and, huddled in my warm sweater, settled back to enjoy the sandwiches I had made for us.

Often, when the boat did come, I'd been asleep, and sometimes I only woke up when I heard the shouts and saw the barrels being lowered down. Then I would fall asleep again and not wake up until our little boat reached the shore. I would crawl out onto the sand and wait there as my father rolled the barrels up into the yard of the factory. Then, he would take my hand and lead me along the path that went to our house. We'd tiptoe in, and he would tuck me into bed. Usually I was fast asleep before my door even closed, my sisters breathing silently beside me.

My memory of those nights is so vivid and complete that I remember every detail of the night that was different — the night my father was killed.

For some time before that, the arguing of my parents had been often and loud. They'd always argued, but never so much or so violently. One Thursday, my father came home from work in the middle of the afternoon. He looked different — angry and even scared. He told my mother that the sugar factory was about to close. Then, he started to drink wine. Usually, he had a little wine with his supper, but this day, he started drinking in the afternoon, which I had never seen before.

As always, my mother was cooking the sauce for supper. Despite the troubles of my father and the fact that she was fighting with him, her hands were sure as she dropped the meat into the sizzling oil. When he realized that she was making Thursday dinner as if nothing had happened at the sugar factory, he started to yell at her. How could she have Zi Antonio for dinner when he was about to ruin them all? She said Zi Antonio had nothing to do with whether the factory stayed opened or closed. I had no idea what any of this meant. I was waiting for my mother to add sugar to the sauce. My father grew more and more angry. Then, he stormed out of the kitchen. I ran after him, but he slammed out of the house. When I went back to the kitchen, I saw that my mother had the little cup of sugar resting on the cupboard. I stepped up, stuck out my finger and reached up to coat it with sugar. To my amazement, my mother slapped my hand so hard that I hit it on the edge of the cupboard and cut it. She didn't even offer to help me. She told me to get out, to wash it off, and to come right back. I did everything she said. A little later, my father came back and went into my parents' room, where he remained.

Zi Antonio did come for supper that night, but there were no jokes. He wasn't even hungry. All we ate was salad, cheese and bread. He and my mother whispered as we all sat at the table. I thought they were whispering to keep from waking my father who had fallen asleep from drinking all that wine. I kept waiting for my father to wake up, for us to go out to the boat. But every time I tried to get up from the table, my mother told me to sit down.

After a long time, my father did wake up, but I knew it was too late for us to go out. It was already dark. My mother now seemed a lot less angry than she'd been. She had even put aside some sauce for my father, and she cooked him macaroni and ladled the sauce onto it. He, too, must have been over his anger, because I could see how hungry he was. He ate it all. Then he went back into the room he shared with my mother, stretched out across the bed and fell back to sleep.

I was heartbroken. All day I'd thought about our trip out to the Palermo boat, and now, clearly, we weren't going. I went to bed myself.

But I had a hard time sleeping. In the middle of the night, I got up to ask my parents if I could get in bed with them until I fell asleep. I crept down the hall. Their door was open, and I looked in. They were lying side by side. A broad ray of moonlight fell straight across my father's face. He had told me again and again that it was bad luck to sleep in the moonlight. Here he was, sound asleep, completely unprotected from the moon. But even more disturbing was the sight of my mother. The moonlight fell on her face, too. She was not asleep. Her eyes were wide open, staring straight up and full of tears that fell down her face, sparkling like diamonds in the pale light.

I knew then, that she was sorry they had fought. I knew, too, that their room was no place for me. I went back to my own room and fell asleep.

Things happened very fast after that. The next day, my father couldn't wake up. The doctor came. Then the priest. He was dead before either got there. They said it was the shock of knowing that the sugar factory was going to close. They said he must always have had a weak heart. They said it was such a shame — a man in his thirties with five children. . . .

Zi Antonio saved us. He told my mother that he would look after us all. He said that his bosses had decided to send him to Canada. He said we could all go with him. My mother wore black clothes all the way to Canada. We had stopped in Rome to get them.

After we got to the new country, our lives settled down. It was strange at first to have Zi Antonio be with us every day, instead of one day a week. It was strange to have a father — he and my mother soon married — who worked in an office every day instead of a factory. And it was strange to live in a real city, instead of a village. But there were so many good things — the school, the museum, the parks, the friends. Before long, I forgot about Sicily. I never, of course, forgot about my father. But it hurt to think of him dying at such a young age. He had been my friend. Now I had other friends. And after a while, I hardly thought about him at all.

Zi Antonio offered to send me to university, but I was rebellious. When I left school, I, like my father, went to work in a factory. It was clean work. If you paid attention and worked quickly, you could make good money. I started on the machines, sewing pajamas. I soon moved up to handstitching dresses, and then, I became one of the senior women. At the time I left, six months ago, I had been making the finest wedding gowns, beading lace that cost almost five hundred dollars per meter.

Two years ago, the orders started to fall off. One by one the women had to be let go. Finally there were only four of us left — the wedding women. Every day for two years, I had gone in thinking it would be my last day, and one day it was. The boss was crying. She didn't even have the money to give us a settlement. The last thing she did was pay the wages she owed us. That was it.

Except for the counselor. The boss gave a little speech about how the government had provided counseling for us all. We could learn to write resumes. We could explore retraining. We could even learn creative writing — to get in touch with our inner selves, she said.

What could my resume say? That I had been sewing for thirty years? For what could I retrain? And as I said, I had already taken a writing course from the government.

The only program left was "Looking Into Ourselves." So it was this workshop that I signed up for, this workshop in which I discovered the secret I had been keeping from my "inner self" all my life.

It happened so simply and so suddenly. I went to the community center where the workshop was to be held. At first everyone was very nervous and embarrassed. But it was all women and pretty soon we started to chat. As the weeks went by, I started to feel comfortable talking to the women in the group, who ranged in age from a little younger than me to a little older.

One night, there were some much younger women there — all sitting together and so pretty, the way my mother was the day she left our village to come to Canada with my step-father.

One of these girls told us that she went to a different group every night in order never to have to spend an evening alone. The silence was total as she told us in a shaky voice that she had been a drug addict.

Now, of course, for women my age, to have a daughter on drugs is the ultimate terror. I had even gone to a lecture once about all the different drugs and the history of where they came from, sponsored by the police.

This girl spoke only a little — laughing and crying as she told us about herself. What she said was that the first time she ever saw heroin, it looked just like sugar. That it sparkled like that and that she had put out her finger and taken a little and tasted it, expecting it to be sweet, but that it was bitter. And that should have told her all she needed to know.

I saw it, then. I saw the whole thing. I saw my father lifting up his arms to receive the barrels of opium from Turkey — just like the police told us about. I saw the factory with its frightening pipes and its strange white product that no one was allowed to eat. I saw Zi Antonio with his fine suits, with the respect, the fear of everyone in our village. And I saw my mother slipping a silk blouse out of a shiny paper bag from Rome.

I picked up my coat and my purse and I walked out of the center and all the way home.

But even then, I had only figured out part of it. It took me until far into the night before I realized what Zi Antonio and my mother were doing every Thursday night. And then, most cruelly of all, I remembered my mother's sharp anger the day I watched her put the secret ingredient into her famous sauce. The day I reached out my finger to taste the sugar as I had done so many times before.

I was sick the next day. All day long I dreamed about my childhood. By the time my husband came home, I could no longer tell what was dream and what was reality.

Perhaps next week, I'll return to the group. I'll tell them I'm depressed about losing my job, that I feel tired, that I'm afraid a woman my age can never find work again. But I'll never speak about my mother. To whom would I tell her story and why? From the day we came to Canada, we lived a law-abiding life. We went to school, then we worked, then we married and we sent our own children to school. Zi Antonio died, and so did my mother. My children have never much wanted to know about the old country.

No, I am the only one remaining who knows the secret of Zi Antonio and my mother. The night I looked in and saw my father so very still that the moonlight on his face could not wake him, I took this secret to myself, without even knowing. Now, because of a few troubled words, I do know. But the secret stays with me. It floats in my mind, detached from all else, the way our little boat floated — a small speck on the waters that lapped the shore of our tiny village, spilled onward toward the bay of Palermo, crossed the Mediterranean, then slipped out to the real sea.

1995 WINNER

ROSEMARY AUBERT
"The Midnight Boat to Palermo"
Cold Blood V

Nominees:

WILLIAM BANKIER
"The Big Lonely"
Cold Blood V

ELIZA MOORHOUSE
"Death of a Dragon"
Cold Blood V

JAMES POWELL
"Midnight at Manger's Bird and Beast"
Ellery Queen Mystery Magazine

PETER ROBINSON
"Lawn Sale"
Cold Blood V

PETER ROBINSON
"Summer Rain"
Ellery Queen Mystery Magazine

Cotton Armour

Cortés has been my model. He really knew how to make people toe the line. You have only to look at the size of his tiny Spanish force and the might of the Aztec Empire he conquered to grant him that. I owe a lot to his influence, up to and including, I must admit, the three years I reigned as President of the Parish League of Women. Three entire years at the top of the parish pile. A record for harnessing control and direction of the parish ladies who preferred to be let loose to wage their petty battles. I can see them now, gloating over their triumphs. How they loved to stake out tiny bits of turf: the altar flowers, the PLOW kitchen, the May procession, the Christmas pageant. But I had them all under my heel for three delicious years. That's right. Me. Don't you forget it.

And don't forget about my year as National Second Vice-President of the National Council of Parish Leagues of Women either. Me again.

That's right. Helen Denniger, Helen Mooney that was, whose mother was only a maid and no better than she ought to have been. That's the one. Helen Denniger, whose father was nothing but a drunk, if he was even who her mother claimed.

Even after I married Walter, long after, the ladies of the parish, they thought they'd never let me forget who I was. Or where I'd come from. Small snubs, a curl of the lip, a turn of the eye. But in the long run it was I who had the ear of the Archbishop, wasn't it.

My career in the politics of church and home was something nobody could have predicted, when you thought of it. Especially when I got packed off to scrub the toilets and sweep the back stairs in the Glebe House when I was no more than fifteen years old. Taking orders from the beak-nosed Housekeeper and told in no uncertain terms to keep out of the way of the priests. No matter what.

I didn't mind. I didn't know any better. And I certainly didn't want to run into any priests. I was scared of them then. But it was there in that Glebe House, that I saw books outside of the classroom for the first time. My job was to dust the tops of the things in the Library and to take each book from the shelves and dust behind it too. I remember sneezing a lot.

There I read Dante and St. Thomas Aquinas and The Lives of the Saints. All enough to convince me that the life I had, which didn't involve believing deeply in anything except getting to the end of the day, was still better than being beheaded or barbecued or crucified upside down or anything like that.

And then I discovered Cortés. And read again and again how six hundred Spaniards with guts and guile conquered the Aztec empire. The whole damn thing. And brought God to the Aztecs, Father Doyle pointed out when he saw me reading about it.

Brought them under control was what I figured. Brought under control hundreds of thousands of strong, well-organized people who didn't much like outsiders. And forced them to change the way they lived. And ended their empire. And claimed their land and riches. And swept away their religion. And more power to those Spaniards, if you ask me.

It wasn't without its light side, the whole thing, the conquest. Throughout the battles, the Spaniards and the Aztecs wore padded cotton armour. I remember thinking at the time, that was pretty funny. What could cotton armour ever protect you from? Depends, I guess, on what you're afraid of. In the case of arrows, I guess it worked pretty well. I thought a lot about that afterwards. Was it just because they believed in it?

Just reading about Cortés changed my way of thinking. I thought about the ladies of the Parish and how they always figured they were a lot better than me, Helen Mooney from nowhere. Their fine clothes reminded me of cotton armour, protecting them from the revealing thoughts of others, if only they knew it. In time I got myself some cotton armour too. But not before I thought a lot about Cortés and his small band of soldiers in Mexico.

How many times did they nearly starve? How many of those soldiers were wounded? How often were they outnumbered? And they never gave up. But the thing that interested me most was how Cortés did it, since he and his soldiers were outnumbered, thousands to one, you know. Through guile, that's how. Always using guile, trickery and playing one group against the other. Just like me, in St. Anthony's Parish.

So you can see Cortés gave me a new perspective on life, knowing I could triumph, against all odds. Little Helen Nobody could become Somebody. I took a night course, and beat out every other student in the class. Me, Helen Mooney, who'd always lurked, tall and gangly, at the back of the classroom. I took another course. Bookkeeping. I still remember the teacher's approval of everything I did. She never could understand how the other night students could get so confused about what the assignment was or what was going to be on the exam, how they made foolish errors because they believed the wrong thing. I owe the technique of trickery to Cortés too.

Within two years, I was able to leave the Glebe House and get a job in the bank, beating out excellent competition that didn't understand about guile and the use of rumor. I learned to dress right. I bought my cotton armour at MacPherson's Ladies Wear. Fashionable. Concealing. Designed to protect the wearer and fool the opposition. It worked too. Two short years of strategy and privation and I married the manager of the bank. Walter Denniger. My Wally. My ambassador into the enemy camp.

But even though I had Wally, I always kept Cortés in my back pocket. Thirty years later he led me to my greatest victory and the sharp sweet three years where every decision was mine. Where the chance to humble and chastise came often but never without the aroma and taste of victory.

Where the troops followed me no matter what unless they wanted to face the consequences.

How often did I smilingly think of Cortés' reaction when I subtly rebuked a lady for insubordination, or raised my eyebrow, and asked for point of clarification during delicate negotiations or turned down the gangly adolescent children of the biggest trouble-makers when they applied to use St. Anthony's hall for their dances.

If Cortés had been alive to see, surely he would have agreed the ladies of St. Anthony's were not unlike the conquered Aztecs, in more ways than one. Right down to the fancy feathers in their hats. Whenever I looked at those ladies in their fine clothes and feathers, I knew they could slip back into human sacrifice as soon as you turned your back.

They made fine enemies.

The memories of their eyes glittering with anger is all that keeps me going these days. Some of them made excellent opponents. Strong and proud. You could smell their cologne. Emeraude or Chanel, back then. Well worth conquering.

Better than that slithering Lila Winthrop, pale and pink, reeking of lily of the valley, always whispering behind her hand, breaking off in the middle of a word when you approached. Pretending to be so kind, so good, so generous, so unimpeachable . . . they said they had no choice but to elect her President in what would have been my fourth year.

No. That Lila Winthrop is more like, much more like, the cancer that invades my body, creeping, growing, pressing, always just out of reach of knife and painkiller. She always lurks in back of my mind, nudging, probing, reminding.

Here comes Mindy with the bedpan. What a wheyfaced cow. What does my son see in her? The woman takes an eternity to do the slightest thing. Is that what hell would be like? Waiting an eternity for the bedpan? But it doesn't matter. What matters is what heaven will be like. I've earned my spot, let me tell you. The evidence of it is everywhere. Three, almost four, years as President of PLOW. Recognition from the pulpit, more times than you could even remember, for fundraising, organizing, making tough decisions, doing what needed to be done.

And more than just that. Dinners with the Archbishop. Receptions with tinkling crystal and fine wine. Didn't I shake hands with the Cardinal on more than one occasion? And think of my role during the Pope's visit. These things will count when the time comes.

"Took you long enough," I say.

"How are you?" she says.

"How do you think? I have a blue grapefruit eating my liver

and I'm just terrific. Have you no feelings? The pain is unbearable."

I like it when her hands shake. That's the secret, just to get her on edge, just rattled enough but not so much she starts to cry and then next thing you know Peter's in the room talking about how much I'll like palliative care. Where they have the resources to look after me.

Resources indeed. He'd do it too. He's just like me. Does what he wants to. Does what he needs to. I'm proud of him.

But I am older and more cunning.

"I have your painkillers," Mindy says with only a small quiver. I smile. Morphine.

"Don't worry," I say. "Things will get better. Soon you'll have my funeral to enjoy."

She gasps. It's lovely.

Her lips tremble. She bites the lower one.

Oh God, don't cry, you idiot woman. Have you no spine? I'd like to smack her, carrying on like that when Peter could step in at any moment.

Of course, she exaggerates her responses. There's some stubbornness deep down, otherwise she'd have given up the big bedroom with the bay window looking out over the birch and maple trees on the front lawn when I wanted it. But she didn't, even though Peter would have been willing. That's how I know she's not everything she pretends to be.

Good, she's got herself in control. Pain is beginning to get me down, sweeping out from the center of the circle. Soaring to flame in my brain. It's hard to breathe when the pills wear out. I don't really have the strength to battle with Peter.

Morphine.

The pills, the pills. Faster, faster . . . need them.

Water. Yes. Don't give in. Just the one, I remind myself. I force myself. Just the one and save the other under the tongue. Until she's gone.

She stays a long time. Lingering by the foot of the bed. Holding the full bedpan. It suits her, this line of work.

I want her out. Out so I can get the second pill from under my tongue and put it with the others. Before it melts. I don't know how much longer I'll be able to keep on saving the second pills. The pain never really leaves me now. I try to stand outside myself and observe my reactions to see what I can do to get control again. But the blast of pain sucks me back into myself. I lose myself to it.

I feel my sheets, warm and wet beneath me. Mindy will have to change them.

But I must do something.

"Call Doctor Graham. Tell him I need a much stronger dosage. The pain is unbearable. Get him on the phone now."

"But Mother . . ."

I want to scream, don't call me mother, you lazy stupid slut, but even in my pain I know it's not a good move. Still I have to get rid of her.

"Or don't call him," I say, "don't call him to relieve my pain." I'm gasping for breath. Imagine knives finding soft places to twist in, it's like that. "The right dosage will only let me live longer, and we all know what a nuisance that would be."

I watch her through half-shut eyes. She always looks like she's been slapped, that one.

"I'll call him," she says.

"You do that."

She turns back when she reaches the door. "Oh, I almost forgot, I was able to reach the friend you asked me to phone. She said she'd love to come and visit you tomorrow. Remember? Lila Winthrop." She smiles when she closes the door behind her.

Of course, I remember. How could I forget? Didn't I ask her to call? Didn't I plan it? Didn't I arrange the whole thing? But, oh, my heart. My head. Lila Winthrop. Tomorrow! Just thinking about that pink and white vulture, flying in to gloat over my living corpse, I have no choice but to swallow the second pill. This time. This one time.

Lila Winthrop. It's only right for me to settle things with Lila. After all, did I not once have the ear of the Archbishop?

It takes eighteen minutes for the second pill to kick in. I know. I've timed it. I count the seconds. There is some satisfaction as I reach one thousand and eighty.

At last I can float on the cloud. Euphoria. Heaven will be like this. The floating. The sense of being well. The absence of pain. I am smiling when I lie there. The feelings last for hours, three, closer to four. Then the long stretching descent again, waiting for the flame knife to conquer my body.

This time it's worth the second pill.

I can finish my plans for Lila's visit.

The doctor is here. I see his face distorted, bending over. I hear his voice, talking to Mindy. Why ask her how I'm doing? What does she know? Scatterbrained would-be do- gooder. Why not ask me? I'll tell him, if he wants to know.

"The medication doesn't seem to be doing the job anymore," she says, twisting her hands.

Yes. That is the right message.

I'm feeling terrific, euphoric, flying through a sky of joy. But I don't want them to know that. Don't let the comfort, the pleasure, take you from your plan, Helen, I remind myself. Remember what you want.

I moan. And thrash.

They turn to look at me and turn away to talk.

Thank you. That tells me what they'd do if I really were moaning and squirming and trashing. If the hot knife were really doing its work.

For good measure, I let out a long, strangled, burbling scream. And try to sit up.

Through eyes more closed than open, I can still watch their reactions. The doctor moves toward the bed. I see Mindy holding back. One of her hands is over her mouth. The other one clutches her breast.

He sits on the edge of the bed.

"Can you hear me, Helen?"

"Of course, I can hear you," I blurt.

His eyes widen.

"In case you're forgetting, my liver's the problem, not my ears." It might be wise to temper my remarks but I feel the arrogant fool has it coming.

"Yes, of course. Mindy tells me the current dose of medication is not doing the job."

"Well, you can see that for yourself. The tumor must be bigger."

He nods. "The dose is already very high, Mrs. Denniger." I notice he's stopped calling me Helen.

"Really?" I say. "Are you afraid I'll become an addict?"

He jerks his head to look at me.

"Or maybe my long-term health will be at risk?"

He narrows his eyes.

I like to toy with them, these priests at the temple of medicine with their primitive totems and potions. I remember how Cortés turned the Aztec priests' beliefs against them, set them up for Christianity. Made off with their gold.

I meet his eyes. "What difference will it make," I say, "if one little old woman cuts out four hours of agony from her life every day? Who will be harmed by that?"

Out of the corner of my eye, I see Peter slip into the room. I hope he will have heard my argument. He likes that kind of thinking. I see him put his hand on Mindy's shoulder. She lays her head on his shoulder. At least she's pale and ugly looking from strain.

"You will have a hard time telling what is real, Mrs. Denniger, with a higher dose."

I bark out a laugh. "Reality is overrated, doctor. Take the word of someone with liver cancer."

I see him watching Peter and Mindy. They are watching him back.

"I think," he says, turning his fish-gray eyes to me, "you would be much better off in a palliative care unit."

You mean, she will be better off if I'm in a palliative care unit.

I say nothing. My heart thunders. I haven't the strength to conquer new territory. I want to stay here with my war trophies. In my own home.

"They have special training. They have the right staff and facilities. You will be much more comfortable there."

"Really," I say. "Staff? Facilities? Is it the same as your family? Can they duplicate the feeling of being in your own home? The memories, the air, the feelings?"

I see Mindy wilt a bit. Why won't I just slink off and die in peace, she's probably thinking, so she can air out the house and burn the mattress and be in charge again.

The doctor compresses his lips. And what is he thinking? That I should have some consideration and die quickly and without fuss surrounded by paid strangers?

Peter's face firms up. I can see his decision written there. I can feel it.

"This is my mother's home," he says.

I see Mindy turn from him and struggle to pull herself together. Smothering the hot tears. Trying to look like it's my best interests she has in mind.

I manage a brave smile through the pain I am not feeling. I reach out and squeeze Peter's hand.

"My home," I whisper and close my eyes.

My plan, I think, will work out fine.

Cotton armour, that's the secret. I have mine. A silky white cotton nightie with handmade lace on the square collar and cuffs. Spotless. Mindy has gone out and purchased new white sheets. With eyelet ruffles and matching pillow cases and coverlet. All with white eyelet ruffles.

Of course, she'd hesitated. Probably thinking what good is it to spend money on the old lady when she can't have more than a month to hang on to life if she's lucky.

"You might as well spend some of my money on me when I'm alive," I said to her. "You'll get enough when I'm dead."

Two spots of red colored her cheeks as she left the room to go shopping. She did not shut the door softly.

I'm sure she was thinking about how much work it would be to get stains from the sheets, but that was not my problem.

Mindy brings the phone to my bed, as requested. When she leaves the room, I order flowers from the florist. A showy bouquet of peach roses, mums and baby's breath. I have them put on Peter's Visa. Why not? Sixty dollars less for Mindy after I'm gone. They ask if I want a message on the card. Oh yes, I say, and give the bishop's name.

I call Peter and Mindy's travel agent. I use the Visa number again to book a tour of the south of France. Two weeks away. Yes, I understand it will be more expensive at such short notice.

I send Mindy out for sachets. And those air fresheners you plug into the wall socket. The scent of roses, I tell her.

It has worked out well. I've had a sponge bath. And scented talc. I have managed to have my hair done. It almost killed me and it cost nearly forty dollars to have that girl come to the house and do my hair in the bedroom, but it was worth it.

Mindy has even ironed my cotton underwear as I requested. She got a look on her face like the trout my husband used to haul from the lake. Didn't want to iron someone else's underwear, I guess. Her problem, not mine. I have the cool, soft, smooth cotton I need next to me. Protection from the treachery and cunning of my rival.

I check the mirror. You can hardly see my illness on my face.

Mindy has set up the silver tea service and china cups. Just within my reach. She goes to sink into the flowered guest chair.

I do not want her hanging around the room while I prepare myself to meet my old enemy.

"Are those the best cookies you could find?" I say. "Don't we have any decent shortbread?"

She scurries from the room and down the hall. Swish, swish. I am alone.

I make myself ready to face Lila Winthrop.

She sits there. Fresh and crisp in her golf clothes. Smiling the snake smile I remember so well. The smile of the good little girl who has gotten everything worked out to her satisfaction, with the help of her orthodontist and her accountant. I can almost read her thoughts. She is thinking I might have conquered her in my parish initiatives, turned her into an unwilling captive, robbed her of glory, especially with the Annual Summer Fête and the Fall Tea and Sale and the Christmas Parish Pageant. Cut off her ways of complaining, turned her allies against her with the right information, the right tones, the right raised eyebrow. Clipped her wings. Until.

Until she triumphed by guile and won the Presidency of PLOW. The worst day of my life. I hated her. I hate her now. I work back in my mind and calculate most likely that's the day it started, the cancer, a small speck, a single cell turned white hot by hate, glowing. Growing.

And look at her. She is certainly thinking she will triumph again in the end because, after all, I am dying of hate and she is off to play nine holes, crisp in her cotton. Pink cotton. A soft deceptive pink, like cotton candy. Very tricky.

But I have cotton too. Cotton armour.

Mindy is back with the shortbread, hovering, even after Lila is seated in the upholstered visitor's chair with the peony design in burgundy and white. Mindy hovers, practically twitching. I can't stand that. She makes me edgy when she hovers. She has already set out the silver service on the campaign table near my bed.

"We don't need anything else," I tell her. "Come back later. You can serve us some fresh tea in about twenty minutes."

Mindy opens her mouth and closes it again. Really, she looks more like a muskie than a trout.

I can hear her polyester swishing as she moves along the hallway. Silly thing. She's never been smart enough for cotton. Wouldn't recognize what it could do for her anyway.

Not like Lila. Lila turns her head when I am speaking to Mindy. It's her little way of letting me know she's much too well bred to listen to orders being given to the help. Fine with me. Out of the corner of my eye, I see her admiring the flowers.

"Aren't they lovely?" I say. "And so fragrant."

Of course she has to lean over and sniff the fragrance. But with the air of humoring me. She must have practiced that look for years. She's much better at it than she used to be. Closer, I think, get closer. Yes.

She has spotted the bishop's name on the card. Her head snaps back. Bingo.

She doesn't see my hand flash over the pink china cup, just high enough, but never touching it.

"Very nice," she says. She doesn't give me the satisfaction of mentioning the bishop's name. Or letting on she's noticed. That's fine. I wouldn't respect her if she did.

And hell would freeze over before I would be so unclassy as to mention it.

"Mindy has left us this very nice tea," I say.

"Yes, indeed." I notice she's looking a little pinched around the mouth.

The cups are Royal Albert. My two favorite from Wally's mother's collection. The pink one has white lacy edges and the blue ones has tiny flowers.

"Which cup would you prefer?" I ask. I make sure she sees me eye the pink one myself. I reach to pass her the blue one just in case she doesn't catch on. She sees all right. She sees my hand shaking too. I actually have to make it shake. I've never felt surer of anything before. Strength floods me.

But I don't let on. Instead, I lean back on the pillow and gasp, as if the effort of reaching for the blue cup has just about done me in.

"I do love pink," she says, as if I didn't know that. "Matches my outfit too."

"It suits you."

She flicks her eyes to my trembling hand.

"May I pour?"

I hesitate. "Of course," I say, pretending to mask my tiny disappointment.

She makes sure I see her strong, steady hands, grip the handle and the lid of the silver pot, pouring with grace and just a little more flourish than the situation actually calls for. She passes me my blue cup with a smile, synthetic pity in her eyes.

As her fingers close around the handle of her pink cup, and she raises it to her lips, I pick up my blue cup and sip. It is all I can do, to keep from howling.

She's lying there, that pink skirt pulled up when she fell. Her mouth is open. Her eyes bulge. You can see her legs, gnarled a bit with lumpy blue veins. Not very pretty.

I smile at that. But internally where such smiles belong.

The only irritation is the sound of Mindy bawling. No sense of proper behavior, that one, never did have.

Peter is conferring with the doctor. They've both let their customary 'I'm in charge here' looks slip a bit. This is bad, this is troublesome and time-consuming, they are thinking. Lila Winthrop's inconsiderate demise will mean a lot of forms to be filled in. A real nuisance.

I slip back into the sheets. I sigh.

Peter and the doctor turn to face me.

I've paid enough taxes in my life, so it's good to see them getting put to work. Fairly quickly, the police figure it out. The drugs of Lila's tea, still pooled in the cup, contain a startling amount of morphine. Enough to knock off the entire block, probably. Paid for in a sea of pain. Dozens of pills held back under my tongue. Dozens of hot knives twisted in my body, to make those pills available, but worth it. Well worth it.

The police have the cup. They will have found only Mindy's and Lila's prints on it. My cup. My favorite china cup. Peter will know that and perhaps mention it to the investigating officer. But never mind, just in case, I have let it slip into the conversation. "But it was my cup, officer, she liked the look of it. Naturally, I let her use it. She was my guest, after all."

Even the doctor with his fish-gray eyes, I know he would rather it be me. Better if I were dead, since I'm a quite a bother now. I can tell he hates to see me when we both know he's help-less against this disease. And, of course, he much prefers Mindy to me. But even he has to admit, I never asked for extra medication. Mindy was the one who asked for the dose.

Mindy, the long-suffering daughter-in-law, waiting on the nasty old lady hand and foot. Why not liberate herself from such drudgery and take a nice little trip or two with the inheritance? I mention to the police officer that Mindy had often talked of going to the south of France. Of course, she will deny it. Because it never happened.

I have many nurses now. Round the clock. Much better if you ask me. They do what they're told. I just have to remember how far I can go.

For days now, I have heard the sound of Mindy's wailing and snuffling. It brings great satisfaction. Who knows what more entertainment will come from all this?

But my day nurse is here, plump and pretty. She gives a love-ly sponge bath. And I'm set up in the big front bedroom now, with the bay window looking over the silver birches and red maples on the front lawn. I can't be expected to stay in the room where such a terrible thing happened to my friend. Peter won't hear of it.

Even the pain is under control, since I don't have to hide one out of every two pills. Everything is much improved.

The nurse sits herself down. She reaches over to hold my

hand. She's the type to be a faithful retainer, this one.

"They're taking her in," she says, squeezing my hand, gently, gently.

"Not really?" I say.

She nods, oozing compassion. She must have had a course in it.

"They're sure . . . she did it?"

"I don't know. But they must be. They're here for her."

I shake my head, as if I'm almost too weak to move. "It was supposed to be me. It was in my favorite cup. She had no reason to want to harm poor Lila."

The nurse squeezes my hand.

No smile mars my face. Cortés would be proud of me.

I pull my eyelet-fringed cotton armour up around me and close my eyes.

I sleep in victory.

1996 WINNER

MARY JANE MAFFINI
"Cotton Armour"
The Ladies Killing Circle

Nominees:

TANYA HUFF
"This Town Ain't Big Enough"
Vampire Detectives

JAMES POWELL
"The Rasputin Faberge"
Ellery Queen Mystery Magazine

JAMES POWELL
"Breakout from Mistletoe Five"
Ellery Queen Mystery Magazine

PETER ROBINSON
"Carrion"
No Alibi

RICHARD K. BERCUSON

Dead Run

Something protruded from the car window. There was a pop, and a second immediately followed. I turned my head to see who was pushing me from behind. No one. But my right shoulder burned. I snapped my head the other way. No one there either.

I raised my hand and felt a little hole in the tee-shirt. It was damp, too. I poked the tip of my middle finger into the hole and suddenly grimaced at the pain. The third, fourth, and fifth pops made me frown. I had a sense of impending discomfort.

I looked back at the car in time to see a wee column of smoke dissolve into the night air. My left middle finger was still tickling the edges of that hole in my shoulder, though the finger knew enough not to foray into it again.

My stomach ached horribly. I coughed once, a chesty sputter which made me wince. Coughs weren't supposed to do that.

There was warmth on the inner part of my bare thighs and my next thought was, "Damn, I've peed in my shorts in the middle of Bayview Avenue." Then, without a hint of warning, both knees buckled in unison. The ache in my tummy worsened and it along with a stabbing pain in my chest collaborated to bend me in half. On my way down to the sidewalk, I could see liquid trickle into the crack.

Another two pops. If the car was still there, I didn't see it and didn't much care. I rolled onto the sidewalk in the tightest imaginable fetal position. My cheeks went wet from whatever liquid I was lying in and it stung my eyes. I hadn't been running long enough for that much sweat to appear. So what was it? Please, not my urine. . . .

I couldn't catch my breath. There was no goddamn air! I sucked in but didn't dare exhale. Whatever was in my lungs needed to stay there. Somehow it was escaping. I could hear it, like listening to the faint pfffffff of air coming out from the pinprick-size hole in a ball. I tried sucking in once more. My chest hurt worse now. Air was leaving me . . . I heaved and gasped . . . no air . . . this wasn't good, not good at all.

So I shut my eyes and tried one more time.

Of course, by now, I was dead.

As if that wasn't annoying enough, events unfolded which made me worry about me. For one thing, being gunned down in the middle of the street just wasn't me at all. I wasn't in a position to so inform the police. It was something they would learn on their own. But let's face it. Any respectable investigator would think the worst about the victim. What nefarious activities could I have been doing to prompt such a loathsome death — drugs, smuggling, loansharking, betting? Typesetting?

At the time of my murder, I was the president of a small printing company. I had a generous salary and a few perks. I was unmarried, lived in a grossly over-priced condo, and drove a Buick without automatic windows. My social life centered on trying to bed one particular woman whose style was both exotic and inconsistent. She was an occasional soirée who seemed to get off on calling me at peculiar hours. Otherwise, I drank with friends, flirted, went out for long runs, played on the company softball team — third base — and invested in mutual funds. A dignified, unencumbered existence.

I lay curled up on the sidewalk in my runner's wear for just a few minutes before the police arrived. I was gratified to learn the liquid was blood, not urine. I also felt better knowing my body was discovered by a responsible taxi driver. He waited till the detectives arrived and told them his first reaction was that I could be a potential fare — drunk and in need of a ride home. The holes in my body apparently convinced him otherwise.

A pair of detectives did the expected walkabout. They surveyed the bushes and shone their flashlights first on me and then on the curb. One of them, a wisp of a fellow, tiptoed around the blood puddles. Meanwhile, a young man videotaped the scene with a large shoulder-mounted camera. It had a lamp attached to it which illuminated the scene like a football field. He then took a series of still photos with a camera hanging from his neck. He took pictures of me and the sidewalk, me with a backdrop of the bushes, and me with the street in the background. Because I was lying with my posterior facing the road, the last one was a bit embarassing.

A man in a lab coat and gloves examined me. With the help of a flunkie, he stretched me out. "Dead less than an hour," he said stating the obvious. "Five shots. All entries from the front — right shoulder, right upper chest, two in the gut, one lower on the left around the spleen looks like." He scribbled in a notebook. "No exits. Didn't die real fast, I'd say."

No, indeed.

The photographer, on his orders, took more photos of the wounds and left. The little detective stood at the edge of my puddles and nodded. Behind him was another detective, taller with arms like kegs that stuck out of a golf short and a belly which was, conservatively, mountainous.

The shorter one addressed the man in the lab coat. "Carl, when can you get to this one?"

"Seems pretty straight forward. I'll let the new guy do it."

He was going to let an intern do my autopsy. What if he missed a bullet hole? What if he lost a bullet? A rookie doing my autopsy.

When the coroner drove off with me in the back, the short detective, Jack, examined my keys which were in my shorts. He held them up for his partner, Charlie the Mountain, to see. "House keys, I s'pose. Three house keys." He pondered for a moment.

For all his largeness, Charlie the Mountain was at least observant, an important faculty in a detective. "Whose house has three locks? Nah. This is either an apartment or a condo. Lobby door key. Two keys for the apartment door."

They remained there for a while longer examining the site, looking for witnesses — there weren't any — and ruminating. Charlie summarized the event thusly: "Here's this guy out for a run at night. Doesn't get far. Someone pulls alongside him and pumps him five times. Five body shots. No head shot. It's prob'ly a hit, a real sloppy hit, but it isn't a hit, y'know? Hard to figure."

They went back to the police station. On the sidewalk my puddle dripped over the curb onto the road.

No one reported me missing, even at noon the next day. My secretary Margie surely wouldn't have called the police. She wouldn't have the sense to call my home. The detectives only learned who I was and where I lived by going to every building within running distance and checking the door keys. Rather than call my company, they examined my apartment. The superintendent, Eldon, followed them from room to room, bless his heart. Bored with the police search through my drawers, Eldon fiddled with my CDs while lounging on my black leather couch, his shoes on the teak coffee table.

The detectives were at least neat. They mumbled aimless comments and picked through closets, delicately fingering my clothes. I was only bothered when they poked into my underwear. Jack, the wispy one, found my electronic organizer in a nighttable drawer. "I have one kinda like this," he said. "Not as much memory though." Naturally not.

Charlie was in the closet and called back, "What?"

Jack walked over to him to show off the gadget. "His daytimer. We should take this back and check out the numbers."

"Phone numbers?"

"Phone numbers, names, some other numbers, too, but I can't make out what they're for." He slipped it into his jacket.

They spent another half hour checking out my place. Eldon was in the kitchen eating my chocolate chip cookies when Jack announced their departure. The super was annoyed, being in the middle of a snack and all, but he saw them out and locked the door. He left the CDs on the coffee table next to the scratch marks from his shoes.

In the elevator, Jack took out my organizer and toyed with it. He inadvertently switched on a button which made each key press emit a ding. It dinged a lot and Charlie snapped at him to put away the toy.

"Lots of brief memos, " Jack half-mumbled to himself.

I knew what he'd found. And not for a moment had I considered those bets grounds for my death. They were small, placed with reputable bookies, and represented a stellar winning record.

Charlie the Mountain and Jack slurped black coffee at a

round formica table in the station. Charlie sat some distance from the table since his belly threatened to overturn it with each expiration of breath. They had printed out the contents of the daytimer and Jack was reviewing the notes he'd scribbled on the fanfold sheets.

"The man gets three k from home," Jack said, "and is gunned down from a car. Five holes. Slow death."

Again the slow death.

"No witnesses. President of a nothing printing firm. Easy life. No drugs or guns. Jazz CDs. No girlfriends, it seems. Phone numbers. Codes. Little memos. No vices really."

Charlie had a sheet of the paper resting on a plateau of his stomach. "My guess is betting. Horses, dogs, maybe even jai-alai."

"Hmm," hmmed Jack. They looked at each other and smirked as if they'd just cracked the crime of the century.

"Jai-alai. Played in Florida, isn't it?" Charlie asked his partner.

Jack nodded. His calls to Margie had already confirmed my bi-annual vacations to Fort Lauderdale. "And the game's played mostly by the Portuguese. Do you think the Portuguese mob is involved?"

Portuguese mob? The only Portuguese mob I'd ever known was the Friday night line-up at the Fernandez Bar and Grill on Park Avenue in Montreal.

Content with their discovery, the detectives headed to the coroner's lab for the autopsy results. Unfortunately, Carl and his new man hadn't yet begun so the detectives stood at the back of the room and watched. This I considered somewhat invasive.

The new guy peeled back the sheet and leaned directly over my chest. "Shot," he said.

Jack nudged his partner and tapped his index finger to his temple. "Sharp lad."

Carl walked the new guy through each step of the autopsy. This wasn't so bad, except the rookie had a book sticking out of his labcoat pocket. You could only see the beginning of the title. "Introductory Pathology: The Scalpel and . . ."

The kid removed the five bullets, though he did drop one on the floor. There was discussion for a couple of minutes on whether it was the bullet from my shoulder or my stomach, but Carl instructed it wouldn't matter in the long run. Carl did the next part. He removed my brain and sliced off a piece. I had no idea this was part of the routine and I was initially rather perturbed. I relaxed when I discovered it was the piece which balances bank accounts.

The two policemen left with a preliminary report which confirmed what everyone knew. The only hint of the unusual was that the bullets were likely fired from some distance away.

Said Charlie in the car, "If you're going to take a guy out, you'd want to be up close to make sure of it. This dude is shot from further away. Not exactly meticulous work."

Frankly, I had never considered murder as being meticulous. Not only that, he was implying that MY murderer was sloppy.

For days, their leads went nowhere. The jai-alai bets were done through a fellow in town, which meant Jack and Charlie were denied a trip to Lauderdale to check out my movements. This would have ultimately proved more frustrating for them since they would have seen how much useless time I spent hanging around country club bars trying to pick up rich women.

They did have other cases to work on but mine was the most intriguing since it involved no obvious answers. In the meantime, Jack and Charlie interviewed Margie and all my employees. Then they heard about my sporadic ladyfriend from Eldon, the super. But all he could provide was a description. He didn't know where to find her any more than I usually did. How many times had I wanted to see her myself only to learn she'd vanished — for days at a time?

About a week after their last interviews on my case, the detectives were called to check into a shooting in the office of a local paper company. The victim was the company's owner and he'd been found by his vice-president, slumped over his desk with four gunshot wounds in the chest. He was an older man, about seventy, with a really familiar name.

In the meantime, I was buried. My company hosted a lovely funeral and printed a flattering obituary in the paper. I was moved. They even named a company award for me which went to the employee who best contributed to the welfare of colleagues outside the workplace. I think it was because I got our softball team to play in some charity events. We'd usually lose.

The preliminary forensics report on the other man's murder indicated he'd been shot with the same weapon as me. Him, four body shots. Me, five body shots. As Jack said, "The running guy was moving. Tougher target." Printing company exec, then paper company exec. This all smacked of conspiracy. Even Charlie suggested the Portuguese mob angle once more.

However, drawing a link between the killings was tricky. The other man didn't exercise, let alone run. He didn't bet and had never been to Fort Lauderdale. He preferred Arizona. I doubt he could spell jai-alai. Perhaps, Charlie the Mountain conjectured, there was indeed a company connection. If there were one, they couldn't find it.

But the coincidence was too striking. Jack poured over his notes on the second killing again. He stopped at one page then opened my file and frantically riffled through the sheets of notes.

"What?" asked Charlie. It was four o'clock in the afternoon and he was attacking a pre-meal snack of carrots and dip.

"Remember the runner's girlfriend? The description the super gave us?"

"Yeah. What of it?" said Charlie

"Doesn't the old guy's wife look like that, sorta?" wondered Jack.

"Maybe. Okay. I guess," answered Charlie scooping gobs of dip onto a carrot stick.

"Now the old man — Mr. Romena — "

The two prattled on while I pondered the implication. No wonder I recognized his name. Romena was the name of my some-time ladyfriend.

"And you think it's the same one the runner was seeing."

Jack nodded.

I had to admit it was plausible. During the investigation of my shooting, they were unable to trace her. I'd assumed she was so broken-hearted about my death that she needed time to herself. She didn't even come to my funeral, but it wasn't unusual for her to disappear for days.

Jack and Charlie called on Mr. Romena's house the next day. Guess who answered the door.

It was Romena, or Mrs. Romena, or whatever. She was wearing a skimpy halter top, knee-length shorts and sandals. Her long dark hair was damp and hung over one shoulder. She looked relaxed and tanned — damn sexy actually — not at all like someone whose lover had been murdered on the street and whose husband had been shot to death in his office.

Jack and Charlie tried not show their surprise. This was particularly hard for Charlie who was as subtle as his stomach. They exchanged pleasantries with her in the doorway.

They brought up my name right away, of course. Romena, however, denied even knowing me. This probably explained her absence from my funeral. Amnesia, perhaps. On the other hand, I was dead and she was now being implicated.

Jack intimated she'd been seen with me in my lobby. She coolly dismissed the notion. He stuck a picture of me in front of her face. Not a hint of recognition. I was getting quite annoyed.

Charlie the Mountain seemed to think she was being straight with them and actually started to apologize for the intrusion.

Jack interrupted. He whipped out the organizer. "Know what this is?"

She shrugged.

"Your boyfriend's electronic little black book," he said waving it before her.

She stared at him, non-plussed. He was persistent, though floundering.

"These things are amazing," Jack told her. Charlie leaned against the wall trying to find the correct center of gravity for him and his stomach. Jack continued. "We got by his password and found out what he kept in here."

She just remained standing in that doorway watching Jack push buttons while little ding-ding noises came from the gadget.

So I took action. I delivered a long, slow, soft, warm steady blow to her left earlobe — a blow reminiscent of other times.

She snapped her head around. Her eyes became large and she shivered. That's when she spilled it all.

Jack and Charlie listened with Charlie frantically trying to scribble down her comments in a notepad which was buried in the fleshiness of his huge hands. When finally she admitted to wanting to keep our relationship secret, Jack muttered, "Ah, yes."

She hesitated for a few moments and Charlie's pen did, too. Again I delivered her the lobe blow. This time she finished the story.

Her plan was to meet her husband — the old guy — for

dinner at a restaurant they frequented. She told the detectives she hadn't wanted the "idiots" she'd hired to know who he was, so she gave them what she thought were simple instructions: watch, follow, kill.

Now I recalled the last time I'd seen her. The very day of my demise. Coincidentally, it was in the same restaurant, one where I often fed my cheesecake fetish. I'd walked in and there she was, sitting alone. A stroke of luck, I'd thought — cheesecake and Romena.

I surprised her and sat down. But she said she was waiting for her mother. Feeling somewhat unwelcome, I got up and left. I was there less than a minute. I was there less than a minute.

Cheesecake and I had an agreement. I could eat it if first I created space in my arteries. After leaving the restaurant, I went home and changed.

A little run would do wonders for my health, I thought.

1997 WINNER

RICHARD K. BERCUSON
"Dead Run"
Storyteller

Nominees:

JANE DIAS
"Too Broke for Bullets"
Storyteller

EDEN ROBINSON
"Dogs in Winter"
Traplines

BRAD SPURGEON
"Murder in the Abbey"
Murderous Intent

EDO VAN BELKOM
"The Piano Player Has No Fingers"
The Piano Player Has No Fingers

SUE PIKE

Widow's Weeds

I t was minus 37 degrees the night in February when my
only son, Blake, froze to death. He and his wife had driven
up from the city earlier that day, leaving their car at the end
of the ploughed road and skiing the final three kilometers
along the shore to the cottage. The last Tess saw of him
was when he went outside around midnight to bring in an arm-
load of firewood.

The coroner ruled the death was accidental, probably caused
by the victim losing his footing on the deck and stumbling over the
low railing to the frozen lake below. The sheer drop would have
broken his bones, but it was the bitter cold that killed him.

I was in the city when it happened and only later heard how
some trappers checking their lines early the next morning had
noticed bush wolves gathered around something near the shore.
They frightened the animals off and one man stayed with the body
while the other two wakened Tess to phone for help.

I never saw the convoy of snowmobiles speeding across the
lake or the paramedics strapping his body to the sleigh. But I
picture it often enough. In my mind's eye I'm standing on the deck
looking down. I see Blake with his legs and arms flung out like
a rag doll tossed to the ice by a petulant child; his skin is trans-
lucent, bruised and torn, his face slicked over with a fine coat
of crystals.

I was picturing it five months later on a warm July afternoon
as I walked along the narrow road that winds behind the three
family cottages on our point. So absorbed was I that I didn't even
hear the car until it was nearly on top of me. I only just managed
to scramble to the verge before the left front wheel skidded to

a stop exactly where my foot had been seconds earlier.

Tess!

My daughter-in-law lowered the window part way and pushed her sunglasses over her forehead.

"Sorry, Isabel. Did I frighten you?" She tilted her head to one side and smiled up at me, and I caught a glimpse of casually elegant riding breeches and a crisp cotton shirt. So it's to be the Princess of Wales today, I thought.

I leaned onto the door and my own sixty-nine year old face glared back at me from the lower half of the tinted window, all pouches and creases under a crooked Tilley hat.

"You're driving way too fast for this winding road, Tess." We'd had this discussion before. "One of these days you're going to kill someone."

"Oh let's not go into that again." Her voice was unperturbed and smooth as the pebbles under my feet. "I'm just anxious to get to the cottage. This is the first I've been able to get up here since Blake had his accident and there's so much to do." She waved a pale hand in the direction of the lake.

I stared at her but said nothing.

"I've been incredibly busy. Settling the estate and dealing with lawyers and accountants. It's all quite daunting."

'Daunting' had a British lilt to it. Very Lady Di.

The last time I'd seen Tess was at my son's funeral. She was Jackie Kennedy on that occasion, the brave young widow greeting mourners in a trim little suit and veiled hat. The only thing missing was a small son to salute the casket, but they hadn't been married long enough for that . . . would never have been married long enough for that, if I knew Tess.

I suppose I was hoping for some change in her since then, some mark of Blake's death written on the perfect planes of her face, but she was as bland and beautiful as ever. Tendrils of fair hair floated down from a loose knot to cling damply to her neck. Her eyes, the colour of blue willow china, were clear and untroubled.

"By the way," she splayed the fingers of her left hand against the steering wheel and began to maneuver the rings into perfect alignment. "I'm thinking of selling the cottage. It's too much upkeep for me to manage by myself."

She looked up at me through her lashes but I kept still.

"My financial advisor tells me this would be a good time to put it on the market. He thinks I can get quite a lot of money for it. Especially if we can sever the property into lots."

"Lots?" My heart lurched. "But you can't do that. This is family land. Blake would never have allowed any of the old property to be broken up."

"Well I'm sorry, Isabel, but Blake's portion is mine now. And anyway, he was coming around to the idea. We talked about it quite often." She blew some wisps of hair out of her eyes. "In any case, he's not here anymore, is he?"

"How many lots?" I was having difficulty getting my breath.

"Lots of lots." She laughed. "Well, as many as will fit, I guess. I know one developer in the city who says twelve building sites would make the deal viable." Tess took a lipstick from her purse and pulled the rear view mirror around so she could apply a fresh coat. She made a little moue with her mouth, blotted it and then flipped the tissue out the window where it fluttered to my feet.

I clutched the edge of the glass hard and forced air into my lungs. My inhaler was in my pocket but I was damned if I'd resort to it in front of her.

"Well, I must go," she turned away and I could feel the window pushing against my hands and then, just as suddenly, it stopped and I was able to unclench my fingers and step back to the verge. "By the way, would you be a darling, and tell Alastair I'm here? I promised I'd let him know the minute I arrived."

Pebbles and dust shot away from the spinning tires and it took every bit of my strength to remain standing until the car was out of sight. Then my knees buckled and I sank down among the buttercups and daisies, wheezing and cursing Tess and the deadly emphysema that sapped my strength and numbered my days on this piece of land I loved so much.

I found my daughter kneeling on the deck of her cottage. She had the porch door off its hinges and was prying the screen from the frame.

"Raccoons!" Lindy sat back on her heels when she saw me. "The kids left a package of cookies lying out last night and the beggars decided to break in for a snack." She wrenched the last of the torn screening away and began to measure a new length from a fresh roll lying at her feet. I picked up the wire cutters from the picnic table and handed them to her.

"I ran into Tess on the road. Or rather, she almost ran into me." I chuckled, hoping to sound more neutral than I felt.

"Mm. I knew she was coming. She called Alastair last night to ask if he'd come over to help her open up the cottage." She had her back to me, her head bent over the door. "By the way, who is she today?"

"Princess Diana, as near as I can tell." I picked up the staple gun and passed it to her when she had the screen in place. "But why Alastair? Being a cottage handyman is hardly his strong suit. Why not hire someone from the village?"

Lindy's shoulders stiffened but she said nothing. I dragged an old wooden Muskoka chair closer to where she was working. The sun was moving behind the cottage now but it was still hot in the shade and my heart was juddering in my chest. I tried to relax, listening to the rhythmic clump of staples biting into wood.

When Lindy finally put her tools down, I patted the seat of the chair beside me. She sank into it and we sat still for a moment looking down at the lake where five teenagers in swimsuits were splashing around. I recognized my two granddaughters and the Crawford kids.

"You haven't wanted to talk about Blake and what happened to him and I've respected that." I turned to her. "But now we must, Lindy. It's important."

"I know, mom. It's just . . ." Lindy began.

"Hi all." Tess climbed the steps to the deck and leaned against the railing. She'd changed out of the jodhpurs and into a high-waisted, low-necked blue dress that reached almost to her ankles. Her hair was down and tumbling in tiny curls about her shoulders. A Jane Austen character, I thought, or perhaps one of the Brontes.

"Aren't you a quaint pair, sitting out here in your old camp clothes." Tess leaned closer, studying each of us in turn. "But look at you! You're letting your skin turn to leather. I'll bet neither one of you has been wearing those sunscreen samples I gave you last summer."

I didn't dare glance at Lindy. Tess had sold cosmetics to help put herself through university. When she married Blake she tried to unload some products on her new in-laws, but found us disappointing customers.

Tess sighed and leaned back again. "And I see you've forgotten to give Alastair my message, Isabel." She smiled at me indulgently then, as if she'd always suspected I was senile. "Never mind, I'll roust him out myself."

She flitted away on her fine leather slippers and we could hear laughter coming from the living room. After a while she reappeared tugging Alastair behind her by his fingertips. I thought he looked extremely foolish and would have told him so except at that moment he had the grace to extricate himself and lean down to give me a kiss.

"Isabel! I had no idea you were here. Can I get you a cold drink?"

But Tess was having none of that. "She knows where the refrigerator is." She reclaimed the fingers and began tugging him off the deck and up the path to her cottage. "We have work to do and if you're very good, I'll give you a cold drink when you're finished."

Alastair shrugged a little sheepishly in our direction before allowing himself to be borne out of sight.

"Don't start." Lindy gave me a warning look.

But I'd been quiet long enough. "What is going on, Lindy? It's not just Blake, is it? What about you and Alastair?"

She took a deep breath. "Does Alastair like being married to a woman who's so consumed with rage over the way her little brother was allowed to freeze to death because his wife didn't happen to notice he was gone?" Her bitterness was frightening. "I'd say probably not, wouldn't you?"

I waited.

"She terrifies me, Mom. She's like that praying mantis Dad found on the woodpile when we were kids. Do you remember? The female was eating the male while he was still copulating with her."

I remembered Rob explaining that people were sometimes like that. Perhaps Blake forgot.

"And now Tess has Alastair over there." Lindy said. "God!

I feel the way Maggie must have felt when Tess first started putting the moves on Blake. Poor Maggie!" She shifted back in her seat. "To have that fey creature sitting in on Blake's Nineteenth Century Poetry class all that year, hanging on his every word, waylaying him in the parking lot to discuss the symbolism in Keats and Shelley. She was so clever and so incredibly gorgeous. And just needy enough to appeal to his male ego."

"Yes but Maggie and Blake were having a bad time right about then." I had to try and make sense of it, for myself as well as Lindy. "Maggie had just had the second miscarriage and she was crying all the time. It seems to me that Blake just allowed himself to be flattered for a bit and then it was too late." I watched a blue heron swoop along the bay and land at the foot of a dead pine tree on the other shore. "But surely Alastair's not attracted to Tess. He's way too smart not to see through her."

"And Blake wasn't smart? Give me a break!" Lindy snorted. "She has this talent for helplessness that men find appealing. If I tried it, Alastair would think I'd flipped. He'd tell me to buck up, like a good girl. But with Tess, he falls all over himself to help her out."

"What do you mean? Has she done this before?"

"Mm. It started right after Blake's funeral. She wanted Alastair to sort through some papers. It made sense at first, with Blake and Alastair in the same faculty. But then it was household things. Would he look at the furnace, that sort of thing."

"The furnace!" I tried to picture my elegant son-in-law squinting at a furnace. If it didn't have a sonnet inscribed on it, I couldn't imagine what he would make of it.

"I know." Lindy tossed her head impatiently. "I'm sure he's never noticed we even have such a beast."

We sat quietly for a while, looking across the water, each lost in our own thoughts. I reached over and took her hand.

"There's something else," I said. "Tess spoke to me when we met on the road. She wants to sell and she's hoping to get permission to sever their twenty acres into building lots. She says she and Blake had talked about doing it before he died."

"Bullshit!" Lindy's hand flew out of mine as she leapt to her feet. Her eyes were wild. "That is total crap! I talked to Blake just a week before he died and he told me then how important the cottage and family land were to him. He sounded depressed and I had the feeling he thought this was the only stable thing in his life."

"You talked to him?" I leaned forward. I didn't think either of us had talked to him since he left Maggie. We were too angry and too proud.

"It wasn't a happy conversation and I didn't want you to know he was feeling so bad." She was pacing the deck now, her arms hugging her chest. "But I know damned well he'd never have sold his part of the property. It was our grandfather's for God's sake!

She sank back into the chair and hugged her knees to her chest. "Alastair thinks I'm being paranoid about Tess." She had her voice under control now. "He believes her story about what happened the night Blake died. He believes she fell asleep and didn't realize Blake was still outside. But Tess would need to get up in the night to put more wood in the stove, just to keep herself from freezing. When I confronted her at the funeral, she did her little-girl-crushed routine and Alastair was appalled and horrified at my lack of tact and sympathy. I don't know when I've seen him so angry."

There was a pause and then she continued in a voice so low I had to lean toward her to hear.

"I never told either one of you I called Tess later. She blustered for a bit, then admitted she'd gone outside that night to get logs for the stove. Said she was furious with Blake for leaving her alone to cope. They'd apparently had a fight and he stormed out in a snit. She thought he was just out walking off his anger. Walking! My God. There was at least twenty inches of snow on the ground and it was one of the coldest nights that winter."

I closed my eyes and I could see Blake again, broken and helpless at the foot of the cliff. Only this time his eyes were open, waiting, watching as his blood turned to ice.

"I couldn't understand what they were doing here in the first place." Lindy said. "Blake and Maggie used to ski in all the time. But Tess? She never struck me as the outdoors type."

"Maybe she was being Amelia Earhart that weekend. The plucky little adventuress." I said, but I knew that wasn't it.

There was a pause and then Lindy began to speak again, her voice tight and agitated.

"Remember last Wednesday, when Alastair took the kids to town?" She went on without waiting for an answer. "I waited until they were off the point and then went over to Blake's cottage to look around. The shutters from the windows overlooking the deck were piled under the cabin. Blake had painted all the shutters last summer but when I dragged those four out into the light they had new scratches on them, as if someone had tried to pry them off. Only whoever did it, didn't have proper tools. It looked like they'd used a piece of wood or something."

I held up my hand to stop her. "But that could have been anyone, prowlers perhaps," I cried.

"I thought of that, but why just their cottage and not yours or mine? And serious thieves would come by snowmobile. That would imply some intention on their part and if that were so, wouldn't they have brought crow bars or something? Whatever was used left splinters and bark behind in the scratches and whoever did it wasn't successful. None of the hooks are ripped out of the wood."

Lindy looked over at me then, her face taut and flushed.

"And something else was weird. All the other shutters were still fastened on and just those four had been removed and put under the cottage. How? Who could have taken them off? Tess says she hasn't been up here since that weekend."

I was silent, thinking, imagining the unimaginable.

"What if it was Blake trying to get back into the cottage?" she said. "What if she locked him out. She might have been trying to teach him a lesson. A lesson he'd never forget."

"She might have pushed him off the deck, I suppose, when he became disoriented." My voice shocked me. It sounded rational except what I was saying was beyond anything I could ever have imagined.

Lindy came over to kneel in front of chair and hug me to her.

"Oh Mom. We must be crazy to be thinking these things." She tried her best to smile. "Surely it can't be as bad as we're imagining."

She didn't look sure of anything though, I thought, as I walked slowly back along the road to the place where it overlooked Blake's cottage. I stood looking down at the deck and out of the corner of my eye I thought I saw his body falling to the ice again. But it was only Alastair and Tess sitting close together on the old wooden glider. She had a hand on his knee and he was talking earnestly to her, his face flushed and animated.

I puffed some of the powdered medicine into my struggling lungs and then turned back toward my own place, remembering as I walked, how things had once been on this point.

When Lindy and Alastair got married seventeen years ago and then Blake and Maggie the next year, Rob and I had the peninsula surveyed and severed into three twenty acre lots. Blake and Maggie had built a winterized home at the neck of the peninsula and we transferred the middle portion with the old family place to Lindy and Alastair. Then, just the year before he died, Rob and I built a small log cottage at the very tip of the point, on a sheer granite cliff high above the lake.

I sank into my favorite chair with a glass of iced tea and a couple of pills and waited for them to take the edge off the pain in my chest.

In the morning I filled the hummingbird feeder and watered the tiger lily plants surrounding the clearing where I park my car. Then I hunted through the bathroom drawers until I found the sunscreen Tess had given me last year and I had never used. I applied a good thick layer and then sat in the soft scented air until I thought she would be awake.

"I wondered if you could come for coffee. I think we have some things to discuss." That was all I said and she agreed to be there at eleven.

When the visit was over I slumped back in my chair and dozed for a while.

The pain in my chest was nearly gone when I woke but there was still something bothering me. For the first time, I hadn't been able to tell who Tess was playing today.

I got out of my chair and looked down at the figure lying on the rocks below. The loose white shift had rucked up over her legs and suntan lotion glistened on the soles of her bare feet. It was the little ringlet of daisies fallen from her head and bobbing gently in the shallow water that gave it away.

Ophelia, I thought. Of course! And I went inside to find detergent and a cloth to wash the oil from the deck.

1998 WINNER

SUE PIKE
"Widow's Weeds"
Cottage Country Killers

Nominees:

JOHN BALLEM
"Rigged to Blow"
Secret Tales of the Arctic Trails

PETER ROBINSON
"The Two Ladies of Rose Cottage"
Malice Domestic 6

ROBERT J. SAWYER
"The Hand You're Dealt"
Free Space

EDO VAN BELKOM
"The Rug"
Robert Bloch's Psychos

Last Inning

Detective Barry Gilbert stared at the twins as the CSU moved the body of Brenda Fowler from the kitchen through the hall and out to the curved driveway. He couldn't rule the twins out; ten years old, the soles of their Reeboks covered with blood, their footprints discovered at the edge of the blood pool. He had a witness; Joe Lombardo had her out in the unmarked Lumina right now, Ellen Cochrane, the next-door neighbor, the woman who called the police. Only where was the gun? Uniformed officers searched the house. He glanced out the big bay window past the curly-headed boys where other officers searched the spacious front yard — a rich neighborhood, Forest Hill, where doctors, dentists, and lawyers lived, an old neighborhood, one of the most prestigious in the city. And looked at the boys again. Angelic? Yes. Identical twins. He was going to have a hard time keeping them straight, Josh on the right, Cody on the left, both in royal blue turtle- necks, both in Levi's 501's, cute, couldn't be killers; but then again . . .

He walked to the kitchen. A kitchen Regina would kill for, lots of room, an island, two ranges, off-white cabinetry, copper-bottomed pots hanging all over the place, a breakfast nook, a large mud-room leading to the back yard, sixteen-foot ceilings, floor of Belgian tile . . . only blood all over the tile now, tissue splattered on the off-white cabinetry, the photography unit still lighting the place with their flashbulbs, other detectives hunkered down taking measurements; sometimes all the activity left him winded, like it was all for nothing, like they played the same game over and over again; there was never any end, never any meaning...

He squatted by the double Pfeiffer sinks and looked at a perfectly delineated set of footprints, had to be size ten men's, a person standing in front of the sink, only the left shoe looked like a brogue or loafer and the right shoe was definitely a jogging shoe, the tread badly worn, practically none left on the heel. Curious clue. Then the boys' prints, at the edge of the of the pool. Cautious prints. A single set each. Explainable prints. Not like the loafer and jogger prints. Someone else had been here, someone had stood at this sink, someone in a loafer and a jogger, and this other someone could have killed Brenda Fowler. Just the same, he couldn't exclude the twins, at least not yet.

"Barry?" Joe Lombardo called him from the front hall.

"I'm in here." He walked carefully to the hall, avoiding the blood.

Joe Lombardo stood there, immaculately groomed, hair tied in a pony tail, a smudge of lipstick on his collar.

Gilbert touched the collar. "What's this? Your latest conquest?"

Joe Lombardo looked down at the collar, frowning. "I paid six bucks to have this shirt dry-cleaned."

"She wanted to mark you," said Gilbert.

"Not funny." Joe glanced past his shoulder to the kitchen; he wasn't impressed; after a while, blood just wasn't impressive any more. "Mrs. Cochrane says she's got a one-o'clock hair appointment. She's got a taxi coming."

"Let's go," said Gilbert.

He found Ellen Cochrane standing next to their unmarked Lumina, looking grumpy, as if the murder of a perfectly innocent nanny, thirty-one years old, meant nothing to her. She had a widow's hump, wore lawn bowling shoes and a white cardigan, and had bifocals dangling from a chain around her neck. He glanced at the bifocals. Thick ones. Not a good sign.

"Good morning, Mrs. Cochrane," he said. "Thanks for calling us."

The old woman peered up at him the same way a mole might peer at the sun, squinting, as if the sight of Detective Barry Gilbert hurt her eyes.

"I'm sorry to pull you away, detective," she said.

She didn't try to hide her sarcasm, but Gilbert played it straight; he was too tired to play it any other way.

"That's quite all right," he said. "Perhaps you can tell me what you saw."

"I'd be glad to," she said, with the tones of a preacher about to blast all the unrighteous sinners of the world. "I saw one of those beastly little boys shoot Brenda Fowler in cold blood. I was standing at my kitchen window." She waved vaguely at the gap between the houses. "I could see it plain as day. I couldn't believe it. Walked right up to her and shot her through the head. The little devil."

Gilbert peered up the side of the house. Mrs. Cochrane's kitchen window did indeed face directly into the Swift's breakfast nook, giving her a clear view of the crime scene.

"Which one did it?" he asked.

She stared up at him, and her face settled, and she didn't look so sarcastic any more, more like a dotty old woman who realized she had made a mistake. "I don't . . ." Her lips came together in an unpleasant pout. "You see, they look so much alike, I always get them . . . perhaps you can have the young man bring them out. If I have a look at them, I might be able to —"

"Joe," said Gilbert.

Lombardo disappeared into the house to fetch the boys.

"I hope you called the boys' father," said Ellen Cochrane.

"He's on his way." He watched the ambulance pull away. Dr. Blackstein would look at the body later, though there was little doubt about how Brenda Fowler had been killed. "Do you know the Swift family well?" he asked.

"I see the boys playing in the yard," she said. "With Brenda. And I see the father now and again. He keeps odd hours."

Joe Lombardo returned with Josh and Cody, looking scared now, tears standing in Cody's eyes, Josh clutching his hands before him, staring at the intricate interlocking brick of the drive.

Ellen Cochrane peered at the boys, fretful, looking from one to the other.

"I can't tell," she finally said.

The boys looked up at her, solemn, silent, waiting to see what would happen. Interesting. A jury couldn't convict. Mrs. Cochrane could point to Cody, but could the jury really be sure it wasn't Josh? One of them did it, but reasonable doubt remained the same for both. Twins. Which to convict? Even with genetic evidence, their DNA was identical. Which to send away as a dangerous young offender? A major obstacle. A possible check on this case. But then there was always the loafer and the jogger.

Gilbert looked at Frank Swift's shoes first, expensive ones, Italian leather, understated, no frills, smooth, quality laces, the only conceit a burgundy sheen highlighting the essential chestnut. The twins were with one of the female officers in the rec-room downstairs. Gilbert and Swift sat in the den, the house quiet, Lombardo wrapping it up outside, the murder now a few hours old, the negative electricity still floating in the air, like a ghost, thick around them, like there had been a magnetic disturbance, a blip on the radar screen, Brenda Fowler's death.

"I was picked up by a business associate shortly after 9:30," said Swift, sitting there bunched on the edge of the full-grain leather sofa, his eyes glassy, inward-looking, as if he were trying to solve Zeno's Paradox.

"Mrs. Cochrane said as much."

Swift was a short man, with close set blue eyes, a full head of black curly hair, and a high forehead.

"I'm sure she did," said Swift. Incredulous creases came to the corners of his eyes and he shifted, the leather squeaking beneath him. "You honestly don't believe her, do you? Josh and Cody loved Brenda."

"But your gun is missing. You keep it locked in a steel case upstairs. And now it's missing."

"Josh and Cody would never kill Brenda," he said flatly.

The game. The endless skirmishing. And always the heightened suspicion, as if everybody was a potential murderer, even Josh, even Cody. Maybe it was just an accident, maybe the boys got their hands on the gun, it went off, Brenda got killed, and now they were too afraid to tell the truth. He couldn't decide on Swift; Swift was many things at once: surprised, relieved, shocked, as if the details of the murder were at once familiar yet strange, as if he were running a movie in the back of his mind, going over the same scene again and again, trying to make sense of it.

"I'll have to take the name of your business associate," said Gilbert.

"Sure."

"Just for verification."

"Domenico Colella."

Swift gave him the address and telephone number.

"What kind of relationship did you have with Brenda?"

But Swift didn't hear, stared at the Japanese vase sitting on the floor in the corner, watching his movie, figuring out his next play, considering possibilities: containment, damage control, cover-up. Didn't hear his question so Gilbert repeated it.

"Brenda's been with us since the beginning," said Swift. "I've known her for ten years. I've always treated her well. She deserves it."

"She's attractive, isn't she? And you're a widower."

Swift's lips bunched. "Brenda's a happily married woman, detective. It's never been that way with us. Even after my wife died."

Still running the movie, could see it in his eyes, but now concerned, about Brenda, about the boys, grasping the enormity of what had happened, how the consequences were going to affect his life.

"You sure it couldn't have been an accident?" Gilbert asked. "The boys somehow got into your gun case."

"How could they? It's solid metal. It's got two locks. I have the only key."

Concerned but cognizant, like he gazed into a crystal ball, divined cause and effect, pieced together circumstances Gilbert could only guess.

"I want to show you something," said Gilbert.

They got up and went to the kitchen.

He showed Swift the footprints, the loafer and the jogger; and now the movie stopped, Swift's brow knitted with mystification, and Gilbert wasn't so sure any more; Swift looked lost, baffled, as if he had given up on Zeno's Paradox.

Gilbert left the boys in the custody of their father over the weekend.

Monday morning, what did he have? As he sat in his office sipping a double cappuccino with one-percent, staring out the window at the congested sidewalks of Chinatown, he couldn't help thinking how next week was his birthday, June 1st, forty-eight years old, time to reflect, to consider what he had made of his life. Choices. Sometimes you had no control over them. He never meant to be a detective, wanted to be an architect, loved the look, shape, and feel of buildings. Loved Swift's house, an old Forest Hill monstrosity, with backstairs for servants, all covered with ivy, and a coach-house out back. But now, like so many buildings and houses in this city, it had become a murder scene. So Gilbert no longer looked at buildings and houses the way an architect did.

He had the twins in the rec-room, watching Ani-Maniacs, when they heard a loud bang from upstairs. Too scared to go up right away. Josh creeps to the foot of the stairs and calls up. No answer. Finally both boys go up together. They find Brenda lying on the south side of the island with a bullet through her head. They accidentally step into pool of blood. They don't call the police themselves. Mrs. Cochrane does. Before the boys get a chance to call, the radio cars are already there. At least that's what they say. But it takes the radio cars twenty minutes from the time of Mrs. Cochrane's call, and that's what he didn't get. With twenty minutes, there should have been a second independent call from the boys. They were ten years old. They knew how to call 911. But they hadn't. And he couldn't figure out why.

What else did he have? The loafer and the jogger, leading to the sink but never away from it. Odd. What happened? No retreating footsteps. Like the jogger and loafer just disappeared.

He heard a knock on his partially open door, and turning, saw a man of about thirty- three, tall, sandy hair, trim moustache, wearing a black suit, black shoes and tie, recognized the man, but couldn't place him.

"Detective Gilbert?" said the man.

"Yes?"

"I'm Constable John Fowler. With 54 division?" Fowler gave Gilbert the chance to nod. "I'm Brenda Fowler's husband."

Gilbert's eyes narrowed; now he remembered, the annual baseball tournament last year, between 54 and 52 divisions; Fowler was a great pitcher, unbeatable, should have played pro.

"I'm sorry about your wife," said Gilbert.

The man's face tightened; he was barely holding himself together.

"Yeah . . . well." He stood in the doorway, looking lost, glanced down the hall, then down at his hands, long-fingered, with freckles. Tears crowded his lower lids and he wiped them away with a quick jerk of his sleeve. He lifted his chin into the air, getting control of himself, and his lips stiffened. "If there's anything I can do . . . anything at all . . . I've been talking to Lombardo."

How to explain to the man he was in no condition to help, that the best thing he could do was take a week off, maybe two, stay with family or friends, and let them get on with the case.

"I didn't know she was married to an officer," said Gilbert.

Didn't know, and now he was beginning to think it might have a bearing on the case.

Fowler's face broke with sorrowful mystification. "Why would anybody want to kill her, detective?" Fowler glanced out the window, where the bustle of Chinatown went on undisturbed by his grief. "She went beyond sweet, she went beyond gentle, we were going to have a family next year, once we had enough for a down-payment on a house. She was good with kids."

Joe Lombardo came to his office just as he was getting ready to visit Domenico Colella. The young detective looked tired this morning, smelled of Chanel Number Five.

"Why do you look at me like that?" asked Lombardo.

"Beds are made for sleeping, Joe. You smell like a cosmetics counter."

"Am I not allowed a personal life?" He dropped a mimeographed sheet on Gilbert's desk. "Did you not have a personal life before you met Regina?"

"What's that supposed to mean?"

"That you should give me a break."

"You love it."

"You're right," said Lombardo, "I do. As much of it as I can get."

Gilbert lifted the mimeographed sheet. "What's this?"

"Did you know Swift had a record?" Lombardo sat on the edge of the desk, his soccer-toned thighs bulging through his pleated dress pants. "Picked up for possession of cocaine eight years ago."

"How much?"

"Two ounces."

"So he walked."

"A fine and probation."

"So you think there might be some connection?" said Gilbert. "I don't. What's two ounces? All these high rollers were shoving that stuff up their noses in the late eighties."

"I don't know," said Lombardo. "It got me checking, that's all. I had Blackstein go through some old files in the Coroner's Office. And he turned up Trudy Swift's autopsy. Cause of death, cocaine overdose. You see a pattern?"

"More than just a life-style?"

"Maybe."

"But no proof," said Gilbert, sighing.

"I'd say the same, if it weren't for the terrible shape Swift's business is in. By rights, he should have gone bankrupt years ago. Import, export, bulk discount clothing, mainly, the kind of stuff you find in bargain stores."

"The kind of stuff you wouldn't be caught dead in," said Gilbert.

Lombardo gave him a wry shrug. "Can I help it if my dad's a tailor?"

"So you think he's shoring up his business by trafficking on the side," said Gilbert.

"Could be." Lombardo's beeper went; he glanced down at the number. "Then again, maybe he turned around when his wife died. I got to go."

Gilbert looked at the beeper. "When I was dating, all I had was a little black book."

Domenico Colella's office was down near the lake-front, not far from the Sunnyside Bathing Pavilion, in an economically depressed and prostitute-infested area known as the Track; not the most prestigious of addresses, grubby old buildings from the thirties, most of the storefront windows covered with years of grime, pigeons huddling in their own filth on second-floor sills. Restaurant supplier. Sold a lot of espresso machines.

Gilbert climbed the stairs and went inside. Looked as if

Colella didn't have much to do, but he made Gilbert wait anyway, out in the dust-choked reception area, with the snake plants growing thick with cobwebs, the secretary looking as if she would be more comfortable working the Track outside in high heels and a short skirt, not sitting in front of a ten-year-old computer.

Colella came out. Short man, bald head, about fifty, brown suit with thick beige pin- stripes, alligator shoes, little pin in his lapel of the Italian flag, green, red, and white. Gilbert showed Colella his identification and badge. Colella could care less.

"I got a full calender, detective, so let's make this quick."

They went into Colella's office. Furniture looked as if it came with the building, from the thirties, still with the patina of the Great Depression, dull browns and greens, chunks of the linoleum tile missing here and there, suffering from dense wax build-up.

Gilbert asked Colella about last Saturday morning.

"I got to the house at nine-o'clock," said Colella. "I had breakfast there, toast, coffee, and orange juice, and Swift and me, we talked business. The kids were downstairs with their Pop Tarts, easy for Swift to fix them something like that."

"What kind of business?"

"Kitchen whites. Aprons. Hats. Pants. That kind of thing. Had this stuff real cheap from China. I thought it might be a good deal. He's had some good deals in the past."

"And what time did Brenda Fowler get there?"

"I don't know. About nine-thirty. We were in the front room having coffee. She let herself in the back door, we didn't hear her, so I can't pin-point it any more than that."

"And what time did you leave?"

"Must have been a little after ten. We left in my car."

"And where did you go?"

Colella frowned. "To look at the whites. Down at his warehouse on Duncan."

"And Swift was with you the whole time?"

Colella leaned forward, looking even more annoyed. "Look, detective. If you think Frank Swift had anything to do with Brenda Fowler's murder . . . I mean why? The kids' nanny. Why would he do that?"

"You tell me."

Colella sat back, his ancient swivel chair creaking. Outside, a streetcar rumbled past, the bell dinging, and six pigeons leapt into the air from the sill, like a mass suicide plunge.

"I'm his alibi, detective. So why don't you stop wasting my time?"

❖

Back in Chinatown, Joe Lombardo came to him with a sheet two volumes thick on Domenico Colella.

"He's been up on trafficking, laundering, counterfeiting, burglary, even murder. No one's made anything stick. He's currently under investigation for a bike-theft ring. Nothing definite yet."

Lombardo took some photographs from the folder and slid them across Gilbert's desk. Grisly photographs. A murder scene, a mother, father, and two children gunned down, the mother, thirty or so, draped over the telephone table in the front hall, the children lying on the floor, the father crumpled on the stairs leading up to the second floor, blood all over the place, like the inside of an abattoir's.

"Colella did this?"

"We think he did. But we don't have any hard evidence. Not enough to prosecute."

Gilbert stared at the photographs. Read the description. Gangland stuff. Just like the Brenda Fowler murder. But Colella was nowhere near the murder scene at the time of the Brenda's killing. Or was he? Swift's silent film, running darkly behind his eyes, distracting him, terrifying him, like he knew something. Yet what about the footprints? A jogger and a loafer, not alligator shoes.

"Did you know Brenda's husband was on the force?" he asked. "John Fowler. I met him last year at the annual baseball tournament. Great pitcher."

"I know the guy," said Lombardo.

"You do?"

"I didn't know he was married to Brenda, though."

"Did you ever see him pitch?" asked Gilbert.

"Oh, sure," said Lombardo. "Ten years ago he almost made the Jays."

"I didn't know," said Gilbert.

"On his good days he's been clocked at 86 miles per hour. He was picked out of high school, went through the Dunedin Single A team, then onto the Double A Knoxville Team, but never managed to make it any further."

"Do you think there's a connection?" asked Gilbert. "The fact she was married to a cop?"

"It's worth considering."

Gilbert's eyes again strayed over the photographs of the slain family. This was what he hated, the game, the endless cycle, everybody knew Colella did it but nobody could prove it, Colella gloating, laughing in their faces, sitting there with a smoking gun that no one could see, least of all a jury. Wiped out a whole family. Wiped out Fowler's family before he could start it. Brenda dead on the kitchen floor. Their only witness, a half blind woman who thought it had to be one of the twins. How was he going to shake this one loose?

"Did you check on Ellen Cochrane?"

Lombardo shrugged. "I called the MTO. She had her driver's license revoked last year." Lombardo gathered up the photographs and put them back in the manila folder. "She didn't pass the vision test."

Dead ends. Games. And Swift with that movie running constantly behind his eyes.

June 1st. His birthday. He didn't know what Regina had planned, but he hoped it would be something that would make him forget all this. He sat on the back patio of the house in Forest Hill, one o'clock in the afternoon, Swift sitting across from him, sipping a wine cooler, nibbling tortilla chips, a work day, the kids at school, but Swift looking as if he didn't have anywhere to go. Shake it loose. Play the game.

"She's blind as a bat," said Swift.

"Yes, but we have other evidence, Frank. We found gunpowder residue on Josh's hands."

"That's impossible."

Of course it was, but this was the game.

"I've got the test results right here, if you want to see them," said Gilbert, lifting his briefcase. "And you want to know what else we found? We found cocaine residue in fifteen different locations throughout your house. I'd hate to see you run into trouble that way again. I think there'd be more to it than just a fine and probation this time."

"I don't get this. Why do you come to me again? I told you everything I know."

From the end of the yard, a squirrel appeared from behind an oak tree and drank from the swimming pool.

"And Mrs. Cochrane isn't our only witness, Frank."

Swift stared at him, then looked away, taking off his Vuarnet sunglasses. "You've got a new witness?"

"That's right."

"And this new witness says Josh did it?"

Gilbert nodded. He was getting somewhere. Swift looked nervous now, his nostrils flaring, as if he were scenting out an enemy, his legs flexing, a small battle playing out across his face, intricate facial muscles at war with one another.

"I don't believe you," Swift said at last.

"I showed you those footprints." Shake it loose. "Someone was there." Play the game. "Someone saw the whole thing."

Forty-eight. Time to think about his life. But he couldn't get away from the game. When he had to fight dirty . . .

"I don't believe it," said Swift.

"I don't believe it, either," said Gilbert, "but until I come up with a better theory, I'm going to have to take Josh into custody. Not very nice for a ten-year-old boy. Especially now, when he won't be able to finish the school year."

"Look, I know Josh didn't do it." He sat forward in the white wicker chair, his forehead creasing with anguish, his face turning red. The squirrel drinking from the pool darted away into the fern garden. "Is there any way we can talk about . . . I don't know, immunity or something?"

"Immunity?" Gilbert's eyes narrowed. "I'm afraid I don't follow you."

"Look, this is very delicate. I could get in serious . . . Brenda got here early on Saturday. It's been very hard for us ever since Trudy died. I've suffered some financial reversals and I . . . it's been hard. And I've had to do some things I . . . just to stay afloat."

Swift turned his head in a sudden nervous movement; the amorphous reflections of the pool danced in his face, same pattern over and over, made by the way the filter jets disturbed the surface.

"So Brenda got here early," prodded Gilbert.

He saw the film rolling behind Swifts's eyes.

Swift lifted his head and looked at Gilbert. "She saw something she shouldn't have seen. We didn't hear her coming, she came in the back door, she's so soft on her feet, and I wasn't expecting her till ten. Before we knew it, she was in the hallway staring at us. She saw a suitcase full of money and a suitcase full of product."

Gilbert contemplated Swift. "Product," he repeated. "Is that what you call it?"

"Sometimes you deal with people you'd sooner not deal with."

"Colella's going to kill you for this, isn't he?"

Swift's eyes grew pensive. And Gilbert had to give the man credit; he was willing to risk his life with a monster like Colella in order to spare Josh the trauma of arrest. But that didn't explain the loafer and the jogger. Or Swift's missing gun. Slow down, Gilbert. One thing at a time.

"So then what happened?" asked Gilbert.

"We drove down to look at kitchen whites."

"So that part of it was true."

"And while we drove Colella asked me all sorts of questions about Brenda. Was she cool? Could we trust her? I just wanted to appease him. I was talking a mile a minute. Both of us had tested some of the product. We were high. And I guess I let slip she was married to a cop." He leaned back in the chair, as if he were winded. He put his hand in front of his mouth and shook his head, incredulous at the enormity of his mistake. "He got quiet after that. Didn't say a word."

Gilbert felt as if he were sliding on ice, as if the firm ground, the direction of a moment ago, was now gone, that his missile was off course.

"And then what?" he said, in tones of growing exasperation.

"We went our separate ways."

"So you didn't see him shoot Brenda?" he asked, unable to hide his disappointment.

"No." Swift looked angry at the suggestion. "I was at work."

"But you think Colella killed her. You think Colella came back here and shot her."

Swift looked at him; his meaning was clear. "Colella's old school. If he sees a problem, he eliminates it."

Gilbert's face settled. "Eliminate," he said, his voice dead. "Is that what you call it?"

He found John Fowler waiting for him back at his office.

Fowler looked paler, thinner, as if he hadn't slept in days, his face expressionless as he asked Gilbert if there'd been any progress on the case. Liked to protect the confidentiality of the case, but in this circumstance he felt he had to make an exception. Fowler was in the club. Fowler was one of them. Fowler was a cop.

"You look at Colella's record," said Gilbert, "you meet him face to face, and you get a feeling about him, like he wouldn't think twice about gunning down those two kids and their mother and father. He doesn't see human beings as human beings. He sees them either as stepping stones or as obstacles. And he takes a long view. He considers all possibilities. That's why he's never caught. He stops trouble before it gets started. I'm convinced he killed your wife."

"But you have no definite proof."

Gilbert stared at Fowler, wishing he could tell him otherwise; a man like Colella had no place on the streets.

"I can't touch him."

"But you think he did it."

"There's lots of circumstantial evidence that says he did."

Fowler's eyes went glassy as he stared at the pewter walrus on Gilbert's desk, souvenir from last year's Alaskan cruise. The young officer then took a deep breath, held it for a few seconds, sat up straight, on the edge of the seat, and exhaled.

"Do you think you can nail him?"

Voice now riding the edge, like he was going to put his fist through a wall.

"I don't know." Gilbert thought of the loafer and the jogger. "There's a few angles we still haven't worked out."

Fowler nodded, a picture of disappointment. "You sound doubtful," he said.

Gilbert felt himself squinting, what he did whenever he was confronted with a particularly sad part of the game. Finally, he put his hands flat on his desk blotter. "I just don't know, John. We'll have to see what happens."

He sat in front of his birthday cake at home, two big candles, one in the shape of a four, the other in the shape of an eight, stuck on a sea of chocolate icing. Regina and his daughters, Jennifer and Nina, sang a discordant Happy Birthday." And all he could think about was Fowler. How he had somehow failed Fowler. How maybe he wasn't cut out for this business after all. Regina had a rack full of mystery novels upstairs, and every one of them seemed so tidy. Nothing was ever so neat in real life.

Later on, a little past eleven, when he was making love with Regina, the blood came back to haunt him, size-six Reeboks, the twins stepping in the edge of pool, indecisive prints, as if they were both so shocked they didn't know what to do. And their story: they came upstairs, and there she was, already dead, they were scared, by the time they finally decided to call the police the sirens were already coming down the street. Yet what about the other prints, the loafer and the jogger? If only he could figure that out.

Like a puzzle. Like a game. And you sometimes got beat in a game. For every inning played, you lost a bit of yourself, but kept yourself going with the thought that somewhere, somehow, you might make a difference to someone.

At half past midnight the telephone rang. It was Joe Lombardo.

"I just thought you'd like to know," said Lombardo. "Domenico Colella has been murdered. In the parking lot behind his building. Bannatyne says he'll hold things for you, if you want to look."

"How do you know all this?" asked Gilbert, impressed by his young partner.

"Keeping track of dates isn't the only thing I use my beeper for, smart-ass."

Down in Parkdale, Lake Ontario stunk, the way it sometimes reeked on a warm night in late spring, thick with algae, like an aquarium with dead fish in it.

At the crime scene, two cruisers with lights flashing blocked the alley leading to the small parking lot, and Gilbert had to walk in, showing his I.D. to the uniformed officer to get by.

Yellow police tape now blocked off the parking lot. Colella lay on his face, wearing the same brown suit of the other day, his feet now pigeon-toed, arms at his sides, hands cupped, palms upward, no blood, at least none that Gilbert could see. Colella's car, a late- model purple Crown Victoria with gold mags, sat parked near the end of the lot. Bannatyne stood talking with some of his officers by a large garbage disposal bin, a flashlight in his hand; Bannatyne, a man about his age, but large, with a wide ruddy face, big gut, thick arms and legs, not wiry and thin like Gilbert.

"Bob!" he called.

Bob Bannatyne looked over. He said a few words to his officers, then joined Gilbert. "Joe said you were questioning Colella in connection with the Fowler murder. I didn't know you had a new one. I've been so busy I haven't kept on top of things."

"Has the coroner been by?"

"Not yet." Bannatyne took Gilbert by the elbow. "Come over here. I want to show you something."

Bannatyne led him to a cube van, badly rusted, splotched with brown primer, looked a bit like a Jersey cow, same kind of markings, with that primer. The big detective got on his knees and shone the flashlight under the chassis.

"Take a look at this."

Gilbert got on his knees and looked under the truck.

He saw a baseball, regulation hardball, sitting there, one half of it covered with blood and a little bit of hair, strands undoubtedly from Colella's head.

"What do you think of that?" asked Bannatyne, getting up, a smile of amazement on his face. "I mean, I've seen a lot of weird murder weapons, but I think this takes it."

❖

Gilbert got to Chinatown shortly after two in the morning, went upstairs to his office. Brooding. Because he shouldn't have told John Fowler about the Colella connection. He went to his desk and turned on his computer. He was tired. He just wanted to go home, there was no place more depressing than division headquarters at two o'clock in the morning. While his computer got itself going, he dug out the hard copy from his file. The game played itself out, always taking unexpected turns, and whether justice was served no one could be sure. He opened the Fowler file and started skimming through.

Couldn't be one-hundred-percent certain that Colella killed her, but now it didn't matter. He picked out any and all reference to Colella as a murder suspect. All that remained was Colella's verification of Swift's alibi. He stroked out any and all cross-references to the other Colella murders. Finally, he crossed out the two mentions of John Fowler.

He then logged on and made the computer edits, deleting all the back-up files. Why did Fowler leave the baseball there? He wasn't stupid. Maybe he didn't have time. Maybe it rolled under the truck, maybe a car came along and he had to get out of there. Wouldn't be any prints. Fowler was a cop. Delete, delete, delete. When Bannatyne came sniffing, he wouldn't find much.

He printed a new copy and shredded the old. And he stopped. Because he knew he was breaking the law, that he was making himself an accomplice, that he was obstructing justice, that maybe, just maybe, Fowler felled an innocent man with his best fast-ball. Gilbert felt torn. Sometimes you had to make up the rules of the game as you went along. If only there were some way he could be certain Colella was Brenda Fowler's killer.

Cody Swift came to his office the next day, ten-year-old boy, all alone, should be in school, looking nervous but determined.

"Cody," said Gilbert, could be Josh, but it turned out to be Cody. Gilbert braced himself; it looked as if the boy had news.

"About the footprints, sir," he said. "The two big ones by the sink? They belong to a friend of mine. I thought I'd better tell you." Cody's eyes became earnest and wide. "He was there. But he didn't do it. He said we shouldn't say anything . . . I mean

. . . even though he didn't do it . . . because he thought if we did, he might . . . he said he might get into trouble. He thought me and Josh might get into trouble. But I think you got to know, don't you, sir? About everything. Even about my friend."

Gilbert lifted a pencil, tore notepaper from his pad, and contemplated the boy.

"And who might this friend be?" he asked.

Cody looked down at his hands, his face coloring.

"His name is Norman," said Cody. "And he lives in the park."

Norman did indeed live in the park, one of Toronto's growing number of homeless, in the heavily wooded ravine section, where he had made a kind of temporary hutch out of old pieces of cardboard and scavenged plywood. One look at him and Gilbert knew he was one of the . . . well, one of the mentally challenged. He wore a green winter parka, black track pants, a jogger on the right foot, a loafer on the left. He cowered as Gilbert and Cody approached through the dense underbrush, and his eyes narrowed with suspicion. He looked about forty-five; his hair was a mess and his face was deeply tanned, pleasantly weathered.

"You don't have to worry, Norman, " said Cody. "This is Detective Gilbert. He's a friend of mine. He wants to ask you why you took my father's gun?"

From his sitting position next to the door of his hutch, Norman peered at Gilbert.

"Do you have the gun anywhere hereabouts?" asked Gilbert.

Norman gave him a shrug. "It's inside."

"Why did you take it?"

Norman turned his head nervously, a jerky, sudden movement, as if he'd been bitten by a gnat.

"Because I know the way you cops work," he said. "Don't think I don't. I go down to Sears and I watch the shows on the TVs there. I know exactly how you work."

"And how's that, Norman?"

"First you find the murder weapon."

"Is Mr. Swift's gun the murder weapon?"

"Josh showed me it before."

"And you used it to kill Josh's nanny?"

Norman's eyes lit up with horror. "No, no, no," he said. "The man killed Brenda. Why would I kill Brenda? Brenda's really nice to me. If I go to the back door, sometimes she'll give me food."

"So you went to the back door last Saturday morning to get some food."

Norman nodded furtively.

"And you saw the man shoot Brenda through the back of the head."

Another furtive nod.

"What did the man look like?"

"I had to do something. I knew you cops would blame Josh and Cody, 'specially because the man took off so fast in his big car."

"You saw the car?"

"So I went inside. And I realized I was walking through blood. And I know how Mr. Swift doesn't like Josh and Cody to track dirt all over the house. So I went to the sink, got up on the counter and washed my shoes off. Then I crawled along the counter so I wouldn't get my feet in any more blood."

Faulty reasoning aside, Gilbert believed Norman's story; the man was an innocent, incapable of lying. Went upstairs and got the gun. Trying to protect Josh and Cody.

"Can you tell me what the man looked like?"

"He didn't have no hair on his head. I saw him shoot Brenda. I was looking through the window. Then I hid behind the bushes when he left."

"Was he tall, short, fat?"

"He was short."

Short, like Colella.

"Did you see the car?" Gilbert asked.

Norman nodded gravely. "A big purple car with gold tires."

Colella's car, the Crown Victoria with the gold mags.

Game over. Never tidy. Still loose ends. Ellen Cochrane, blind as bat, not seeing Norman, even though he was standing right in front of her. Gilbert stood at his office window looking down at Chinatown, where the bustle went on as usual, a double espresso warming his hands, no longer feeling so bad about

Colella. What to do about Frank Swift? Swift loved his children, Gilbert could see that in the man's eyes; but Swift's judgement was fundamentally bad, and he might in the long run hurt Josh and Cody. He would have to think about it. Then there was John Fowler. Just forget about John . . . if Bannatyne nailed him, that was that. But so far, Bannatyne hadn't asked for the case file. Bannatyne was overloaded with a hundred other cases. Just like they all were.

He took a sip of his espresso, relishing the thick bitter liquid as it slid down his throat. A win, a loss, or a draw? He pondered the question as the sun buttered the street below. This one felt like a win. And so there was no point in adding Norman's name to the case file. Add Norman's name, and it might steer Bannatyne toward Fowler. And that would be a shame. Because justice was done. Colella would never destroy another family, born or unborn. Norman wouldn't have been a credible witness anyway. Colella could afford top- notch help; Norman would have been destroyed on the witness stand.

So that was that. He smiled. Kept himself going by thinking that somehow, somewhere, he made a difference to someone. Maybe to an unborn family. Lights out. The crowds had left the stands. And it felt like a win. Just had to keep it that way. He took the case file from his desk and wedged it between a hundred others on the shelf. Still an open case, at least in the official record. But there it would sit, untouched, closed as far as Gilbert was concerned . . . buried in the dust of the game.

1999 WINNER

SCOTT MacKAY
"Last Inning"
Ellery Queen Mystery Magazine

Nominees:

BARRY BALDWIN
"Do You Take This Man?"
Ellery Queen Mystery Magazine

J. S. LYSTER
"The Hunter of the Guileless"
Storyteller

JAMES POWELL
"Strangers on a Sleigh"
Ellery Queen Mystery Magazine

WAYNE YETMAN
"Getting Ahead"
Storyteller

Arthur Ellis Award Winners and Nominees

(Winners are indicated by an asterisk *)

1984

Best Novel

WILLIAM DEVERELL ❖ *Mecca* ❖ McClelland & Stewart
ERIC WRIGHT ❖ *The Night the Gods Smiled* ❖ Collins *
TED WOOD ❖ *Dead in the Water* ❖ Scribners

Chairman's Award for Lifetime Achievement
(subsequently renamed the Derrick Murdoch Award)
DERRICK MURDOCH

1985

Best Novel

WILLIAM DEVERELL ❖ *The Dance of Shiva* ❖ McClelland & Stewart
HOWARD ENGEL ❖ *Murder Sees the Light* ❖ Viking/Penguin *
DOUGLAS GLOVER ❖ *Precious* ❖ Bantam/Seal
JOHN REEVES ❖ *Murder Before Matins* ❖ Doubleday
ERIC WRIGHT ❖ *Smoke Detector* ❖ Collins

Best Non-Fiction

MARTIN FRIEDLAND ❖ *The Trials of Israel Lipski* ❖ Macmillan *
GEORGE JONAS ❖ *Vengeance* ❖ Collins
DAVID PEAT ❖ *The Armchair Guide to Murder and Detection* ❖ Deneau
EDWARD STARKINS ❖ *Who Killed Janet Smith?* ❖ Macmillan

Derrick Murdoch Award
TONY ASPLER

1986

Best Novel

MAURICE GAGNON ❖ *The Inner Ring* ❖ Collins
ANTHONY HYDE ❖ *The Red Fox* ❖ Viking/Penguin
JOHN REEVES ❖ *Murder With Muskets* ❖ Doubleday
ERIC WRIGHT ❖ *Death in the Old Country* ❖ Collins *
L.R. WRIGHT ❖ *The Suspect* ❖ Doubleday

Best Non-Fiction

MAGGIE SIGGINS ❖ *A Canadian Tragedy* ❖ Macmillan *
(There were no other finalists in this category.)

The Derrick Murdoch Award
MARGARET MILLAR

1987

Best Novel

TIMOTHY FINDLEY ❖ *The Telling of Lies* ❖ Viking
ALEXANDER LAW ❖ *To an Easy Grave* ❖ St. Martin's
EDWARD O. PHILLIPS ❖ *Buried on Sunday* ❖ McClelland & Stewart*
MEDORA SALE ❖ *Murder on the Run* ❖ Paperjacks **
TED WOOD ❖ *Fool's Gold* ❖ Scribners
ERIC WRIGHT ❖ *A Single Death* ❖ Collins

*(** Although there was technically only one fiction category,
a prize was awarded to Medora Sale for Best First Novel,
which subsequently became an annual event.)*

Best Non-Fiction

MARTIN FRIEDLAND ❖ *The Case of Valentine Shortis* ❖ Uni. of Toronto Press
MICHAEL HARRIS ❖ *Justice Denied* ❖ Macmillan
ELLIOTT LEYTON ❖ *Hunting Humans* ❖ McClelland & Stewart *

The Derrick Murdoch Award
THE CWC DRAMA DEPARTMENT

1988

Best Novel/Gilbey Prize

JOSEPH LOUIS ❖ *Madeleine* ❖ Seal
ANNA PORTER ❖ *Mortal Sins* ❖ Irwin
CAROL SHIELDS ❖ *Swann: A Mystery* ❖ Stoddart *
ERIC WRIGHT ❖ *A Body Surrounded* by Water ❖ Collins

Best Non-Fiction/Sleuth of Baker Street Prize

JAMES DUBRO & ROBIN ROWLAND ❖ *King of the Mob* ❖ Viking/Penguin
EDWARD GREENSPAN & GEORGE JONAS ❖ *Greenspan: The Case for the
Defense* ❖ Macmillan
GARY ROSS ❖ *Stung: the Incredible Obsession of Brian Molony* ❖ Stoddart *
CARSTEN STROUD ❖ *Close Pursuit* ❖ Viking/Penguin

Best First Novel/Worldwide Library Prize

LAURENCE GOUGH ❖ *The Goldfish Bowl* ❖ Gollancz *
SUSAN MAYSE ❖ *Merlin's Web* ❖ Irwin
PETER ROBINSON ❖ *Gallows View* ❖ Viking/Penguin

Best Short Story/Amphora Prize

TONY ASPLER ❖ *Murder by Half* ❖ from Cold Blood: Murder in Canada
JAS. R. PETRIN ❖ *Magic Nights* ❖ from Alfred Hitchcock Mystery Magazine
JAS. R. PETRIN ❖ *Prairie Heat* ❖ from Alfred Hitchcock Mystery Magazine
TED WOOD ❖ *Pit Bull* ❖ from Cold Blood: Murder in Canada
ERIC WRIGHT ❖ *Looking for an Honest Man* ❖ from Cold Blood: Murder
in Canada *

The Derrick Murdoch Award
J. D. SINGH AND JAMES REICKER

1989

Best Novel/Gilbey Prize

WILLIAM DEVERELL ❖ *Platinum Blues* ❖ McClelland & Stewart
LAURENCE GOUGH ❖ *Death on a No. 8 Hook* ❖ Gollancz
PETER ROBINSON ❖ *A Dedicated Man* ❖ Viking/Penguin
CHRIS SCOTT ❖ *Jack* ❖ Macmillan *

Best Non-Fiction/Sleuth of Baker Street Prize

MICK LOWE ❖ *Conspiracy of Brothers* ❖ Macmillan *
MARTIN O'MALLEY ❖ *Gross Misconduct: the Life of Spinner Spencer* ❖
  Viking/Penguin
DAVID STAFFORD ❖ *The Silent Game* ❖ Lester & Orpen Dennys

Best First Novel/Worldwide Library Prize

ELISABETH BOWERS ❖ *Ladies' Night* ❖ The Seal Press
JOHN BRADY ❖ *A Stone of the Heart* ❖ Collins *
BRENDAN HOWLEY ❖ *The Stalking Horse* ❖ Random House
SCOTT YOUNG ❖ *Murder in a Cold Climate* ❖ Macmillan

Best Short Story

WILLIAM BANKIER ❖ *One Day at a Time* ❖ from Ellery Queen Mystery
  Magazine
JAS. R. PETRIN ❖ *Killer in the House* ❖ from Alfred Hitchcock Mystery
  Magazine *
JAMES POWELL ❖ *Still Life with Orioles* ❖ from Ellery Queen Mystery
  Magazine

1990

Best Novel/Sleuth of Baker Street Prize

JACK BATTEN ❖ *Straight No Chaser* ❖ Macmillan
JOHN BRADY ❖ *Unholy Ground* ❖ Collins
WILLIAM DEVERELL ❖ *Mindfield* ❖ McClelland & Stewart
LAURENCE GOUGH ❖ *Hot Shots* ❖ Gollancz *
PETER ROBINSON ❖ *The Hanging Valley* ❖ Viking/Penguin

Best Non-Fiction/Mostly Mysteries Prize

VICTOR MALARAK ❖ *Merchants of Misery: Inside Canada's Illegal Drug Scene* ❖ Macmillan

LISA PRIEST ❖ *Conspiracy of Silence* ❖ McClelland & Stewart *

Best First Novel/Worldwide Library Prize

MAYNARD COLLINS ❖ *Death on 30 Beat* ❖ Deneau

KEITH MCKINNON ❖ *The Rempal Inquest* ❖ Highway Book Shop

JOHN LAWRENCE REYNOLDS ❖ *The Man Who Murdered God* ❖ Viking/Penguin *

Best Short Story/Parker Prize

WILLIAM BANKIER ❖ *One Day at a Time* ❖ from Cold Blood II

ELAINE MITCHELL MATLOW ❖ *Safe as Houses* ❖ from Cold Blood II

JAMES POWELL ❖ *Burning Bridges* ❖ from Ellery Queen Mystery Magazine

JOSEF SKVORECKY ❖ *Humbug* ❖ from The End of Lieutenant Boruvka *

ERIC WRIGHT ❖ *Kaput* ❖ from Mistletoe Mysteries

The Derrick Murdoch Award

ERIC WILSON

1991

Best Novel/Sleuth of Baker Street Prize

JOHN BRADY ❖ *Kaddish in Dublin* ❖ HarperCollins

LAURENCE GOUGH ❖ *Serious Crimes* ❖ Viking/Penguin

BRIAN MOORE ❖ *Lies of Silence* ❖ Lester & Orpen Dennys

JOHN LAWRENCE REYNOLDS ❖ *And Leave Her Lay Dying* ❖ Viking/Penguin

PETER ROBINSON ❖ *Caedmon's Song* ❖ Viking/Penguin

L.R. WRIGHT ❖ *A Chill Rain in January* ❖ Macmillan *

Best Non-Fiction

PETER EDWARDS ❖ *Bloodbrothers: How Canada's Most Powerful Mafia Family Runs its Business* ❖ Key Porter

J.L. GRANATSTEIN & DAVID STAFFORD ❖ *Spy Wars: Espionage and Canada from Gouzenko to "Glasnost"* ❖ Key Porter

ELLIOT LEYTON ❖ *Sole Survivor: Children Who Murder Their Families* ❖ Seal

SUSAN MAYSE ❖ *Ginger: The Life and Death of Albert Goodwin* ❖ Harbour Publishing *

JOCKO THOMAS ❖ *From Police Headquarters: True Tales from the Big City Crime Beat* ❖ Stoddart

Best First Novel/Worldwide Library Prize

JAMES BURKE ❖ *Fatal Choices* ❖ Knightsbridge
DAVID LAING DAWSON ❖ *Last Rights* ❖ Macmillan
CARSTEN STROUD ❖ *Sniper's Moon* ❖ Viking/Penguin *

Best Genre Criticism/Reference

BERNARD DREW ❖ *Lawmen in Scarlet: An Annotated Guide to*
Royal Canadian Mounted Police in Print and Performance ❖ Scarecrow
ANNE HART ❖ *Agatha Christie's Poirot: the Life and Times of Hercule Poirot*
❖ Pavilion
DONALD A. REDMOND ❖ *Sherlock Holmes Among the Pirates: Copyright and*
Conan Doyle in America, 1890 - 1930 ❖ Greenwood *

Best Short Story

JOHN NORTH ❖ *Out of Bounds* ❖ from Cold Blood III
JAS. R. PETRIN ❖ *Man on the Roof* ❖ from Cold Blood III
SARA PLEWS ❖ *Blind Date* ❖ from Cold Blood III
JAMES POWELL ❖ *The Tamerlane Crutch* ❖ from Cold Blood III
PETER ROBINSON ❖ *Innocence* ❖ from Cold Blood III *

1992

Best Novel/Sleuth of Baker Street Prize

LAURENCE GOUGH ❖ *Accidental Deaths* ❖ Viking/Penguin
PETER ROBINSON ❖ *Past Reason Hated* ❖ Viking/Penguin *
L.R. WRIGHT ❖ *Fall From Grace* ❖ McClelland/Bantam

Best Non-Fiction

OWEN D. CARRIGAN ❖ *Crime and Punishment in Canada: A History* ❖
McClelland & Stewart
WILLIAM DEVERELL ❖ *Fatal Cruise: the Trial of Robert Frisbee* ❖ McClelland
& Stewart
JAMES DUBRO & ROBIN ROWLAND ❖ *Undercover: Cases of the RCMP's*
Most Secret Operative ❖ Octopus
DEAN JOBB ❖ *Crime Wave: Con Men, Rogues and Scoundrels from*
Nova Scotia's Past ❖ Pottersfield Press
WILLIAM LOWTHER ❖ *Arms and the Man: Dr. Gerald Bull, Iraq and the*
Supergun ❖ Doubleday *

Best First Novel/Worldwide Library Prize

PAUL GRESCOE ❖ *Flesh Wound* ❖ Douglas & McIntyre *
DAVID PARRY & PATRICK WITHROW ❖ *The Jacamar Nest* ❖ Macmillan
LESLIE WATTS ❖ *The Chocolate Box* ❖ General

Best Genre Criticism/Reference

MARTIN L. FREIDLAND ❖ *Rough Justice: Essays on Crime in Literature* ❖
University of Toronto Press
WESLEY K. WARK ❖ *Spy Fiction, Spy Films and Real Intelligence* ❖
Frank Cass *

Best Short Story

GAIL HELGASON ❖ *Wild Stock* ❖ from Great Canadian Murder and
Mystery Stories
JAMES POWELL ❖ *Santa's Way* ❖ from Ellery Queen Mystery Magazine
JAMES POWELL ❖ *Winter Hiatus* ❖ from Ellery Queen Mystery Magazine
PETER SELLERS ❖ *This One's Trouble* ❖ from Alfred Hitchcock Mystery
Magazine
ERIC WRIGHT ❖ *Two in the Bush* ❖ from Christmas Stalkings *

The Derrick Murdoch Award
WILLIAM BANKIER, JAMES POWELL AND PETER SELLERS

1993

Best Novel/Sleuth of Baker Street Prize

GAIL BOWEN ❖ *The Wandering Soul Murders* ❖ Douglas & McIntyre
LAURENCE GOUGH ❖ *Fall Down Easy* ❖ McClelland & Stewart
PETER ROBINSON ❖ *Wednesday's Child* ❖ Viking/Penguin
MEDORA SALE ❖ *Pursued by Shadows* ❖ Scribners/Maxwell Macmillan
CARSTEN STROUD ❖ *Lizardskin* ❖ Bantam *

Best First Novel/Worldwide Library Prize

ROY FRENCH ❖ *A Sense of Honour* ❖ Hounslow
MARGARET HAFFNER ❖ *A Murder of Crows* ❖ Crime Club/HarperCollins
DOUGLAS MARSHALL ❖ *A Very Palpable Hit* ❖ Douglas & McIntyre
SEAN STEWART ❖ *Passion Play* ❖ Beach Holme *
BETSY STRUTHERS ❖ *Found: A Body* ❖ Simon & Pierre

Best Non-Fiction

WARREN KINSELLA ❖ *Unholy Alliances: Terrorists, Extremists, Front Companies and the Libyan Connection in Canada* ❖ Lester

RICK MACLEAN, ANDRE VENIOT & SHAUN WATERS ❖ *Terror's End: Allan Legere on Trial* ❖ McClelland & Stewart

KIRK MAKIN ❖ *Redrum the Innocent* ❖ Viking/Penguin *

GREG WESTON ❖ *The Stopwatch Gang: the True Story of Three Affable Canadians Who Stormed America's Banks and Drove the FBI Crazy* ❖ Macmillan

Best Short Story

WILLIAM BANKIER ❖ *Wade in the Balance* ❖ from Criminal Shorts

HOWARD ENGEL ❖ *Custom Killing* ❖ from Criminal Shorts

GAIL HELGASON ❖ *Fracture Patterns* ❖ from Grain

NANCY KILPATRICK ❖ *Mantrap* ❖ from Murder, Mayhem and Macabre *

TED WOOD ❖ *Murder at Louisburg* ❖ from Cold Blood IV

1994

Best Novel/Sleuth of Baker Street Prize

JOHN BRADY ❖ *All Souls* ❖ HarperCollins

HOWARD ENGEL ❖ *There Was an Old Woman* ❖ Viking/Penguin

WILLIAM GIBSON ❖ *Virtual Light* ❖ Seal

JOHN LAWRENCE REYNOLDS ❖ *Gypsy Sins* ❖ Harper Collins *

GREGORY WARD ❖ *Water Damage* ❖ Little Brown

L.R. WRIGHT ❖ *Prized Possessions* ❖ Doubleday

Best First Novel/Worldwide Library Prize

BEVAN AMBERHILL ❖ *The Bloody Man* ❖ Mercury Press

JANE BOW ❖ *Dead and Living* ❖ Mercury Press

STUART LANGFORD ❖ *Deadlock* ❖ Voyageur

GAVIN SCOTT ❖ *Memory Trace* ❖ Cormorant *

CAROLINE WOODWARD ❖ *Alaska Highway Two-Step* ❖ Polestar Press

Best Non-Fiction

VERNON FROLICK ❖ *Descent into Madness: the Diary of a Killer* ❖ Hancock House

GRAEME S. MOUNT ❖ *Spies & Spying in the Peaceable Kingdom* ❖ Dundurn

CARSTEN STROUD ❖ *Contempt of Court: the Betrayal of Justice in Canada* ❖ Macmillan

DAVID R. WILLIAMS ❖ *With Malice Aforethought: Six Spectacular Canadian Trials* ❖ Sono Nis *

Best Juvenile Novel

LINDA BAILEY ❖ *How Can I Be a Detective if I Have to Babysit?* ❖ Kids Can

JOHN DOWD ❖ *Abalone Summer* ❖ Raincoast *

JENI MAYER ❖ *Suspicion Island* ❖ Thistletown

Best Play
(the only year this award has been offered)

TIMOTHY FINDLEY ❖ *The Stillborn Lover* ❖ Blizzard *

DAVID FENNARIO ❖ *Doctor Thomas Neill Cream* (Mystery at McGill) ❖ Talonbooks

DAVID FRENCH ❖ *Silver Dagger* ❖ Talonbooks

Best Short Story

JAS. R. PETRIN ❖ *East End Safe* ❖ from Alfred Hitchcock Mystery Magazine

JAMES POWELL ❖ *The Fixer-Upper* ❖ from Ellery Queen Mystery Magazine

ROBERT J. SAWYER ❖ *Just Like Old Times* ❖ from OnSpec *

ERIC WRIGHT ❖ *The Casebook of Dr. Billingsgate* ❖ from The New Mystery

ERIC WRIGHT ❖ *The Duke* ❖ from 2nd Culprit

1995

Best Novel/Sleuth of Baker Street Prize

PETER ABRAHAMS ❖ *Lights Out* ❖ Mysterious Press

GAIL BOWEN ❖ *A Colder Kind of Death* ❖ McClelland & Stewart *

JOHN BRADY ❖ *The Good Life* ❖ HarperCollins

JOHN LAWRENCE REYNOLDS ❖ *Solitary Dancer* ❖ HarperCollins

L.R. WRIGHT ❖ *A Touch of Panic* ❖ Doubleday

Best First Novel/Worldwide Library Prize

SPARKLE HAYTER ❖ *What's a Girl Gotta Do* ❖ Soho *

SUZANNE NORTH ❖ *Healthy, Wealthy & Dead* ❖ NeWest

MICHELLE SPRING ❖ *Every Breath You Take* ❖ Pocket Books

Best Non-Fiction

SYLVIA BARRETT ❖ *The Arsenic Milkshake* ❖ Doubleday

STEPHEN HANDLEMAN ❖ *Comrade Criminal* ❖ Michael Joseph

ROBERT D. HARE ❖ *Without Conscience* ❖ Pocket Books

MICHAEL HARRIS ❖ *The Prodigal Husband* ❖ McClelland & Stewart *

WADE HEMSWORTH ❖ *Killing Time* ❖ Viking/Penguin

PHONSE JESSOME ❖ *Murder at McDonald's* ❖ Numbus

Best Juvenile Novel

ANN AVELING ❖ *Trouble on Wheels* ❖ Scholastic

LINDA BAILEY ❖ *Who's Got Gertie and How Can We Get Her Back?* ❖ Kids Can

JAMES HENEGHAN ❖ *Torn Away* ❖ Viking/Penguin *

Best Short Story

ROSEMARY AUBERT ❖ *Midnight Boat to Palermo* ❖ from Cold Blood V *

WILLIAM BANKIER ❖ *The Big Lonely* ❖ from Cold Blood V

ELIZA MOORHOUSE ❖ *Death of a Dragon* ❖ from Cold Blood V

JAMES POWELL ❖ *Midnight at Manger's Bird and Beast* ❖ from Ellery Queen Mystery Magazine

PETER ROBINSON ❖ *Lawn Sale* ❖ from Cold Blood V

PETER ROBINSON ❖ *Summer Rain* ❖ from Ellery Queen Mystery Magazine

The Derrick Murdoch Award

JIM AND MARGARET MCBRIDE

1996

Best Novel/Sleuth of Baker Street Prize

WILLIAM DEVERELL ❖ *Street Legal* ❖ McClelland & Stewart

ALISON GORDON ❖ *Striking Out* ❖ McClelland & Stewart

LAURENCE GOUGH ❖ *Heartbreaker* ❖ McClelland & Stewart

PETER ROBINSON ❖ *No Cure for Love* ❖ Viking/Penguin

L.R. WRIGHT ❖ *Mother Love* ❖ Doubleday *

Best First Novel/Worldwide Library Prize

MEREDITH ANDREW ❖ *Deadly by Nature* ❖ Mercury Press

TERRY CARROLL ❖ *No Blood Relative* ❖ Mercury Press

HARRY CURRIE ❖ *Debut for a Spy* ❖ Rivercrest
JOHN SPENCER HILL ❖ *The Last Castrato* ❖ Constable * (tie)
D.H. TOOLE ❖ *Moonlit Days and Nights* ❖ Cormorant * (tie)

Best Non-Fiction

JACK BATTEN ❖ *Mind Over Murder* ❖ McClelland & Stewart
MICHAEL HARRIS ❖ *The Judas Kiss* ❖ McClelland & Stewart
LOIS SIMMIE ❖ *The Secret Lives of Sgt. John Wilson* ❖ Greystone *

Best Juvenile Novel

MARTHA ATTEMA ❖ *A Time to Choose* ❖ Orca
ROY MACGREGOR ❖ *Mystery at Lake Placid* ❖ McClelland & Stewart
ROY MACGREGOR ❖ *The Night They Stole the Stanley Cup* ❖ McClelland
    & Stewart
NORAH MCCLINTOCK ❖ *Mistaken Identity* ❖ Scholastic *
MORDECAI RICHLER ❖ *Jacob Two-Two's First Spy Case* ❖ McClelland
    & Stewart

Best Short Story

TANYA HUFF ❖ *This Town Ain't Big Enough* ❖ from Vampire Detectives
MARY JANE MAFFINI ❖ *Cotton Armour* ❖ from The Ladies Killing Circle *
JAMES POWELL ❖ *The Rasputin Faberge* ❖ from Ellery Queen Mystery
    Magazine
JAMES POWELL ❖ *Breakout from Mistletoe Five* ❖ from Ellery Queen
    Mystery Magazine
PETER ROBINSON ❖ *Carrion* ❖ from No Alibi 1997

Best Novel/Sleuth of Baker Street Prize

MARGARET ATWOOD ❖ *Alias Grace* ❖ McClelland & Stewart
MARTIN S. COHEN ❖ *Light from Dead Stars* ❖ Coteau
SPARKLE HAYTER ❖ *Nice Girls Finish Last* ❖ Viking/Penguin
PETER ROBINSON ❖ *Innocent Graves* ❖ Viking/Penguin *
FRANK SMITH ❖ *Fatal Flaw* ❖ St. Martin's

Best First Novel/Worldwide Library Prize

C.C. BENISON ❖ *Death at Buckingham Palace* ❖ Bantam *
ANNE M. DOOLEY ❖ *Plane Death* ❖ NeWest
NANCY RICHLER ❖ *Throwaway Angels* ❖ Press Gang
RICHARD J. THOMAS ❖ *Gas Head Willy* ❖ Ginger Press

Best Non-Fiction

BRIAN DEMERT ❖ *Graham Greene Thrillers and the 1930s* ❖
McGill/Queen's University Press

HOWARD ENGEL ❖ *Lord High Executioner* ❖ Key Porter

DON HUTCHISON ❖ *The Great Pulp Heroes* ❖ Mosaic Press

JEAN MONET ❖ *The Cassock and the Crown* ❖ McGill/Queen's University
Press *

MERILYN SIMONDS ❖ *The Convict Lover* ❖ McFarlane Walter & Ross

Best Juvenile Novel

LINDA BAILEY ❖ *How Can a Frozen Detective Stay Hot on the Trail?* ❖
Kids Can *

DAVE GLAZE ❖ *Who Took Henry and Mr. Z?* ❖ Coteau

JAMES HENEGHAN ❖ *The Case of the Blue Raccoon* ❖ Scholastic

MARY ANN SCOTT ❖ *Ear Witness* ❖ Boardwalk/Dundurn

Best Short Story

RICHARD K. BERCUSON ❖ *Dead Run* ❖ from Storyteller *

JANE DIAS ❖ *Too Broke for Bullets* ❖ from Storyteller

EDEN ROBINSON ❖ *Dogs in Winter* ❖ from Traplines

BRAD SPURGEON ❖ *Murder in the Abbey* ❖ from Murderous Intent

EDO VAN BELKOM ❖ *The Piano Player Has No Fingers* ❖ from The Piano
Player Has No Fingers

1998

Best Novel/Sleuth of Baker Street Prize

ROSEMARY AUBERT ❖ *Free Reign* ❖ Bridge Works

C.C. BENISON ❖ *Death at Sandringham House* ❖ Bantam

WILLIAM DEVERELL ❖ *Trial of Passion* ❖ McClelland & Stewart *

JOHN SPENCER HILL ❖ *Ghirlandaio's Daughter* ❖ McClelland & Stewart

PETER ROBINSON ❖ *Dead Right* ❖ Viking/Penguin

ROBERT J. SAWYER ❖ *Illegal Alien* ❖ TOR

Best First Novel/Worldwide Library Prize

JIM CHRISTY ❖ *Shanghai Alley* ❖ Ekstasis Editions

LYN HAMILTON ❖ *The Xibalba Murders* ❖ Berkley Prime Crime

MAUREEN JENNINGS ❖ *Except the Dying* ❖ St. Martin's

ALLAN LEVINE ❖ *Blood Libel* ❖ Great Plains Fiction

KATHY REICHS ❖ *Déjà Dead* ❖ Scribners *

JOHN W. SIMPSON ❖ *Undercut* ❖ Mercury

Best Non-Fiction

PATRICIA PEARSON ❖ *When She Was Bad* ❖ Random House *

ANDREAS SCHROEDER ❖ *Cheats, Charlatans and Chicanery* ❖ McClelland & Stewart

DAVID STAFFORD ❖ *Churchill and Secret Service* ❖ Stoddart

Best Juvenile Novel

LINDA BAILEY ❖ *What's a Daring Detective Like Me Doing in the Doghouse?* ❖ Kids Can

NICHOLAS BOVING ❖ *Maxim Gunn - the Demon Plan* ❖ Taurus

NORAH McCLINTOCK ❖ *The Body in the Basement* ❖ Scholastic *

ROY McGREGOR ❖ *Terror in Florida* ❖ McClelland & Stewart

CORA TAYLOR ❖ *Vanishing Act* ❖ Red Deer College Press

Best Short Story

JOHN BALLEM ❖ *Rigged to Blow* ❖ from Secret Tales of the Arctic Trails

SUE PIKE ❖ *Widow's Weeds* ❖ from Cottage Country Killers *

PETER ROBINSON ❖ *The Two Ladies of Rose Cottage* ❖ from Malice Domestic 6

ROBERT J. SAWYER ❖ *The Hand You're Dealt* ❖ from Free Space

EDO VAN BELKOM ❖ *The Rug* ❖ from Robert Bloch's Psychos

The Derrick Murdoch Award

HOWARD ENGEL AND ERIC WRIGHT

1999

Best Novel/Sleuth of Baker Street Prize

GAIL BOWEN ❖ *Verdict in Blood* ❖ McClelland & Stewart

NORA KELLY ❖ *Old Wounds* ❖ HarperCollins *

SCOTT MACKAY ❖ *Cold Comfort* ❖ Carrol & Graf

CAROLINE ROE ❖ *Remedy for Treason* ❖ Berkley Prime Crime

JEAN RURYK ❖ *Next Week Will Be Better* ❖ McClelland & Stewart

MICHELLE SPRING ❖ *Standing in the Shadows* ❖ Ballantine

Best First Novel/Worldwide Library Prize

LIZ BRADY ❖ *Sudden Blow* ❖ Second Story *
PETER CLEMENT ❖ *Lethal Practice* ❖ Fawcett Gold Medal
KAREN DUDLEY ❖ *Hoot to Kill* ❖ Ravenstone
MEL MALTON ❖ *Down in the Dumps* ❖ Rendezvous
KERRI SAKAMOTO ❖ *The Electrical Field* ❖ Alfred A. Knopf Canada

Best Non-Fiction

STEVIE CAMERON ❖ *Blue Trust* ❖ McFarlane Walter & Ross
DEREK FINKLE ❖ *No Claim to Mercy* ❖ Viking/Penguin *
DAVID PACIOCCO ❖ *Getting Away With Murder* ❖ Irwin Law
BILL SCHILLER ❖ *Hand in the Water* ❖ HarperCollins
ALISON SHAW ❖ *A Friend of the Family* ❖ McFarlane Walter & Ross
RUDY WIEBE & YVONNE JOHNSON ❖ *A Stolen Life* ❖ Alfred A. Knopf
    Canada

Best Juvenile Novel

KIM ASKEW ❖ *Surfers of Snow* ❖ Fitzhenry & Whiteside
SHEILA DALTON ❖ *Trial by Fire* ❖ Napoleon
NORAH MCCLINTOCK ❖ *Sins of the Father* ❖ Scholastic *
ROBERT SUTHERLAND ❖ *The Secret of Devil Lake* ❖ HarperCollins
MARY WOODBURY ❖ *The Intrepid Polly McDoodle* ❖ Coteau

Best Short Story

BARRY BALDWIN ❖ *Do You Take This Man?* ❖ from Ellery Queen Mystery
    Magazine
J.S. LYSTER ❖ *The Hunter of the Guileless* ❖ from Storyteller
SCOTT MACKAY ❖ *Last Inning* ❖ from Ellery Queen Mystery Magazine *
JAMES POWELL ❖ *Strangers on a Sleigh* ❖ from Ellery Queen Mystery
    Magazine
WAYNE YETMAN ❖ *Getting Ahead* ❖ from Storyteller

The Derrick Murdoch Award
TED WOOD

Canadian Winners of International Crime Writing Awards

EDGAR ALLAN POE AWARDS

Mystery Writers of America (MWA)

Grand Master Award

1957: VINCENT STARRETT
1973: ROSS MACDONALD (a.k.a. KENNETH MILLAR)
1982: MARGARET MILLAR

Edgar Award

1955: MARGARET MILLAR, *Beast in View* (Best Novel)
1973: PAUL B. ERDMAN, *The Billion Dollar Sure Thing*
(Best First Novel)
1977: GEORGE JONAS AND BARBARA AMIEL, *By Person Unknown*
(Best Fact Crime)
1981: L.A. MORSE, *The Old Dick* (Best Paperback Original)
1985: L.R. WRIGHT, *The Suspect* (Best Novel)
1988: TIMOTHY FINDLEY, *The Telling of Lies* (Best Paperback Original)

HAMMETT PRIZE

North American Branch of the International Association of Crime Writers
1998: WILLIAM DEVERELL, *Trial of Passion*

JOHN CREASEY MEMORIAL AWARD

(Best Crime Novel by a Previously Unpublished Author)
Crime Writers Association (U.K.)
1983: ERIC WRIGHT, *The Night the Gods Smiled*

MACAVITY AWARD

Mystery Readers Journal (Mystery Readers International)
1998: PETER ROBINSON, *Two Ladies of Rose Cottage* in Malice
Domestic 6 (Best Mystery Short Story)

SHERLOCK HOLMES AWARDS

Sherlock Holmes: The Detective Magazine
1999: SPARKLE HAYTER (Best Comic Detective) for ROBIN HUDSON

About the Authors

ROSEMARY AUBERT brings an insider's perspective to her crime fiction through her background as a criminologist. She has provided public education and produced videos for clients such as Correctional Services of Canada. She also has diverse experience as a writer with several successful romance novels, as well as poetry and journalism, to her credit. Her first crime novel, *Free Reign*, was short-listed for the 1999 Arthur Ellis Award for Best First Novel. "The Midnight Boat to Palermo," from *Cold Blood V*, was her first published crime fiction.

RICHARD BERCUSON is a writer and teacher living in Ottawa. He has had numerous short stories, including "Dead Run," an Arthur winner, published in *Storyteller* magazine. A former sportswriter, Richard has contributed articles to various hockey and coaching publications as well as writing for the *Ottawa Citizen* and several weekly newspapers.

EDWARD D. HOCH is unique in the world of crime fiction. He has, since 1955, devoted himself almost exclusively to the art of the short story. He has almost 1,000 published stories to his credit and more than two dozen different series characters. His work has appeared in every issue of *Ellery Queen Mystery Magazine* since May, 1973. A resident of Rochester, New York, and a longtime member of the Crime Writers of Canada, Ed's mystery writer/detective hero Barney Hamet has solved mysteries at various crime writing events in his career. In "The Unpleasantness at the Arts & Letters Club," he solves one at the annual Arthur Ellis Awards banquet itself, and sets both the scene and the tone for what's to follow.

NANCY KILPATRICK is known primarily as an accomplished writer of horror fiction and dark fantasy. In that genre she has published dozens of short stories; novelized the recent musical stage production *Dracul*; edited several anthologies; and written a number of vampire novels, including *Near Death* and *As One Dead*. Under the name Amarantha Knight, she has also published a series of erotic horror novels. "Mantrap" — one of her few works of pure crime fiction — is a powerful example of mood, pace, and skilful plotting.

SCOTT MACKAY is a native of Toronto, where he lives with his family. His writing resume is varied, including the successful thriller, *A Friend in Barcelona*, the science fiction adventure, *Outpost*, and the Arthur Ellis-nominated police procedural, *Cold Comfort*. He has been a frequent contributor to *Ellery Queen Mystery Magazine* and is an active member of the Crime Writers of Canada.

MARY JANE MAFFINI is an anthology editor, mystery writing teacher, and part owner of Ottawa's Prime Crime mystery bookshop, as well as being an accomplished short story writer. Her stories, displaying a unique ability to blend crime and humor, have appeared in *Ellery Queen Mystery Magazine* and the anthologies *Cold Blood V*, *The Ladies' Killing Circle* and *Cottage Country Killers*. She's co-editor of the forthcoming anthology, *Menopause Is Murder*, and her first novel, *Speak Ill of the Dead*, was published in 1999 by Rendezvous Publishing.

JAS. R. PETRIN lives in Winnipeg and is a regular contributor to *Alfred Hitchcock Mystery Magazine* — where "Killer in the House" appeared — as well as anthologies such as the Cold Blood series. His work is diverse, ranging from stunning exercises in pure suspense to humorous tales of whimsy to the dark and bizarre. His stories have been reprinted frequently, recorded in audio books, dramatized for television — and nominated for Arthurs on several other occasions.

SUE PIKE lives in Ottawa and is quickly becoming one of Canada's most respected writers of short crime fiction. She is a member of both the Crime Writers of Canada and the Ottawa-based Ladies' Killing Circle. This Arthur-winning story first appeared in the Ladies' second anthology, *Cottage Country Killers*. "Widow's Weeds" was inspired by the beautiful and terrifying wilderness surrounding Sue's cottage in Eastern Ontario.

PETER ROBINSON is perhaps the most acclaimed crime writer Canada has ever produced. His exceptional series of novels about Yorkshire Dales Inspector Alan Banks, most recently *In a Dry Season*, has earned him international recognition — as well as Arthur Ellis Awards for Best Novel for both *Past Reason Hated* and *Innocent Graves*. His first novel, *Gallows View*, was nominated for the British Crime Writers Association's John Creasey Award, and *Wednesday's Child* was nominated for an Edgar Award by the Mystery Writers of America. His short stories have been collected in the book *Not Safe After Dark*, and he has also published two non-series thrillers.

ROBERT J SAWYERS's Arthur Ellis Award for Best Short Story is just one of many international honors he has received in recent years. His science fiction writing has garnered top prizes in Japan, France and Spain — in addition to the coveted Nebula Award from the Science Fiction Writers of America. Many of his novels — as well as "Just Like Old Times," an Arthur-winning story — brilliantly interweave elements of crime and mystery along with SF. Prime examples include *The Terminal Experiment*, *Illegal Alien,* and *Flashforward.*

JOSEF SKVORECKY is one of Canada's most highly regarded literary figures. Born in Czechoslovakia and for many years a resident of Toronto, his many critically-acclaimed novels include *Dvorak in Love* and the Governor General's Award-winning *The Engineer of Human Souls.* He is also the creator of police detective Lieutenant Boruvka, who, in collections of stories, such as *The End of Lieutenant Boruvka* and *Sins for Father Knox*, brings deep humanity to the solving of crimes in a Prague under Communist domination. Josef's most recent crime novel, *Two Murders in My Double Life*, was published in 1999.

ERIC WRIGHT is one of Canada's most honored crime writers with four Arthur Ellis Awards to his credit. In 1984, Eric captured the inaugural Arthur for the first Charlie Salter novel, *The Night the Gods Smiled.* Two years later, he won again for *Death in the Old Country.* He has also won twice for Best Short Story — the first time for this story, "Looking for an Honest Man," from *Cold Blood: Murder in Canada.* In addition to the popular and ongoing Charlie Salter series, Eric also chronicles the adventures of female private eye Lucy Trimble and Toronto cop Mel Pickett. And he has recently published a volume of memoirs called *Always Give a Penny to a Blind Man.* "Two in the Bush" is the second of Eric's Arthur-winning stories, a deft and brilliantly plotted tale of crime in the Christmas season.